THE MATTRESS HOUSE

Also by Paulus Hochgatterer in English translation

The Sweetness of Life (2008)

Paulus Hochgatterer

THE MATTRESS HOUSE
A KOVACS & HORN INVESTIGATION

Translated from the German by
Jamie Bulloch

MACLEHOSE PRESS
QUERCUS · LONDON

First published in Great Britain in 2012 by

MacLehose Press
an imprint of Quercus
55 Baker Street
7th Floor, South Block
London W1U 8EW

First published in German as *Das Matrazenhaus*
by Deuticke im Paul Zsolnay Verlag, Vienna, 2010
Copyright © Deuticke im Paul Zsolnay Verlag, 2010

English translation copyright © 2012 by Jamie Bulloch

The translation of this book is supported by
the Austrian Federal Ministry of Education, Arts and Culture

A CIP catalogue record for this book is available
from the British Library

ISBN (HB) 978 0 85705 028 1
ISBN (TPB) 978 0 85705 029 8

10 9 8 7 6 5 4 3 2 1

Designed and typeset in Minion by Libanus Press, Marlborough
Printed and bound in Great Britain by Clays Ltd, St Ives plc

Revenge, revenge! Timotheus cries,
See the Furies arise!
See the snakes that they rear,
How they hiss in their hair,
And the sparkles that flash from their eyes!

"Alexander's Feast", JOHN DRYDEN

HOW IT MUST HAVE BEEN

It is windy. As if propelled by rubber bands, the pelicans shoot upwards, squawk, plummet back down with bent wings, and slice through the surface of the water. When, a little later, they resurface somewhere else, they stretch out their bills and shake their throat pouches, emptying the entire contents into their gullets. Then they ready themselves to take off again. Once in the air the flock, maybe two hundred birds in all, breaks out in every direction as if it were disbanding for good, only to re-form moments later into a dark cloud. This process repeats itself hundreds of times. When the offshore winds blow, the birds often linger above the section of beach between the loading dock in the harbour and the long, grey building of the railway works.

The woman does not like these animals. They are loud, and they stink when you get close to them. With a quick jerk of her shoulder she adjusts the yellow cloth bag on her back, without stopping reaches down to pick up the girl who has been walking beside her the whole way, and sits the child on her left hip. The little girl is still for a moment, but then starts chuckling and waving her arms about. She points to a pair of red-backed shrikes hopping through a thistle bush, a wooden shed painted with faces, and an old man sitting asleep in a plastic chair. Her voice slightly raised, the woman utters a few sentences over and over again with a particular urgency, as if she were telling short, serious stories. The girl babbles. Sometimes she appears to be paying attention, sometimes not. Before beginning the steep climb up to the road the woman tightens her grip on the child's body, nods to the sky and says something which might be, "Now you've got to be quiet." The girl crosses her arms and leans her head against the woman's chest.

The wind blows ochre swirls of dust across the road. Some distance away cars are veering right to overtake a herd of goats. A lorry laden with crates of vegetables gives a loud honk of its horn. This does not bother the goats in the slightest. The man herding the animals is wearing an eyepatch. Two long bamboo canes are balanced on his shoulder.

The girl raises her hand to grab the hem of the woman's blouse and starts twisting it between her fingers. The woman shakes her body in irritation. When the girl shows no sign of stopping, she puts her on the ground. For a while the two of them wander behind the herd of goats, and then turn into a wide street lined with hoardings. The girl sticks out her arm to point at a mobile phone advertisement; the woman says something and laughs. Embarrassed, the girl bends over, picks up an orange drinks carton and then throws it away again. The woman watches it skittle along the road. Out of the corner of her eye she can see a huge bank of cloud rolling over the hills beyond the city. She takes the child's hand and quickens her pace.

They pass the entrance to the corrugated-iron sheds of a haulage company, and then just beyond a row of newly painted houses they come to the rectangular courtyard of a building decked out with flags. A bunch of people are sitting on the lower part of a flight of steps that sweeps up to the entrance. A man walks to and fro in front of them, waving his arms theatrically. Perpendicular to the steps, he has placed three baskets in a row: one longish and box shaped, and two round ones. Squealing with delight, the girl lets go of the woman's hand and makes to run over to the people. The woman grabs the child's shoulder and restrains her. The girl whines in protest, struggling to free herself from the woman's grasp. She calms down only when the woman lifts her up and walks over to the gathering. The man, short and thin, with an abnormally large head, looks at the girl and raises a finger. The girl tries to hide her head behind the woman's neck; the woman pacifies the child with soothing words and then points to the man and his three baskets. The man lifts the lid of one of the round baskets, reaches his arm in, and pulls out a snake, maybe thirty centimetres long. With his thumb and forefinger he holds the creature just behind its small, triangular head, and presents it to the crowd. The snake is pale green, with two rows of bright-yellow markings on either side. The man climbs a few steps, throws back his head, and slowly begins to push the snake up his right nostril. The crowd shriek; some of them turn their heads away. When all that remains to be seen of the snake is the tip of its tail, the man opens his mouth, inserts his left forefinger, pushing it past his blackish-brown teeth, and pulls out the head in one swift movement. He takes a bow as the crowd howls its approval.

The girl grabs the woman's blouse again. Slowly, she pushes the first three fingers of her other hand further and further into her mouth. The woman gazes into the distance, beyond the roofs of the city, as if assessing the wind. She does not look at the child until she begins to choke violently. Without a word she pulls the girl's hand out of her mouth. There is still time. It is going to rain, but they have almost reached their destination.

The man with the large head beckons the woman and girl over. The girl closes her eyes when the man invites her to look inside the basket. The woman smiles and says something like, "Don't be afraid." The man bends down and whispers something in the girl's ear. Then he feels inside his jacket pocket and presses a round object into her hand. The girl puts it straight into her mouth. The woman shakes her head, but does nothing more. Perhaps she thinks it is a sweet.

They walk, quicker than before, first along a line of plane trees, then on a much-worn path up a shallow incline. Now and again the woman looks around. The clouds tower high above the city. To the east the chimneys of the power station rise like gigantic columns. The pelicans have vanished. The girl runs between the tamarisk bushes growing beside the path, making soft, cheerful noises. When a vermilion-painted house looms before them, the girl moves to the woman's side and takes her hand.

The servant who opens the door leads them through a sparsely furnished hall into a glass annexe with wide doors that give onto the garden. Three people stand there talking in a foreign language: two men in suits and a woman with a pink handbag. When they notice the woman and the girl they fall silent. One of the men – he is short and fat – approaches them and rests his hand on the child's head. The girl cowers. The other man pulls an envelope from the inner pocket of his jacket and gives it to the woman. She lets go of the girl, walks over to a round, mosaic table with a jug and some glasses, and opens the envelope. She takes out the money, lays it in front of her, and counts it into a new pile, note by note. She then puts the money back, and clutches the envelope. She slides the yellow cloth bag from her shoulder, waits for a moment with both arms splayed, and then leaves the room smartly without a backward glance.

The girl just stares. The cloth bag is on the floor, two or three metres away. Nobody says a word.

Outside, the woman walks through the wind. She may be laughing. She may be also screaming. The first drops hit the dust hard.

ONE

She stands in the doorway, looking into the classroom, and knows that things are going to get difficult again. It's like this every few weeks.

She puts down her bag carefully. It's not my fault, she thinks, the bell rang two minutes ago, the children are riotous, and in the middle of it all there's a sick person sitting on the desk talking about heaven. It's really not my fault.

She tries to stay calm, and lets her eyes scan the wall to the left: the whiteboard; the cupboard with the craft materials; the trees in blossom, twenty-one of them, one for each child, some drawn, some cut from magazines; the large map of Austria with the red hare that Lena drew in the bottom right-hand corner; Phillip's footprints on the wall, the left one 120 centimetres from the floor; the roll-down chart of school handwriting – the headmistress has insisted on it being in the classroom; the windows through which she can see the roofs of the town and, through the right-hand one, just in the corner, a fragment of the lake.

Bauer looks at her, laughs, waves and has no intention of stopping. If nothing else, he seems to be in good form. But then, totally out of the blue, he starts singing at the top of his voice. She tries to identify the song. She can make out *On the water*, but nothing else. Julia and Sophie are singing along with him, just as loudly.

She claps her hands. "That's enough, my lovelies," she shouts. "Now it's my turn!" "Hello Stella!" Bauer says. "Have you come to

11

join in my lesson?" "I'm Protestant," she replies, although this is not true. "You're lying," says Bauer. "May I?" she asks. "Please?"

"Only if you tell me what God looks like."

"An old man with a white beard."

"Correct. And what does he carry around with him?"

"A book and a lightning bolt."

"Wrong! A guitar, of course!"

She pictures an angry old man smashing a guitar against a whiteboard and, as she stands there, surprised at herself, Manuel tugs on her sleeve. He shows her a drawing. "We did pictures of God," he says proudly. Given how poor the boy's graphomotor skills are, it is not a bad attempt, particularly the guitar – a spiral with parallel lines going sideways, one to six. His arithmetic is excellent.

Bauer leaps from the desk, dances the two-step towards her, and plants a kiss on her cheek. The children laugh. "My favourite teacher!" he says. "O.K., O.K.," she says. "Now, will you put your things away, please?"

"Do you think God has a walking stick?" He circles her and asks whether God wears vests or reading glasses, whether he's a vegetarian, smokes a pipe, and whether he's more of a car or motorbike man. "Motorbike," she says, "and he's got trouble with his lumbar column." He pauses, and before he can butt in she says that when God had his last medical check-up they discovered that his prostate was not working properly. What is more, his psychiatrist was not at all pleased as he was failing to take his medicine regularly.

"You are one mean feminist of a schoolteacher," Bauer says, and she worries that Manuel, who is standing open-mouthed beside her, will want to know what feminists and prostate results are.

While Bauer looks for his shoes, she directs the children back to their seats. One of them is missing. "What's happened to Felix?"

she asks. Bauer looks around, puzzled. "He went home," Julia says.

"Wasn't he feeling well?"

"Yes, he looked perfectly fine."

She tries to catch Bauer's eye. "Would you mind giving me an explanation? Felix did *what*? Went *home*?"

"What's wrong?" Bauer says. "He only lives two streets away."

My class, she thinks, this is my class, and is somewhat surprised both by her proprietary attitude, and by the fact that her infinite patience for her fellow human beings – the bedrock of her personality, which without doubt made her ideally suited to such a career – has crumbled within seconds.

"Say that again please! You let him go *home*? *Alone*?"

"He does it quite often. He always comes back after a quarter of an hour. I've signed him out."

"Signed him *out*?" Now she is yelling. All her suspicions about this professional Catholic group are confirmed – dishonest, lazy and, when push comes to shove, irresponsible to the very core. "A six-year-old child is signed out of an R.E. lesson and our pastor thinks nothing of sending him out onto the street alone. Just like that!" Bauer purses his lips, keeps his head down and takes his jacket off the hook. The children avoid her gaze, too. I'm losing it, she thinks, that hardly ever happens. Chubby red-headed Leonard comes up to her. "I'll go over and see if he's fallen asleep," he says. She takes his hand and does not reply. "How long has he been gone?" she asks. Bauer looks at his watch. "Forty minutes," he says.

"And you weren't even aware of it?"

"No," he says. "When I'm in a certain frame of mind, there's quite a lot I'm not aware of. You know that."

Yes I do, she thinks. She goes to the back of the classroom to Felix's desk on the left-hand side. When she stoops to take a look inside his tray, she realises that Leonard is still holding her hand. "He's left everything here," she says. "He took his water bottle,"

Leonard says. "He's got a new silver water bottle with a black dragon on it." From the tray she takes a large exercise book with a red protective cover. English. A hat. A cat. A bat. Drawing a bat is difficult, she told the children, more difficult than a cat. With the tip of her forefinger she follows the words, the drawings, too. What a terrible hat, she thinks – like a molehill. And yet it comforts her to look through the exercise book. "He can't draw," Leonard says. "Kids in kindergarten could do better than that."

Bauer is standing in front of the whiteboard, gawky, pale, his legs twitching. L.D.R., she thinks, Long Distance Runner, that's what some of them call him. His colleagues say he spends every spare minute running – around the lake, along the river, up into the mountains, sometimes for several hours at a stretch. And listening to music while he runs. Now he is humming. "You've got a nerve," she says. He shakes his head slowly. "I know," she says, "I'm sorry." She puts the book back. The tray to the right is empty. It belonged to a girl who left only a few weeks after school started. That happens in the first year. Susi – a quiet, thin girl with wild black hair and an old-fashioned name. Felix liked her. "What are we going to do now?" Bauer asks. There is a sentence on the board behind him: *The hare has long ears.* She wrote it well over an hour ago. "You're going to stay right here and look after the class. I'll go and fetch Felix. Leonard can come with me."

They walk along the corridor, cross the hall where the children spend break-time, and climb the steps to the main entrance. She has to be careful not to trip. I'm scared, she thinks. She can see through the arched fanlight that the sun is shining outside. She knows that as they go out onto the street she will be dazzled momentarily, and she can already smell the subtle scent of lilac. They might bump into Friederike, who always starts two hours later on a Tuesday, and maybe also catch a glimpse of the tame guinea fowl that belongs to the junk dealer whose office is opposite.

14

As she reaches for the door handle it is pulled away from her. A small, dark figure stands in the white rectangle of the doorway. Leonard is the first to speak. "What took you so long?"

TWO

The black Porsche Cayenne, which has been tailgating him for a kilometre and a half, flashes its lights for the third time, swings out to the left, screeches past and, without dropping its speed, shoots straight by the bright green newspaper stand they are always waiting behind. Twenty seconds later he sees the highly satisfied face of a policeman peeping above a radar gun, and he knows it's going to cost the other man around three hundred euros, maybe even more. Whatever happens, there'll have to be some grovelling at the police commissariat: I really can't do my job without a driving licence, Herr Inspektor, I'm sure you understand.

Raffael Horn guided his Volvo uphill, first through the pine forest, then alongside the wide open space which was half rape field, half meadow this spring. He was driving extra slow as the trailer was swinging alarmingly on the tight bends and lifting off the road surface at the slightest bump. Meanwhile, he replayed the scene a few times in his mind as if it were a short film: Lissoni puts his foot down, overtakes, and drives into the radar trap. There was no doubt about it, *schadenfreude* was one of the few things that made life tolerable. But you'd have to be a bit of a psychopath or have been through a good course of analysis to admit to it without feeling bad.

Lissoni had been head of the casualty department for six months. From day one he had made it plain that colleagues whose daily activities did not involve drills, bone saws or transfusion

16

pumps would not be taken seriously. Horn had been his enemy for five months and two weeks. It had nothing to do with the Porsche. Lissoni had decreed from on high that he would not dream of sending anyone from his department to the child protection group – if a child suspected of being abused arrived in casualty, the fact would be reported and that would be that. The matter was not up for discussion, irrespective of how things had worked in the past. Lissoni was blond and had a sunbed tan; he wore white Ralph Lauren polo shirts and a chunky signet ring. You could rely on him to serve up the clichés.

The area outside their house was empty. Horn put the car into reverse by pressing down on the clutch several times. For a while now this had been the only way of engaging the reverse gear. As the garage had told him tersely: Twelve years up and down mountain roads, what do you expect? But he still liked the Volvo, and after he had given Irene the compact off-road Suzuki for her forty-fifth birthday she had stopped harping on about it, too. He manoeuvred the trailer close to the edge of their front garden, got out, and removed the tarpaulin. The resinous smell coming off the heap of bark mulch filled his nostrils. He breathed in deeply. It's spring, he thought, the air is fresh and I've defeated an opponent.

He fetched a rake, shovel and wheelbarrow from the shed, removed a couple of broken twigs from the lawn, and began to unload the mulch. He spread some under the currant bush, under the rhododendrons, and in amongst the honeysuckles, roses and hydrangeas. The two wisterias, which Irene adored and he did not, got some as well. I'm shovelling bark mulch into a wheelbarrow and enjoying it. If someone had told me that fifteen years ago, I'd have said they were mad. He thought about real country people, Lisbeth Schalk, for example, and the bunches of wild flowers she regularly brought onto the ward, some pink, some yellow, some a

17

mixture of bright colours. Raimund called her an elfin princess, and to be honest there were worse ways of describing a psychologist. "But I haven't got pointy ears," she said. "Yes you have," Raimund replied, and she felt her ears to check. Lisbeth Schalk looked as though she had walked straight out of one of those sentimental "*Heimat*" films. Her psychological test results were not as dazzling as her bunches of flowers, but that was another story.

Horn trod down the bark chippings around the walnut tree he had planted in the autumn. Finished. He was hot. He rolled up his shirtsleeves. About a third of the mulch was left. He uncoupled the trailer and pushed it across the lawn to the rear wall of the shed. He tipped out most of the mulch and used the shovel for the rest. He shaped it into a neat cone. But even this would not be good enough for Irene. A garden with a heap of bark mulch was not a perfect garden.

"You'll get blisters on your hands." Tobias was leaning against the corner of the barn, wearing a smug grin. "Not something you've ever been in danger of in the last few years," Horn replied. "Where have you come from, anyway?"

"I go to school, remember? Seventh year."

Horn threw the shovel onto the trailer. "Give me a hand," he said. Together they manoeuvred the trailer into the garage. Tobias groaned several times as if in pain. Fathers of adolescent sons ought to be granted the right to make occasional use of corporal punishment, Horn thought – the odd stroke with a willow stick, now *that* wouldn't be bad. He closed the garage door. A large butterfly flitted towards them and landed for a second on Tobias's chest. "A pearl-bordered fritillary," Horn said. Tobias shrugged. There's something I've overlooked, Horn thought as they crossed the gravel to the house. He could not work out what it was.

"Are you hungry?"

Tobias shook his head.

"Are you unwell?"

"What? Because I'm not hungry? There's a point at which you stop being hungry all the time, like everything in life."

Horn rummaged through the bread drawer. Two hard rolls and a pack of bread for toasting which was now cultivating small bluish-green spots of mould at one end. "Actually, it's a good thing you're not hungry," he said. "I knew it," Tobias said.

"What did you know?"

"That I wouldn't get fed properly in this house."

"Get out of here!"

"Now I'm being booted out, too."

"Out!"

Horn filled the water container of the espresso machine and inserted a pod. He heard Tobias shuffling out of the room. He's getting on my nerves, he thought, and I've no interest in what he's doing, whether it's French or Latin or Physics. I'm deliberately not asking him and I know that's bad. He pressed the button, the espresso machine hummed and, when it was finished, spat furiously. He stirred a spoonful of sugar into his coffee and thought for a while. Then he went out of the front door, sat on the bench and looked down at the town. No newspaper, no book, nothing but a cup of coffee, he thought – like an old man; all I'm missing is the cat. He looked around. No sign of her. Up in one of the spruces at the edge of the forest a hawk sat motionless.

He thought about the argument he'd had that morning with Kren, the businesslike director of the hospital. It had been about staff numbers, specifically about the possibility of a third specialist for his department. In the end Kren had said he was sorry, but one had to bear in mind that, purely from a P.R. angle, psychiatric patients were not an asset to the hospital. At this, Horn had stood up. "The problem is that human beings in general are not assets, not even you, Herr Direktor," he had said, slamming the door behind him. Alongside his job, Kren was deputy regional secretary of the Business Party, went hunting twice a year with the mayor, and had a tendency towards obsessive–compulsive disorder. Let him throw me out, Horn thought. He imagined trying to explain it to Irene: "Listen, please don't be shocked, but they fired me today." She would narrow her eyes at him and ask, "How am I going to satisfy my need for luxuries now?"

The sky above the town was gloomy and edgy. The towers of the abbey church seemed to sway, as did the steel chimneys of the woodworking factory, and several times he had the impression that water from the lake was sloshing over the promenade. Perhaps it's just my eyes, he thought, maybe I've had a cataract for years without knowing. Christina, his ward sister, advised him at least once a month to go to an eye specialist. He could not bear being mothered like that and hardly ever replied.

Irene picked up the phone when he rang a second time. "Could you get some bread on your way home, please?" he said. "Tobias is starving."

"That's technically impossible."

"Nonsense! It's easy; you just have to try to imagine it."

"I mean the shopping, not Tobias starving. I've got two more pupils and then orchestra practice afterwards. Had you forgotten?"

She had told him, now he remembered perfectly. They had been having breakfast and she had told him: Easter Saturday, evening concert, Mozart's "*Requiem*", and Bruckner's "*Te Deum*", and he had said, "What a depressing programme!" Her retort was that the psychiatrist obviously had no clue about the emotional charge of music.

"What do you mean *forgotten*?" he said. "You didn't mention any rehearsal."

"We were having breakfast. You made a totally ignorant remark

20

about Anton Bruckner's naivety and I lost my temper. Memory still failing you?"

Horn said she was making it up; he had to chair the relatives' group that evening. He explained how he'd just been contemplating two rock-hard rolls and some mouldy sliced bread, and she replied that, like it or not, he would have to go to the Prinz bakery himself on his way to the hospital. "That means I've got to leave ten minutes earlier," he said.

"Oh, you poor thing!"

"When are you back?"

"That depends on the tenor."

"The tenor, I see." So that was her way, he said, of thanking him for doing his utmost to protect her garden from being overrun by pernicious weeds. He, too, would find a tenor and use him as an excuse for coming home late in the evenings. Why don't you do that? Irene Horn said. Seeing as you're such a bisexual. Anyway, she added, it was common knowledge that nobody could handle a sexual relationship with a female cellist, least of all a tenor, and so the whole thing was pretty daft full stop.

The cat was sitting outside on the windowsill, meowing resentfully. "She's right, Mimi," he said. "Forget the tenor; I'll get myself a soprano with sticky-out ears." He opened the window. The cat rubbed itself along his forearm, purring loudly. When he tweaked her neck she spun around hissing and sank her claws into the back of his hand.

There was something funny going on. A load of bark mulch left over, bread rotting in the drawer, fantasies about resigning, forgetting Irene's appointments, and church spires swaying in the distance. His son was being patronising and distant, and now even his pet was attacking him. Irene would probably say he was attaching far too much meaning to all of this, and he would reply that attaching meaning to things was his job.

21

Horn washed out his coffee cup. The cat toyed with the jet of water, behaving as if she had never been cross with him. "Devious little bitch!" he said quietly. She purred and looked right through him. She's got a squint, he thought. He had never noticed it before. He wondered whether he should take the car or his bike again, but in the end he decided to walk. The front tyre of his cross bike was losing air unpredictably – sometimes almost all of it in one go, and at other times nothing for kilometres – and he did not want to get straight back into the Volvo.

He crossed the back garden and knocked on the door to Tobias's bedroom. There was no response so he opened it. Tobias was lying sideways across the bed, snoring. A blob of saliva had collected at the corner of his mouth. Horn watched him for a while. He's got my build, he thought, he's got Irene's freckles, he's truculent and he stinks. I'm trying but failing to drum up some affection for my son. The cat leapt onto the bed and curled up behind his knees. None of that bothers you, Horn thought.

*

In spring, the path which cut across the winding road and led in a straight line into town, was habitually overgrown with weeds and bushes. It was only when people started to make a fuss that Martin Schwarz, the farmer who lived a little further up the hill, would come down with his strimmer and clear the path. As he got caught several times on young bramble stems, Horn cursed, and then became aware that a tune had filled his head, a short passage from Bruckner's "*Te Deum*". *Sanguine, sanguine* – these were the only words he could remember, but he was able to hum a few bars more. He imagined some nuns gazing heavenwards in ecstasy, then Padre Pio with his hands swathed in bandages, and finally he saw in his mind Sabrina, the red-headed sixteen-year-old who had been admitted to his ward, and who each day for the past week had sliced open another part of her body, needing each time

22

to be stitched up. There's nothing lovelier, she had said, than the moment just after you've made the cut, when the body pauses briefly, as if it were thinking, you can see the gash, pure and white, and the blood doesn't start flowing for a second or so. This was why she had no time for burns, even though she was a smoker. "You reek of burning and there's not a drop of blood," she had said. When she was offered alternative ways of reducing the tension she just laughed or tapped her forehead. Everyone else could bite into chilli peppers or smash their fists into bags of sand; she wasn't that nutty. "But who's going to want you later on, if you're covered from head to toe in scars?" Sonia, the young social worker, had said, and Sabrina had answered, "Who's wanted me up till now?"

Irene hated stories like this. "My existence is an idyll," she said. "You're the one in charge of fear and horror." That's how it was: *Sanguine, sanguine.* He dealt with girls disturbed in early childhood who harmed themselves, while she sat in stuccoed halls, playing her melancholic solos with eyes closed and the tip of her tongue between her teeth. "I don't know anybody more consistently in denial than you," he would sometimes say, and she would reply that if he saw music as a form of denial then she wouldn't argue with him. "Do you think Michael sees it like that?" he said, and tears welled up in her eyes. There was something irreparable between those two; Michael's moving out had not changed the situation one bit. They hardly ever spoke, and whenever they met it always went the same way: within minutes Irene would start nagging him, and Michael would go red in the face and clam up.

He had plenty of time so he left the main road and took the path to the wildlife observation centre. Behind the dark-brown wooden building he turned left and walked eastwards along the lake outlet and the first section of river. Coots and great-crested grebes were making their way through the reeds. There was a yellow dinghy in a side channel. In it sat a man with a baseball cap, performing bizarre contortions and taking photographs. Horn felt the urge to creep up on him and push him into the water, but at that moment two joggers trotted by, both wearing pink – one was more salmon, the other more shocking pink – and the feeling had passed. There's still hope, Horn thought, my wickedness is dispelled by young women jogging in springtime.

Next to the reed bed was an area of raised bog, from which peat had once been cut. Now it was in flower with cotton grass, willowherb and irises. Signs put up by the Furth Nature Conservation Authority requested visitors to watch out for grass snakes and ground-nesting birds, and to stick to the marked paths. I would like to see a bittern, just once, Horn thought, a wild boar in its natural habitat and a bittern. Where did the goals in our lives come from? In many cases it was impossible to determine.

The hospital stood on a rocky hill directly across the river. When building the extension two years previously they had put in some glass-covered steps down to the promenade, which had no doubt cost a fortune and were quite clearly too steep for invalids.

The first view of the lake was from a platform half-way up the steps. The air was still hazy; it was hard to make out the houses in Moosheim to the west. Horn took off his jacket. It was muggy, like in summer. He bumped into Jakob Fuhrmann, a squat, bald-headed operating theatre assistant. "Someone on your ward's yelling their head off," he said. "Thanks," Horn said, and was immediately irritated. Fuhrmann was a union representative and saw himself as a kind of policeman for the hospital. The man made his way down carefully, step by step. I'll give him a shove, Horn thought, my fist between his shoulder blades. He pictured arms flailing to either side, Fuhrmann swaying wildly and his massive body tilting ever further forward, finally falling and hitting the ground with a hideous thud. There's nothing better for one's mental health than a good old aggressive fantasy, his former supervisor Aichhorn had once said. Then he had been devoured by cancer.

As he pressed the button for the lift, Horn wondered whether he should go straight up to the ward or not. It was probably Schwind who had been doing the yelling, the schizophrenic forklift-truck driver who, in his worst phases, was tormented by the conviction that at any moment someone would come to take him to his execution. It may also have been Fehring, the junkie, who for several days had been in a complicated withdrawal from a number of substances. Both could make a lot of noise when they were in a bad way. So what? The relatives' session never started on time anyway.

The door to P2 was locked. That was not good news. Horn fished out his key and listened. To begin with he could not hear any shouting. In the day room a few patients were sitting down to their evening meal. Daniel Fehring had pushed his plate away and was staring at the silent television. "Didn't you like it?" Horn asked. "I'm not hungry," Fehring said. "You know that food helps with withdrawal," Horn said.

"Junkies don't eat much." Fehring yawned.

"Are you tired? That's a good sign."

Fehring looked awful, with a grey, shrunken face. He also had swollen eyelids – this was new. Once or twice a year he came for physical drug withdrawal, whenever his girlfriend threatened to leave him. Afterwards it would usually only be a few days before he was back on them again.

Horn walked along the corridor to the office. Karin, the youngest nurse, a skinny girl with very blonde hair, was sitting at the computer and hammering away at the keyboard. She seemed tense. "What's up?" he asked. "Sabrina," she said.

"Sabrina? The usual?"

"Yes, the usual. And she's put it on the web."

"What do you mean she's put it on the web?"

The girl had slashed her forearm with a razor blade while her room-mate took photographs, and had put the whole thing on the Internet using the patient computer. She had also provided a written commentary: This was how much the psychiatry department in Furth cared for its patients, and anyway, doctors couldn't give a toss about human misery, etc., etc. Her room-mate had been paid to take the snaps and then spilled the beans, which Sabrina had objected to.

"So then she started screaming," Horn said.

"What do you mean? She didn't scream."

Horn explained that outside they'd heard someone yelling. He told her about his conversation with Fuhrmann. All of a sudden Karin smiled. "It was Raimund," she said. "He was the one shouting." He'd been pretty angry that the bloodbath had been posted on the Internet, and when he discovered that Sabrina's commentary mentioned him by name, he slightly lost it.

"What did she write about him?"

"That he's a nerd with a ponytail."

Now it was Horn's turn to smile. Karin raised her head. "Yes it's true, I know," she said, "but she wrote something else, too."

"What?"

She stood up, went to the filing cabinet containing the patient histories and pulled out Sabrina's file. "You'll find it under 'Current'," she said.

There were seven printouts from the Internet, each one a photograph with comments. A drawing of a red heart with a razor blade in the middle. *They don't understand anything in here.* A girl sitting on a white-tiled bathroom floor, looking as buried in thought as someone giving themselves a shot of heroin, and slitting her lower arm. *You could kill yourself here and nobody would give a fuck.* Two close-ups of the cuts. *The core of existence. A kind of heaven.* Two sentences written on the wall in blood: *I'm dying* and *Fucking*

Furth. The girl lying on her back in a pool of blood, her eyes closed and arms stretched out. *Something for Raimund to jerk off to, the nerd with the ponytail who always gets a hard-on when I cut myself.*

Sanguine, sanguine, Horn thought, and he also thought of Irene – it was a safe bet that the image of blood dripping from a girl's forearm never crossed her mind as she played her Bruckner. He put the file back and stood up. "Can I talk to Raimund?" he asked.

"Christina sent him home. He'd totally lost the plot," Karin said.

"What about Sabrina?"

"In a deep sleep. Hrachovec sedated her."

Male solidarity, Horn thought. She humiliates her primary nurse and the duty doctor pumps her full of drugs. He probably wouldn't have done any different. Sometimes all you could do was show who's boss, even if it didn't look especially pretty on the outside.

He decided against calling Hrachovec and left the ward. As passed the day room he saw that Fehring had fallen asleep in his chair. The television was still on with the sound turned down. Something unpleasant scratched at the furthest corner of his consciousness. He could not identify what it was.

*

Four people were there. Frau Kirschner and the Reintalers were chatting at a table in the waiting area, Kurt Frühwald sat apart from them, and the grey-haired man who had first turned up a fortnight ago was leaning against a wall, tapping at his Palmtop with a stylus. Horn could not remember the man's name; this had been happening to him rather a lot lately.

A strange collection of people, he thought. Mothers, fathers, husbands, all of them looking as if they were straight out of a photograph, their faces flat, shoulders a little too low. Why am I here? he thought. Why don't I sit and watch the hawk? Or enjoy the rhododendron flowers? Or imagine my wife playing the cello, with glowing ears and the tip of her tongue between her teeth?

The light in the day room was flickering slightly. This annoyed Horn. He had forgotten to report it to the in-house electrician. In a few minutes' time someone would say: *The light's still flickering*. It was inevitable. It was not just one light, but all of them, he was glad he had noticed that. Someone's tapping into us, he thought, I'll say that someone's siphoning off electricity from the hospital and we can't work out who or where. He chose to wait.

More men than women, he said as he opened the session – we've never had that in a relatives' session before; generally, men are not so involved. Maria Reintaler laughed. *Involved*, what a joke, she said, and anyway it was a draw, two-all, because her husband was nothing more than an accessory. He only came along because he didn't know what to do with himself at home on his own. Now Sophie Kirschner was laughing, too, and Max Reintaler said, "True." He was one of those men who, if he spoke at all, tended to speak in one word-sentences: Yes. No. Cheers. Pissoff. True. Running a small firm that installed electrical items, he had become something of a specialist in photovoltaics, and could be confident that his customers did not have the faintest idea what he was up to. His wife had managed the office for him until about a year ago, when her mother was first afflicted with a rapidly advancing form of dementia, so now she devoted all her time to looking after her. Horn asked the other men whether they, too, felt like accessories. Maria Reintaler said she didn't care about the others, but her bloke definitely was one, here and even more so at home, she was at the end of her tether, nobody could imagine what it was like, and it didn't seem to affect her dear husband in the slightest. She was coming to this group in the hope that somebody, finally, might read him the riot act, it was not on for her to have to shoulder the entire burden of caring for her mother, not to mention the housework and the bookkeeping she still did for the company. Max Reintaler was wearing light-brown corduroy trousers, a checked shirt and a chunky chain around his neck. As Reintaler gazed into the distance, Horn was sure that he was thinking about condensators, cable cross-sections or solar panels, and that everything his wife was saying was going in one ear and out the other like a spring breeze. In a way I can understand him, Horn thought, she'd drive you up the wall. She had dominated the last two sessions with her lament, and he had no intention of letting it happen again. "What sort of care allowance does your mother get?" he asked. Maria Reintaler raised an eyebrow and gasped. "Why?" she asked. "What's that got to do with it?" There were times when Raffael Horn could feel duplicity and hypocrisy swell up inside him like a soft, sweet mass, and he was incapable of doing anything to stop it. He had just wondered, he said, whether she might not be getting enough allowance for her mother, and therefore couldn't hire professional help. There was now a broad range of mobile nursing available, he added, particularly in the psychiatric sector. No, she didn't want that, Maria Reintaler said, getting agitated. Nobody knew her mother as well as she did, and anyway, each time she came into contact with strangers she'd get more and more panicky. Frau Reintaler was now sitting bolt upright, prodding the air with her index finger as she spoke.

"Obviously all you care about is the money!" Kurt Frühwald said very quietly, almost incidentally.

"I beg your pardon?" she spluttered.

"Level seven, isn't it?" Frühwald said. "The maximum plus a supplement for increased medical costs."

"And? She's entitled to it!"

"No-one's disputing that."

"Exactly. So what are you after?"

"Justice," Kurt Frühwald said, "just sometimes I'd like a little bit of justice, that's all."

29

"*Justice?* – Nobody's to blame for what happened to your wife!" Any moment now, Horn thought, she's going to leap up and go for his throat. Maria Reintaler's face was puce, her hands clutched the seat of her chair. Kurt Frühwald looked completely relaxed. He's smiling, Horn thought, he's actually smiling. Frühwald was a bald-headed man of medium height who swam across the lake and back again several times a week, from the boat jetty at the wildlife obser-vation centre to the point where the stream at Fürstenau flowed into a waterfall, a distance of more than three kilometres. He didn't need to do it for his ego, he would say if somebody asked him, he was doing it for his wife. She weighed seventy-five kilograms, was as strong as an ox, and completely unpredictable. Eleven years ago, Frühwald's wife had suffered a serious injury to her skull. As a result she was unable to walk and her personality had completely changed. Her husband had taken her away from hospital at the earliest possible opportunity, taught her how to use a wheelchair, and then looked after her predominantly on his own. To begin with he had taken unpaid leave; later he gave up his job as a bank employee and set himself up as a freelance insurance broker. That gave him the flexibility he needed to care for his wife. Immediately after the accident he had given his son, five at the time, and their two-and-a-half-year-old twin daughters to his wife's mother. They still lived with her.

"'Nobody' isn't right," Frühwald said.

"What do you mean?" Horn asked, even though he knew the answer.

"That little brat my wife chased after – he's entirely to blame."

"Not again," Frau Kirschner sighed.

"I'm sorry," Frühwald said, "but I'm not going to change my opinion."

"He was only a little boy!"

"So what?"

Margot Frühwald had been playing a game of "We are jungle

30

animals" with her group of children on the strip of lawn behind the kindergarten. Everything had gone according to plan until Moritz Leitkamp took his role as a leopard one stage too far. The five-year-old had fixed on Nina Rohrer, who was a gazelle, as his victim, and had pounced with his claws at the ready. Nina fled, Moritz pursued her, and Margot Frühwald had chased after him to prevent any greater mischief. She did not see the rim of the inflatable paddling pool, caught her foot, stumbled, and hit her head against the edge of the concrete plant trough. She spent several weeks in a coma, and her life was only saved when an intracranial pressure probe was applied just in time. "What's your wife's level of paralysis?" the grey-haired man asked bluntly. Frühwald spun round towards him. "Her what?" he asked.

"Her level. Cervical spine, thoracic spine, C five, C seven, T something. You know."

"She doesn't have a level," Frühwald said. "My wife doesn't have your average paralysis." In her case it had been an epidural haematoma, bleeding between the skull and the brain which had put such pressure on the cerebral cortex that part of it had been destroyed. "The Gyrus precentralis," the man said. How did he know that? Frühwald asked, it wasn't the sort of thing you just came out with – if he was a doctor then he should tell them all, not keep it a secret. No, the man said, he wasn't a doctor, but he couldn't help having an interest in medical matters, especially those to do with the central nervous system. I don't like him, Horn thought, even if he says he *couldn't help* it. I don't like the way he taps at his Palmtop, and I don't like the way he says *Gyrus precentralis*, *medical matters*, and *central nervous system* – with the arrogance of someone who's half educated, *and* with a slight north-German accent.

What did he mean he *couldn't help* it, Frühwald asked somewhat uncertainly, what did that have to do with his being in this relatives' group? He had a mentally ill wife and a difficult daughter.

31

The man looked around the room. Nobody said a word. Why did he say *mentally ill*, Horn wondered, he's attention-seeking, and I still don't like him. I'm sorry, Frühwald said at last. "No reason to be," the man said. "Your wife is paralysed and mine has paranoid schizophrenia. We've both been dealt our fair share."

"Where's she being treated?" Frühwald asked.

"In Graz," the man said. "Someone was recommended to us."

They've found each other, Horn thought – men who are suffering on account of their wives. The group is fulfilling its function. Graz is a beautiful city, Elfriede Kirschner said, nice people, the Schloßberg with its beautiful view, and good doctors. It wasn't surprising his daughter was being difficult, she said, having a paranoid schizophrenic must be a terrible burden on the whole family, especially the children.

Foster daughter, the man said, strictly speaking she was a foster daughter, from a province in south-west India, which threw up problems of its own, of course. For instance, her younger sister hadn't been able to cope with it in the end – the reorientation, the social dislocation and the latent xenophobia which still existed here. She'd gone into decline, both mentally and physically, and when his wife became ill they'd had to send her back. The older one was still here and doing almost nothing else but indulging in oppositional behaviour. She wasn't speaking to him or his wife any more, went to school as and when she fancied, and spent entire days shut away in her room. He was part of this "pray and work" society like most of the rest of them, and having to put up with trying circumstances was water off a duck's back to him. But right now he no longer had a clue what to do. He's beginning to let his guard down now, Horn thought, when he feels helpless he casts off his arrogance.

"How old is she?" Elfriede Kirschner said.

"Thirteen," the man said. "And two months."

After this they spoke briefly about the difficulties of being an adolescent, a little more about the difficulties of being the parents of adolescents, but they spent most of the time recalling how it had been when they themselves, aged thirteen, had shut themselves off in their rooms all day long, not communicating at all with the adult world, not even with obscene gestures. Kurt Frühwald spoke of his grandfather's powerful status and Maria Reintaler of how unbearably conservative her mother had been in some things, hairstyles for instance. In the middle of all this Elfriede Kirschner suddenly said she felt awful but she'd forgotten the name of the man, the foster father, and she hoped this wasn't the first sign of dementia. "Possner," the man said, "Armin Possner." His wife was called Erika and his daughter Fanni, in case anybody was interested. The mood had relaxed, Horn was happy with the level of communication and mutual burden-sharing from the group, and at the end of the session he remarked how surprised he was that nobody had complained about the flickering light. "We're discreet and well mannered," Max Reintaler said. The others laughed.

*

When Horn turned on his mobile again it showed two missed calls. Tobias and an unknown number. Tobias never called. All of a sudden Horn was worried. The words *epidural haematoma* and *Gyrus precentralis* flashed through his mind.

"Is there anything wrong with Irene?" he asked.

"What makes you say that?" Tobias's voice was faint.

"Why are you mumbling? Have you been asleep again?"

"Just shut up. It's Mimi." Horn felt hot again.

"What's wrong with Mimi? Has she been run over?"

"Christ, you've got disaster on the brain. She looks weird and sometimes she makes these movements like she's stoned."

"Stoned?"

Her leg keeps on giving way, Tobias explained, it was just her right hind one, he'd been watching. You noticed it particularly when she was trying to negotiate obstacles. The thing with her eyes was even stranger. When he looked at her he could tell something was wrong, but he didn't know what. "She's squinting," Horn said.

"What makes you say that?"

"It was the impression I got. She's also irritable."

"True. So what does that tell us?"

"How am I supposed to know?"

"You're the doctor. Expert in all kinds of nutters and drunks."

There are fundamental physiological differences between cats and human beings, Horn said, we need a vet here. As it didn't sound life-threatening he should wait until he got back. Tobias grunted and hung up, just like that. Moron, Horn thought.

He walked home via Gaiswinkler Straße and Achenallee. The sky above the town was flecked with orange fleecy clouds. To the south-west the rim of the Kammwand mountain was shining white. Seats had been set out in the gardens of the housing development and the first lanterns lit. I'm desperate for Irene, Horn thought, for her voice, the noises she makes as she moves through the house. I want her to be there when I get home. I'd like to share a glass of wine with her and put my nose in her hair. She's my wife. It makes me nervous when there are tenors around her.

He had just turned off the main road when his mobile rang. "Has she bitten you? Or is her leg giving way again?" he said. The voice at the other end did not belong to Tobias. Nobody had bitten her, thank God, the woman said, and she hadn't recently come across anyone whose leg was giving way either. Her name was Eleonore Bitterle, she was a policewoman, and if she wasn't mistaken, he was a psychiatrist who understood children. If that was what she thought then there must be some truth to it, he said. "What do you think about this?" she asked. "A child gets beaten, on his face, on his back, on his arms, and when he's asked who did

34

it, he says: Something black." Horn said nothing. "Any ideas?" she said after a while. "Something black beats up a child," he said. Nothing else came into his mind. The boy was seven years old and due to be questioned the next day. Might he be able to come along to police headquarters? "In the afternoon," he said. "Three o'clock."

The sun had now vanished. It was difficult to make out the terrain, so Raffael Horn decided against the shortcut. Who would go around beating up seven-year-olds? Stupid question, he thought. Then he thought of Tobias, lying asleep on his bed, the blob of saliva at his lips, and how he had called because he was worried about Mimi. Tobias had been tired, he thought, and even more facetious than usual. Again something niggled at the back of his mind. It was connected with what his son had said about the cat. All of a sudden he knew what it was. He quickened his pace.

THREE

It was many years since he had needed an alarm clock. No matter what time he had gone to bed the night before, the following morning he would watch the dawn creep into his bedroom, through the gap beneath the door, through the tiny holes in the roller blind at the window. He knew that trying to go back to sleep again was pointless, so he had trained himself not to even think about it. He lay on his back, stretched his legs and thought about all kinds of things, about the mood in his team, about what was happening on the drug scene in Furth, and about whether the Weghaupt boy had been pushed from the scaffolding or not. Charlotte, his daughter, had been in touch, too. She had been away for a year and a half and had not given a reason for wanting to come and see him. Like all sixteen-year-olds she probably needed money.

Kovacs reached his arm out to the right and felt around the empty side of the bed. Marlene wasn't there. Sometimes there were things you knew, but still you had to make sure. That's what children did, and nobody thought anything of it. She spends at least every other night here, he thought, she cooks for me, she plans our holidays, and I need to try summoning her to cope when she's not here; that's what it's come to. After his wife had left him for a dapper-looking chap from Upper Austria he had sworn he would never let himself get into another relationship. He started drinking, beer mainly, eating rubbish, and in the end he was chucking his guts up on a daily basis. A walrus-faced internist pushed a tube down his throat, said "gastritis", and strongly urged him to find a psychotherapist and change his life. He went to Szarah and Lefti's, ate red lentil soup and yoghurt with fresh coriander, and changed his tipple to peppermint tea. Psychotherapy could go hang as far as he was concerned. Nine months later while investigating a burglary he met Marlene Hanke, the owner of the only second-hand shop in Furth. Even though she had been extremely cautious following the end of her own marriage, she eventually allowed herself to enter a businesslike relationship for the purpose of mutual sexual gratification. It worked pretty well; sex once or twice a week with the usual ups and downs. Without noticing it, he had become quite fond of her, and one day it was no longer her breasts and smooth incisors which were the chief objects of his desire, but the rolls of fat on her hips, the way she clenched her fists when she was angry, and her wonderfully tinny laugh. Or after we've made love, the way she rolls onto her side and pushes her back towards me invitingly when she sees that I'm lying here wide awake at night, Kovacs thought, and I can snuggle up to her for a more appealing type of insomnia. This was precisely what he was missing at that moment. I'll give her a call, he thought, and he felt like a small child that wants its mother immediately. He pulled back the blanket. If there was one thing he did not need in life right now it was a mother.

*

At the fountain outside the housing blocks of the Walzwerk estate a young, dark-haired man was sitting asleep. Kovacs did not wake him. It was warm enough. The man, drugged up to the eyeballs, was probably a crony of Sharif Erdoyan, the Sheriff. If you ever asked any of them a question none of them knew a thing. *Cinn* perhaps, Kovacs thought, the new herbal drug. Someone from his team should get onto it, Sabine Wieck would be best: she could do

37

with boosting her reputation. Anyway, the other two were hopelessly overworked – George Demski with the international child porno-graphy business, which meant he was forever dashing all over the place; and Eleonore Bitterle, who still seized on the minutest thing and, if in doubt, made it a matter for the Furth criminal police.

The streets were empty. Kovacs drove westwards along the northern side of the lake. When he reached the edge of town he put his foot down. At half past three on a Thursday morning his colleagues in the traffic department would still be snoring, for certain. At the entrance to the village of Waiern he overtook a moped which was swerving from side to side. The rider was wearing a black half-face helmet. Judging by his clothes he was an older man. Kovacs stopped in the car park by the landing stage. A spring night peopled with suspicious characters, he thought: a young Turkish lad under the influence of drugs, a drunk old man and an unwashed criminal commissar. He looked up at the sky. The old favourites: Daneb in Cygnus, Altair in Aquila and, almost at the zenith, Vega in Lyra. Insomniacs like him were able to see the Summer Triangle already in April.

A dirt track led through a strip of sparse meadow to the dinghies. They were secured by chains to a low concrete wall. Kovacs undid his padlock, fetched his boat, threw in his rod case, net and tackle box, and jumped aboard. As soon as he had set up the oars and taken the first stroke he started to feel good.

The wind was still and the lake was a smooth expanse before him, like a mirror. He rowed out to the middle, towards the Sankt Christoph lighthouse. Apart from the first signs of the dawn in the east, it was still dark. He switched on the headlamp, opened the plastic box, and took out a white rubber fish with golden speckles. He assembled the shorter of the two rods, fastened on the multiplier reel and attached the lure to the line. Then he flicked open the lock and cast. Everything was the same as usual: the short, sharp plop as the weighted head of the rubber fish hit the surface of the water. Then imagining it descending, determined and energetic, in a long, oblique line. He counted to nine, flicked back the lock, and began to row carefully. Others counted to ten or thirteen or twenty; from childhood he had harboured the idea that multiples of three were magical. Three, nine, twenty-seven – these were his numbers. He manoeuvred the boat westwards at first, broadly following the axis of the lake, and then took a wide arc back towards the northern shore. This was the most likely spot for predators – pike, sander and char. He kept checking the line tension with his finger. Every few hundred metres he reeled in the lure and cast again.

"Why don't women go fishing?" he asked Marlene once, and her reply was that it obviously had something to do with a specific male disorder, and in any case, women didn't find it so easy to bludgeon living things to death. He had once read that hunting was all about aggression and angling about sexuality; that was about as smart as saying that the whole of life was about sexuality. The simpler truth was that women got cold easily and never stopped talk-ing; neither of these was particularly desirable for going fishing. He did not say this to Marlene, not least because she had recently attended a frightfully expensive filleting course run by a celebrity chef, just to please him.

It was getting cold. This was probably why such thoughts had entered his head. The sky above Furth was turning a delicate shade of yellow, and close to the shore a thin layer of mist had settled above the water. There were no other boats to be seen. He was casting more frequently now, parallel to the shoreline, and each time he reeled in again quickly. This kept his circulation going.

He felt the bite after he had stopped expecting one, just by Waiern, at a spot where a narrow stream flowed into the lake. The

39

lure moved horizontally at first, and then plunged straight down. The pull was so strong that Kovacs had difficulty loosening the reel lock to prevent the line from snapping. A sander, he thought, a powerful bugger. He was delighted. It could not be anything else. The salmonids in the lake, char and trout, took it half a metre down at most and could never summon such force; pike could be substantially bigger, but were passive in a struggle and gave up easily; while carp never went for rubber lures in the first place.

What he finally hauled onto the boat in his net was a huge chub, silver and shining, as thick as his forearm, and maybe three-quarters of a metre long, with eyes the size of thumbnails. Still Kovacs felt dissatisfied. True, he had never caught such a splendid white fish, but these creatures had millions of bones. "A non-predatory fish that behaves like a predator deserves to die, you know that," he said, dropping the beast to the floor of the boat. The chub made a rasping sound. "You can speak, can you?" Kovacs asked. He put on a cotton glove to give himself a better grip, and took the long-handled hook remover from his box. The rubber lure was in fairly deep, but it came out of the gullet relatively easily. "There you go," Kovacs said, lifting the creature with the net and heaving it back into the lake. The fish shimmered red in the rising sun before vanishing into the depths.

*

Kovacs took a hot shower, put on fresh clothes and made a pot of tea. Before leafing through the newspaper he called Marlene. I feel bad doing this, he thought, but I have no choice. "Are you in the shop already?" he asked. What on earth did he think she might be doing in the shop at half past six in the morning, she replied, perhaps he could enlighten her. And she might also point out that he had rung the landline, her flat indeed, so unless he'd installed some crafty diverting equipment his question was doubly strange. "I'm going senile," he said. "I'm sorry." She said senility didn't come into it; he was merely exhibiting fundamental husband-like qualities: being clingy and behaving like a zombie. And this behaviour was getting more extreme.

"A zombie? You're pissed off with me."

Pissed off was not quite right, she said, at that very moment she had her tights on her left leg, but not yet on her right – in case he wanted to know the precise details – so she was not pissed off, but in a rather delicate state of limbo. "I caught a chub," Kovacs said.

"A what?"

"A chub."

She was silent for a few seconds, then said, "Hold on a second. Just so I know. A criminal or a fish?"

"Fish," he said.

"So what? You're always catching fish."

"Not chub."

Did this mean that a chub was the albacore tuna or blue marlin of Lake Furth? Could you only eat it by risking your life, like the pufferfish? Would he mind explaining what was so special about this fish?

"He's an imposter," Kovacs said. "A *what*?" Marlene asked. "A non-predator that sort of thinks it's a predator, and which sometimes eats its own fry."

"Don't like the sound of that," she said, and he replied that nature had punished it by giving it so many bones that it was totally unsuitable for eating, so on that score she had nothing to fear. "That's a relief," she said. So, to recap, he had called to tell her about a fish he had caught but wouldn't eat because of its complicated personality and excess of bones.

"Exactly," he said. "Did you kill it?" she asked.

"No."

"No? Do you mean it's still swimming around, trying to dupe the other fish and eating its own children?"

41

"That's right."

"Excellent, Herr Commissar!"

It's a spectacular fish nonetheless, Kovacs thought. But there was something else he had to tell her.

"What's that?"

"Charlotte's coming."

"Charlotte? When?"

"Tomorrow, I fear."

"*Tomorrow*? Great!" She was assuming he'd come up with something for that weekend which, if her memory served her correctly, they had planned to spend together. Having said that, she pointed out that she was only acquainted with Charlotte from photographs, and he knew the score with daughters of divorced fathers and their new girlfriends. Kovacs suddenly felt a fit of giggles bubbling up inside him, without a clue where it was coming from. "You could always go fishing," he said before snorting with laughter. "I'll lend you my boat." She hung up.

Kovacs poured himself a cup of tea. As he buttered a slice of bread he pictured Marlene putting on her tights, combing her hair, and uttering a steady flow of short, irate sentences. I'm a wretched father, he thought, and I love this woman.

*

He walked along past the Walzwerk estate towards the centre of town. The morning traffic had not yet built up. I feel like an officer on the beat, he thought, the operational side of law and order. He liked living in this area, even if the basic idea of social integration which was the premise behind the Walzwerk project had not really worked. The three former factory buildings were inhabited by Bobos between the ages of twenty-five and forty, most of them with an attachment to the proletariat that was more sentimental than anything else. They pranced around their loft apartments and penthouse flats, while the former workers' quarters were home to the underdogs: people on social benefits, migrant families and single mothers, all with exactly the same story – alcohol, domestic violence, if you divorce me you'll never see me again, child benefit. The first lot installed new alarm systems or C.C.T.V. cameras every week; the others would smash their car wing mirrors. Kovacs was very grateful not to belong to either of these groups. Because of his job he earned the respect of everyone on the estate, even the members of the Turkish underground who kept their distance from him. Given that he had bought his flat in Hall B just after the development had been launched, when prices were still reasonable and there was no sign yet of the smarty-pants set with their free-standing Philippe Starck bathtubs and holidays to Vietnam, he was clearly not one of them either.

The young man who had been sleeping by the fountain a few hours earlier had gone; he was probably in bed by now. What was *cinn*? A kind of herbal crack? Or just ground cinnamon bark, as some people claimed? Cinn from cinnamon? The drug scene worried Kovacs. Although the Sheriff said he had everything under control, for a while now he had appeared nervous. Some-body else was pulling strings in the market, and nobody had a clue who it was. It had started in people's flats with cocaine that was especially pure and twenty per cent cheaper than the norm, followed by events: raves and large birthday bashes and parties. Apart from the cocaine, different types of ecstasy had popped up, the classic round tabs, green ones stamped with pictures of clowns, or purple lozenges with tiny elephants on them. The people at ChEckiT, the drugs advisory service, were amazed at the quality, or rather the chemical manufacture of the narcotics, as they called it, and the Sheriff had put himself on a war footing. Now not a single party took place without his people on duty, he had eyes and ears everywhere, and yet the alien gear still turned up, each time, as if from nowhere. Sometimes someone would say that Keyser Soze,

43

the bloodthirsty avenger from "The Usual Suspects", must be the brains behind it all. The Sheriff did not find this funny.

The barriers came down just before Ludwig Kovacs reached the level crossing. A bad omen, he thought, at the same time feeling ashamed for being so superstitious. He climbed over the bar and crossed the tracks. A woman with grey hedgehog-like hair stared at him angrily from her Fiat. He gave her a friendly nod. Idiot, he thought, I'm police. As he passed the abbey he met a group of Benedictine monks. He recognised one of them, Joseph Bauer. They said he was a complete nutter. Apparently he listened to music on his iPod while celebrating mass. He claimed it helped banish his acoustic hallucinations. Even so, two years ago Bauer had played a key role in solving the murder of an old man. Back then Kovacs had not thought him mad at all, quite the opposite in fact. It was only at the funeral that he had behaved a little oddly.

Kovacs crossed the triangular Rathausplatz and walked down the short avenue of chestnut trees that led off it. Then he took the turning towards the lake. Crates of cherry tomatoes and heads of lettuce were being unloaded outside the supermarket. Yesterday's menu at *La Piccola Cucina* had included sea bass on a bed of rosemary potatoes and lamb ravioli; it was written on the board by the entrance. Hunger. He wondered whether it was his turn to bring breakfast. No, it was not.

*

When he opened the door to the commissariat he was met by the smell of coffee. "Want one?" Eleonore Bitterle's voice. "Please." He went into his office, slipped off his jacket and took his notepad from the desk. Always the same routine, he thought, every day, like an obsessive old man. He perched on the windowsill and started to think. He would normally use this time before the morning meeting to organise himself and decide what was important and what was not. In the new housing development in north Furth, two flats had been burgled and cleared out, right in the middle of the morning. The usual things had gone: jewellery, watches, a laptop, some cash. The only odd thing to have disappeared was a collection of model cars from the fifties. The burglars had opened the door without making a scratch. At the station there had been a second incidence of a man asking some schoolgirls whether he could photograph them naked. It would only take half an hour and he would pay them 50 euro. Staying calm, the girls had taken out their mobiles, and the man had run off. He was shortish, stout, middle-aged and wore green-rimmed glasses – the girls had given a precise description. And finally there was the Florian Weghaupt business. The young builder's apprentice had fallen sixty metres from scaffolding while carrying out insulation work on the facade of the Neptun insurance company offices. He had struck the edge of the pavement and died on impact. A passer-by had claimed that the man toppled over the railing with his arms stretched out in front of him, shouting something; she was quite sure she'd seen a second person standing right behind him before he fell. This contradicted the statement given by Weghaupt's two colleagues, who said that all three men were busy lagging and filling on different levels; each man had been allocated his own floor and nobody was near anybody else.

"There you go." Eleonore Bitterle put a cup of coffee in front of him, black with a touch of sugar. "You should read your e-mails today, just for once," she added. Kovacs looked up from his notepad. "How far has George got with the Weghaupt case?" he asked. "No idea," she said. "He flew to Berlin yesterday evening; you ought to know that." It's true, Kovacs thought, I really am going senile. About a year ago George Demski had joined an international working group to combat child pornography. He had been summoned to Berlin because of a meta-analysis he had produced of criminal psychological studies on biographies of abusers. The article, which

45

he had published in a sociology journal, was the by-product of a correspondence course that he had been doing for years at a Belgian university. Whenever he was asked what, in fact, he was studying, he would say "everything", and if anybody tried to delve a little deeper, he would scowl. While Demski was committed and brilliant at his job, he had of late increasingly been neglecting his day-to-day work "I'll give him a call," Kovacs said. "Good luck," Bitterle replied. Arms crossed, she was standing in the doorway, lanky and gaunt, her grey hair in a bun. She suffered most from Demski's absence. He had been her partner, her alter ego, especially after her husband's death when she had more or less cut off contact with other people. The two of them were known as Maigret and Mrs Brain, he on account of his French mother, she because of her analytical mind. Now he was in Berlin and she was lonely.

"What was that about e-mails?"

"Read them, please."

"Why?"

"My God!" She rolled her eyes. It was to do with Stephan Szigeti, she said.

"The plastics man?"

"Yes, him." Istvan Szigeti had come to Austria from Hungary in his mother's belly, an inter-uterine immigrant, as he was wont to say. He was born and grew up in Vienna, studied petrochemistry, and worked for several years as a university assistant with polyhalogenated polymers. Finally, after an argument with the head of his institute at the university, he left Vienna and rented an empty warehouse in Furth's industrial estate. Nothing happened for a while, then he brought in machines on an ancient juggernaut – where from, nobody knew – employed a handful of labourers, and after a few months started manufacturing petrol canisters. The firm now employed one hundred and eighty people and was producing all sorts of plastic containers, from tiny bottles for eye-drops to oil tanks. Whatever people had to say about a rags-to-riches story, he was a successful man, and nobody held it against him that when he started the company he changed his name from Istvan to Stephan with a "ph".

Szigeti had called early the previous evening, Eleonore Bitterle explained. He was completely beside himself. His son had been beaten at school, in the face and on the back, something had to be done immediately. Was it a teacher or another pupil? she asked. Neither, he replied, and when she asked whether it might have been the caretaker, he started screaming down the phone. People never took him seriously, he was fed up with the impertinent, wishy-washy cynicism in this country, he wanted to speak to her supervisor, immediately – the usual, basically. With a great deal of patience she had calmed the man down and eventually discovered that, although the incident had happened in lesson time, nobody was sure exactly where it had occurred, probably somewhere between the classroom and the Szigetis' house, and that the boy himself had not said anything except that he'd been beaten by something black. No, he wasn't injured, not physically anyway, he was sitting on the floor of his bedroom, shell-shocked, obstinately playing with his Gameboy. She said she didn't know whether it should be a case for the criminal police department, and he said he understood that, but insisted that his son be questioned, and whatever happened he was going to press charges against the unknown person. To be on the safe side, she had spoken to Raffael Horn and asked him for some expert advice, so that later on nobody could claim that all the police were capable of was re-traumatising children.

Eleonore Bitterle stood there in her pleated trousers and a white, long-sleeved blouse; yet again she was prudence personified. In theory a godsend for any man, Kovacs thought; in practice a godsend for me. He took a sip of his coffee.

"What's that got to do with my e-mails?"

"Szigeti sent it in writing, in four versions, each one more detailed than the next, to me, to you and to Eyltz."

"To Eyltz?"

"Things that get sent to the chief of police are bound to be dealt with more rapidly – he's on the right track there. Perhaps they hunt together."

Not all men hunt, Kovacs thought, some go fishing. A brief glance at Eleonore Bitterle's green eyes was all it took to convince him that she wouldn't be the least bit interested in what he'd caught an hour ago, a chub, a trout, or a shark. Philipp Eyltz, the town's chief of police, wore dark-blue blazers with gold buttons, hand-stitched shoes and a signet ring bearing his family's coat of arms. He loved to gloat over his collection of hand-chased hunting rifles mounted on a wall in his house, but was only ever seen out hunting if there was a press photographer in the vicinity.

"So what did Eyltz say?" Kovacs asked. "Top priority," Bitterle said. Of course. One of those spoilt brats from a frightfully important family gets the hiding they've probably long deserved, and suddenly there's intervention from on high. Kovacs could feel himself getting angry. She interrupted him. "Just think about what you're saying – I'm dead against children being hit." Kovacs took a deep breath and raised his hands in conciliation. "And the boy isn't even seven," she said. My daughter's sixteen, he thought, and in the past five years there were probably two occasions when I might have hit her . . . in theory.

The front door was pushed open and they could hear what sounded like a heated discussion. "Who's bringing Sabine today?" Kovacs asked. Bitterle put her head back, glanced into the corridor and just had time to take a step backwards before Mauritz, all hundred plus kilos of him, appeared in the doorway. "I'm not doing it!" he bellowed with a crimson face. "Wouldn't even consider it!"

48

"Forensics is being difficult," Kovacs said. "What am I supposed to do?" George Demski had left him written instructions, which he regarded as an impertinence in itself, Mauritz said, "and now this!" "Now what?" Kovacs asked. "Weghaupt," Sabine Wieck hissed from behind Mauritz, and grimaced. He didn't know the details, Kovacs said, either Weghaupt jumped or he was pushed, that was the only question. Exactly, Mauritz said, agitated; despite the fact that the scene of the incident had been photographed thoroughly the first time around, now Demski had had the scaffolding sealed off and was instructing forensics to look at the whole thing again. "And?" Kovacs asked. "I'm not doing it," Mauritz barked. "I'm not going up there!" "Is this a body mass problem?" Kovacs asked. Mauritz did not answer.

"Or one of coordination?" In the background Wieck covered her eyes. "Fear of heights?" Bitterle asked. "Yes, of course! Stop giving me that stupid look!" He had suffered from it since he was a child, Mauritz said, it had got better over time, but he still couldn't cope with scaffolding and church steeples, and he asked them to please stop pretending they'd never heard of it. "The Hitchcock film where James Stewart climbs up the tower at the end," Kovacs said.

"'Vertigo'."

"There's a blonde at the top."

"Kim Novak."

"Is she dead?"

"Of course she's dead."

"How do you know all this?"

"I'm a single woman who sometimes gets bored," Bitterle said. "So I watch old films that don't have happy endings." If the husband you love dies of bone cancer, Kovacs thought, then you probably do tend to watch old films with unhappy endings. He asked whether there was any hint at the scene that someone else was involved. As good as none, Mauritz replied. *As good as* was crap, Kovacs said, and Mauritz replied that, O.K., there was no sign, no evidence of a physical struggle, no footprints belonging to anybody else. "Was everything examined carefully?" Kovacs asked. Mauritz mimicked biting into his knuckles. "Calm down," Kovacs said. "I know you weren't there." There were some things you had to do yourself if you wanted to be sure. And he definitely didn't have vertigo. He stood up, pushing his chair back to the wall. "What are you doing?" Mauritz asked. "I'm going," Kovacs said.

"Are we that awful?"

"Yes."

"Don't be silly. What are you really doing?"

"I'm going to climb the scaffolding. Someone's got to do it."

"But you're not forensics."

Kovacs did not reply. I'm the boss of a forensics officer with vertigo, he thought. By sealing off the "crime" scene Demski had once again been satisfying his all-consuming need to be absolutely sure, whereas in fact everything had happened as it appeared: the guy had stumbled, slipped and that was it. He certainly hadn't been thinking about Mauritz. He put on his jacket. As he left the room he turned again to Bitterle. "What did Szigeti say about his son?" he asked. "How did he describe him sitting on the floor? Shell-shocked and petulant?" "Obstinate," Bitterle said. "Not petulant. Shell-shocked and obstinate."

"Shell-shocked and obstinate," Kovacs repeated. He thought of Charlotte. It didn't matter whether they were six or sixteen, children were ghastly.

FOUR

I've got a sister. I asked how old she was and they told me she was three and a half. Apparently she comes from the same city as me. I asked what her name was and they said: Susi. I tried using it but she didn't answer to it. They said it's like with a little cat, she has to get used to it first. In our language I said, "My name is Fanni." She closed her eyes and replied with a single word: "Switi". She's thin and tiny and she's got frizzy hair. She keeps closing her eyes. She's got to stop doing that. Keeping your eyes open is the only thing that really matters. It took me a while to understand that.

It's raining. She seems to like it. She's standing on the steps outside the house, looking up at the sky and laughing. The water runs down her neck from her earlobes, in two small streams. "I'll show you everything," I say. She takes my hand.

We walk along Fürstenaustraße towards the lake, past the big houses with sloping gardens and dark glass circles above the doorbells. Those are cameras. "Rich people live here," I say. I don't know if my sister knows what rich means. "We're rich," I say. We've got a glass circle above our doorbell, too. To the left the path branches off into the gorge. A sign says: PROCEED AT YOUR OWN RISK. Beneath the writing are pictures of a baby in a pram, a man in a wheelchair and an old lady with a walking stick. There's a red line through all three of them. I liked that from the moment I first saw it.

Switi stamps in all the puddles. The higher the splash the louder she laughs. It's summer so it doesn't matter. We walk around the long bend until we get to the first viewing platform. Ahead of us is the bluish-green pool from which the stream gushes down, straight into the lake, that's what it looks like. We can hear the whooshing. But we'd have to go further to see the waterfall. I'm going to save it for another time. I point to the Kammwand. "This is what it's like here," I say. "Up there are the mountains, and down there you've got the lake. Back home it's different: up there's the rain, and down there's the thick mud." She looks at me with wide eyes, almost as if she's understood what I'm saying. "There's one thing that's the same," I say. "The town's all around. It's smaller here, but you don't always notice that." Then we turn back.

I stop at the top of the hill. On your left you can see the cliff that looks like an owl. If you're lucky you can hear a train travelling through the mountain at this place. I listen. There isn't one at the moment. The umbrellas are up in front of the hotels, white, bright green and orange. I read her the names of the hotels: Wertzer, Fernkorn and Abendroth. "With a 'th'," I say. "But you won't understand that till you can read." The dwarf goats in the enclosure beside the Fernkorn push against the fence as we walk past. She doesn't seem to notice them. She's looking at the lake the whole time.

At the snack bar in the marina I ask her whether she'd like an ice cream. It takes her a while to understand what I'm saying. She nods and closes her eyes. I get strawberry and chocolate, two cones. "Have you got visitors?" Gino asks. "No," I say, "she's my sister." "I've never seen her before," he says. "What's her name?" "Switi," I say. "Switi," Gino says, "that goes with the ice cream." I don't ask why *Switi* goes with the ice cream. Gino comes from Reggio di Calabria and says his dad's a mafia boss who runs half of Italy. I don't believe a word of it. I'm not even sure he comes from Italy. The ice cream's yummy, that's all that matters.

We walk along the jetty as far as the concrete pillars with the iron rings. Ducks are swimming below us, three big ones and five little ones. One of the big ones has put her foot on her back; it looks funny. Switi points at the ducks and makes rasping sounds. Ahead of us two boats are going back and forth, one with a row of blue dots on her sail, the other with orange stripes. They'll be looking for me, I think, they'll knock on the neighbours' doors and phone around. There'll be a mixture of fear and anger in their faces.

On the way back I tell her the story of the maharaja's daughter who runs away from her parents' palace because she feels like a prisoner. She makes hundreds of friends who protect her from her terrible father and mad mother. When her father's soldiers come near she hides in a pelican's pouch. Although it smells horribly of fish, nobody can find her there. When the pelican takes off and flies around in the sky he opens his bill a little, and through the gap she can look down upon the city, the houses, the beach, the power station with its chimneys, and at the palace she will never return to. Switi doesn't take her eyes off me. I'm sure she understands every word, even though I'm not as fluent in our language as I was. Neither of us cares that her chocolate ice cream is melting and dripping down her T-shirt.

I show her the pharmacist's sign as we walk past it. You can see two dromedaries, a big one and a little one. I haven't got a clue why a pharmacy in Furth am See, of all places, should be called the Dromedary Pharmacy, but sometimes things stray into places where they don't belong. Dromedaries have one hump, normal camels have two – I learned that from this pharmacy. Furth's also got a pharmacy near the station in Bahnhofstraße, but that's just called Station Pharmacy – it doesn't teach you anything. When the door opens suddenly and someone comes out I get a fright. It's Frau Wirth, the lady who runs the kindergarten. Everyone she's taught calls her Tante Lea. I never had her. But she still knows me.

53

"Well, well, who have we got here then?" she asks. That's what child abductors on the telly ask. "I didn't know you had a sister," she says, "what's her name?" "Susi," I say. "Hello, Susi," she says. "How lovely that there are still people who call their daughters Susi." She asks whether Susi will go to kindergarten, and I say I think so.

I wonder to myself what sort of medicine Frau Wirth might have got from the pharmacy – an asthma spray, valium, or ointment for varicose veins. When we turn the corner by the district court I ask Switi whether she, too, thinks that Tante Lea's hair is like a bicycle helmet – stuck onto her head somehow, and making you want to give it a good thump.

When we reach the end of the wall by the abbey she holds out her arms to me. I lift her up and carry her for a while. I can't go for long but she seems happy. We cross the railway line and climb the hill towards the Walzwerk estate. I tell her how Ümid showed me his brother's shisha and how he said he'd used it too, which is a total lie, of course, and how he said his brother would kill him if he found out, and he would have to kill me too, unfortunately, if I told anyone a word of what he'd said. I don't even know Ümid's brother.

On Fürstenaustraße, just before the place where you get a view of our house, we turn left. "From now on it's a secret," I say. "Escape route number one." I've got a thing about escape routes; I've always got to have one, at home, at school, even when we're at the swimming pool. Here we go: start off in the cul-de-sac, go past the florist's and those four houses that all look exactly the same, as far as the yellow factory building with the sliding gates, the windows with small panes and the entrance that nobody knows except me. Head right, as far as the end of the building, and then don't go around the corner but through a gap in the elder bushes and onto a path which starts along the edge of a bank, then there's a wooden board over a small stream, and finally up and across the slope behind the gardens. First there's the one that belongs to Kubiks, the optician, and his wife; then the garden that belongs to old Findenegg with his checked shirts; and, at the end, the one that matters. I stop, put a finger to my lips, and listen. Nothing. They seldom use the garden when the weather's bad. And anyhow, the sheds block the view from the house. I'm ducking nonetheless. At the fourth section of fencing you can push the diamond-mesh to one side and bend it up far enough for someone like me to slip through pretty comfortably. It's even easier for Switi.

On the grass under one of the damson trees is a bird I've never seen before: big, light brown, with black-and-white stripes on its wings. As we go past it raises its beak and fluffs up the feathers on its head. I clap my hands. It takes two hops to the side, over to the square of concrete with the iron ring that's overgrown with weeds, but it doesn't fly away. Switi's not interested. She sits on the wet grass, closes her eyes and rests her head on her knees. I lift her up and carry her to the back door. I open it carefully and listen once more. Again, nothing. I take her hand and lead her to the bedroom. "Stay here," I say. She nods. I tiptoe into the bathroom and fetch the large Lisa Simpson towel with the saxophone on it, so I can dry her. When I come back she's lying on the floor by her bed, asleep. I sit on my beanbag and watch her breathing. "Later I'll show you the house," I say. "Only the ground floor to begin with; not upstairs yet."

FIVE

"You're my saviour," he says softly. Her eyes are closed and she is picturing him looking through her skylight at the treetops and, beyond them, the sun rising at that very moment.

She can feel her lower lip trembling slightly as she breathes. "Are you talking to me or your god?" she asks.

"I didn't want to wake you," he says.

"You didn't. What's the time?"

"Ten to six."

"I've still got a bit of time to save you, then." She opens her arms and turns towards him. He plucks a strand of hair from the corner of her mouth. "You don't take me seriously," he says. "Of course I do," she says. Devils, witches, demons and bucketloads of fear, always the same, she thinks – of course I know I'm your saviour, and of course I take you seriously. She pulls him down on top of her and breathes hot air into the hollow of his collarbone.

"Spring is sort of an imposter," he says. "It makes you feel like everything's going to turn out alright." "But it does," she says feeling for the edge of his shoulder blade. "Someone like you should know that better than anyone."

"Someone like me knows that it's not true."

"Not again. Here, put your hand on my neck."

She can feel his fingertips on the spinous processes of her neck vertebrae. "There's no guarantee," he says. True, she thinks. She imagines them soaring above the clouds, fringed with red from the morning sun, and flying away over the town and the lake, nothing in sight to be frightened of. "I'm going to doze for a couple more minutes," she says, and as she nods off she snuggles up close to him. Sometimes he says that it's simple to drive away his madness; all he needs to do is feel her from head to toe, as many square centimetres of bodily contact as possible, and she likes this, even if it is just another of his psychotic notions.

*

For breakfast he wolfs down spoonfuls of cottage cheese, as always. He maintains that this is the best way for him to stomach his medication. She sits there, taking the occasional sip of her coffee, and looking at him. He makes me feel good, she thinks, it's as simple as that. When he sits there in the morning light, pale and a little slouched, shovelling these little white balls into his mouth, he makes me feel good; the same when he calls and just says "you", and he even makes me feel good when he puts his hand on my neck. Sometimes it's the mad stuff that makes you feel happiest, she thinks, the stuff that makes other people roll their eyes or tap their heads in disbelief.

"What are you thinking about?" he asks.

"Believe me, you don't want to know," she says.

"Why not?"

"You might get angry."

He scoops up a portion of cottage cheese with the spoon and offers it to her. "O.K., O.K." she says, throwing up her hands in submission. "I just had this thought, strange as it may seem, that sometimes it's the mad stuff that makes you feel happiest." He puts down the spoon and stares at her, wide-eyed. "You see," she says, "you're getting angry already." "Rubbish," he says. People were forever mistaken in believing that it was the mad stuff that must make you feel dreadful. On the contrary, he says, it was every-thing else that made you feel dreadful: the people around you,

57

particularly your so-called nearest and dearest, your own history, everything which people might pretentiously call the world or reality. "Then you reconfigure yourself internally and everything becomes bearable," he says.

She nods. Or you go to bed with a Benedictine priest who is a certified Grade A nutter, she thinks.

She remembers how it all began the previous September. She was in the staffroom with a colleague, Ursula Leeb, paying close attention while a number of things were being explained to her, as she was still new to the place, and then at five to eight this monk burst in, singing the "*Dies Irae*" at the top of his voice, and explained that the first day of term was inevitably a day of wrath. She remembers Ursula saying she needn't be scared, he had these episodes, and then he did three or four laps of the room, alternating between singing and greeting his colleagues. When he got to her he paused, looked into her eyes for a second and said, "A new one." He moved on and she felt the relief a patient does following a medical that turns out to be far less intrusive than feared. When she was on her way to her classroom a little later he was waiting in the corridor. "I'm there for anybody who needs help," he said. She had enough composure to ask what gave him the idea that she needed help. It wasn't rocket science, he said, the sleeve of her sweater had ridden up her arm, that's what gave him the idea. She looked down at her forearm and immediately felt blood rush to her face. Not long afterwards she told him the whole story.

"Who actually knows about us now?" she asks.

"My psychiatrist," he says.

"Who else?"

"Don't know. I don't think anybody does."

"How on earth is that possible? What about the abbot, for example? Or your colleagues? Whenever you spend the night with me you miss choral prayers the following morning."

"I used to miss them even before I started spending the night with you."

She takes his word for it and she also believes him when he says that the other padres do not envy his relationship with her. Each one of us has our contacts, he had once explained, some are women, some men. A few of them have children. The order pays, that's it. He scoops the remaining cottage cheese out of the pot with a piece of white bread. She thinks that in moments like these he comes across as perfectly calm and orderly. Some day she will ask him whether he would like to have a child of his own.

*

The bus is half empty. They are earlier than usual. She does not care if people see them together. Young teacher seduces Benedictine priest, she thinks; but that's far from the truth. They sit in one of the back rows. He rummages around in his bag, humming all the while. She grabs his arm. "That's what you were singing a few days ago when we had that spat in the classroom, remember?" He looks confused.

"When Felix went missing."

"You're right." He takes out his iPod, puts the headphones in her ears, does a quick search, and presses play.

Spirit on the water / Darkness on the face of the deep / I keep thinking about you baby / I can't hardly sleep.

"Who's this?" she asks. "God," he says. "His Holy Bobness."

"Stupid question, sorry."

"'Modern Times'," he says, "his last album but one."

God's last album but one, she thinks, he's really lost it. He nudges her in the side. "Why are you grinning?"

"Now you've disturbed my listening," she complains. "There was something about pain." He pulls the headphones out of her ears, and tucks the iPod back into his bag. She knows it is pointless to ask what's wrong. He's toppling over the edge, she thinks, he's plummeting into the abyss and freezing up, from one moment to the next. Nobody's going to save him from that.

They cross Severin bridge, then follow a loop heading westwards along Waldzeller Straße, Rohrweg and back along Seestraße to Rathausplatz. He spends the entire time looking silently out of the window. As soon as they get off she grabs him by the sleeve of his coat. "What are those monks called, the ones who take a vow of silence?" she asks. He turns to her. "Trappists and Carthusians" he says quietly. Then he starts laughing. He's good for me, she thinks, he's so good for me.

*

They are in the large square by the abbey. On the outer wall of the nearest garden a dove is strutting around in circles. "I'll listen to it some other time," she says, holding up her hand when he opens his bag again. He shakes his head. No, not the iPod, he had forgotten to show her something else, a drawing from the last lesson he took with her class.

A dark wave, just one, with a ball on top, she thinks as she takes a look at the piece of paper, a sort of Gaussian normal distribution curve, or perhaps someone in a cape, their arms sticking out to the side. He says they were given the task to draw something to do with Easter, after all Easter was quite soon. Most of them had come up with hares or eggs, as he had expected them to, only Britta did something different. Britta? she asks, and he says, yes, Britta, that was the name of the skinny blonde girl in the front row on the far left, who loved talking about her guinea pigs. To start with she had sat there motionless, bent forward stiffly, and when he asked her, "Maybe do a chicken?" she had shaken her head without saying a word. Then she had grabbed a fat crayon and drawn this, quickly and deliberately.

She frowns. "It's not a guinea pig," she says after a while. No, he says. He had asked Britta what the curve was supposed to be, and she'd said without a moment's hesitation: an owl, a black owl, and he instantly knew that it couldn't be anything else. A brown owl could be black, just for once. "I'm sure she didn't say *owl*," she says, "but *awrl, plack awrl.* She can't say *owl*, even though she sees the speech therapist twice a week." "You're really quite pedantic," he says. "Sometimes it gives me the creeps." She was right, of course, the little girl had not said *owl*, but *awrl*, or maybe even *oowl*, depending on her particular speech impediment, but still it was obvious that it *was* an owl and, in any case, that was not so important.

"So, what are you saying?" she asks.

He says he's certain she heard it from Felix, otherwise what she said made no sense. "What makes no sense?" she asks. "What else did she say?" That she had been beaten on her back, he says, on her back, shoulders and head. The black owl had used a stick to beat her.

It's the small things, Horn thought, it's the things you'd imagine
were trivial. Names you forget, new sweaters you don't show enough
appreciation for, the walking speed you don't try to keep up with.
Sometimes just the adjectives you omit: *wonderful, prudent, grip-
ping.* Or the rolls I've forgotten to buy yet again, he thought. If I
don't drop to my knees in contrition, it's all over. In the end she
yells at me and I criticise her for all those things I've always wanted
to criticise her for.

He had left home ten minutes earlier than usual, seething with
anger and without having had any breakfast. He knew where he
could shove his idea of going to Scotland in the summer, too, she
had shouted after him. Islay, Skye and the Highlands, nothing
more than a thinly disguised piss-up – not with her, thank you very
much. Fine, not with you, he had answered and slammed the car
door behind him. Since then he had not been able to get images of
Irene out of his head, first of her diving between manta rays and
porcupinefish off one of those Maldive islands, and then of her
having sex on a bed strewn with flowers in an air-conditioned
bungalow, both these activities taking place with a dark-haired,
slightly too short tenor with an Italian grandmother and a spare
tyre around the waist. Fine, if that was what she wanted!

He looked around. The meeting room was gradually filling up.
Hrachovec was sitting on his right, spreading a croissant with
apricot jam. He seemed in a good mood, but he had been like that

continually ever since he had landed the junior doctor job. Natalie Bernert, the ergotherapist, stretched her extraordinary long neck over the table, chatting as ever to Renate Mutz, the social worker. Lisbeth Schalk was wearing a new, egg-yolk yellow Moncler jacket and took a couple of seconds longer than normal to sit down. Günther and Vessy looked tired, but so they should after a night shift. Last to come through the door was Leonie Wittmann, rings around her eyes, and her fists clenched. She fell into the vacant chair beside Horn. Two irate women in the same morning – how am I supposed to deal with that? he thought.

Basically, everything had been quiet until just before three, Günther reported. Sabrina had slept through thanks to her extra medication, Fehring had taken himself to bed, and evidently none of the others had been minded to get up to any mischief. Until this Marcus came in and the delicious peace was disturbed. "Which Marcus?" Horn asked. A young man, Hrachovec explained, twenty-one years old, a timber engineering student from an ordinary family. Nobody knew why he had tied a length of climbing rope to the chandelier hook on the sitting-room ceiling in the middle of the night, placed his neck in an amateurish noose and then kicked a chair from under him. He probably hung there for a while, for a few seconds at least, becoming hypoxic, until the hook could take the weight no longer, and the young man came crashing down with the crystal chandelier. "Who heard him first?" Horn asked. "His mum," Vessy said. "Mums always hear those sorts of things first."

"And?"

"She came into the room and laughed," said Vessy, turning red. "Then she asked if he'd hurt himself," Hrachovec added. He took a bite of his croissant. "She did *what*?" Horn said. "Laughed," Günther said. The woman, who seemed to have a big screw loose herself, told them that she'd found the whole thing a bit like a Monty Python film – a suicide everything conspires against, including the

63

ceiling hook – it was just so funny, surely they could see that? In any case Marcus had said that he wasn't in any pain, and she could see at once that he hadn't lost consciousness at any point. "It's Marcus with a 'C'," Vessy said. "Marcus with what?" Horn asked. "With a 'C', as in Caesar," Günther said. "Please don't write it with a 'K'!" Vessy muttered something in Russian, and Hrachovec, who had swallowed his mouthful, said that fortunately the neighbour from the flat below had come up soon afterwards. As he enquired about the cause of the noise, he caught sight of the man sitting on the floor, the crystal chandelier and a length of rope beside him, and ignoring the woman's protests he immediately called for an ambulance and the police.

It had been tricky from the moment they arrived on the ward. The woman had revealed that her son had the occasional strange turn, probably as a result of the cocktail of alcohol and energy drinks that he kept on knocking back, but really, they didn't want to embarrass themselves, nobody here had a death wish, least of all her son, so all this talk of being admitted to hospital must be some kind of mistake. Marcus kept on gazing up at the ceiling, as if this were a nervous tic of his, and when asked whether he would stay on the ward voluntarily, he had shaken his head and finally uttered a single sentence: "I'm a laughing stock."

Horn turned to his right. "And then you came in."

Leonie Wittmann replied that, for better or for worse, the telephone had rung at ten to four, the very point which determined whether her night's sleep would be relaxing or not. But what did it matter? On call was on call, no matter what the clock said. In the car her anger at this mother of a laughing stock, who was totally in denial, had risen to such a level that when she arrived at the hospital the only options open to her were either to give the woman a good thump, or else to keep a lid on her aggression and see the whole thing through, coolly and according to the letter of the law. "She

64

said precisely one sentence, did our consultant," Günther said, grinning. Horn looked at Leonie Wittmann out of the corner of his eye. When there's that hint of irony in her face she's quite beautiful, he thought, despite her straw-like hair and predator's teeth. There was an expectant silence. "What, do you really think I can remember?" she growled finally. One sentence, Horn thought, I bet it began with *Please be aware that* . . . "What?" Leonie Wittmann asked. I'm thinking aloud again, without knowing it, Horn thought. "I just wanted to make a suggestion," he said.

"What suggestion?"

"About the sentence you might have uttered."

"And?"

"I bet it began with *Please be aware that* . . ."

"Maybe it did. But what else?"

"Haven't got a clue."

"Please be aware that your authority ends here, your son will be treated according to the provisions of the mental health act, and Furth district court now has full jurisdiction. Goodbye, see you tomorrow, it's four o'clock in the morning," Günther said. Leonie Wittmann thanked him with a nod of her head. "That's exactly what I said." The woman had been escorted out and the son given something to eat, she said. She herself had stayed there; it wasn't worth going home.

"So what's the background?" Horn asked.

"A long period of despair," she said. "As always. What twenty-year-old hangs himself from a hook on the ceiling? – Someone who's been sentenced to an early death by life. He can sense it, and there comes a point where he stops trying to fight it." Horn said nothing. He imagined Leonie Wittmann coming into a room in which a young man was hanging from the ceiling, very calmly walking up to him, grabbing him around the waist, and lifting him up while somebody else removed the noose from his neck. He imagined her letting him slide down until she was supporting him under the armpits, his head sinking onto her shoulder with half-closed eyes, and the vivid realisation that nothing more could be done. That's why I've wanted her, Horn thought, because she can do things like lift people out of nooses.

Horn had not regretted for a second his recommendation that the hospital employ this short woman, who already in her job interview had been remarkably prickly and determined to reveal nothing about her private life. That was nine months ago and they still knew very little about Leonie Wittmann – she had done part of her training in a specialist forensic clinic in Hamburg and the rest at an adolescent psychiatry department in eastern Switzerland; she was divorced; and she had a grey parrot by the name of Schopenhauer, who apparently could cite entire passages from *The World as Will and Representation*. Some people claimed she was a psychoanalyst, others spoke of a daughter studying sculpture in Vienna who made large art objects out of waste packaging. Neither of these assertions had been verified. Besides, I can't picture her together with a man, Horn thought.

"What's he doing now?" he asked. Leonie Wittmann was confused. "What's who doing?"

"This Marcus chap. What's he up to?"

"He's sleeping," Hrachovec said. "I gave him an infusion with a few vials of diazepam. Click – he went out like a light!" Hrachovec brushed croissant crumbs from his shirt. Click, Horn thought – there comes a point in your psychiatric training where you need to be certain that you've got things under control; putting people to sleep is the quickest way to achieve this. A jab, a little infusion or, if it's not complicated, a few bitter drops, and they're in your hands, snoring away. Whenever Hrachovec was on the night shift, half the ward would still be asleep the following morning. Lisbeth Schalk and a number of nurses did not approve. Horn had decided to let it go. As a psychiatrist you were also an anaesthetist, simple as that. Hrachovec had become a perfectly decent psychiatric anaesthetist; he logged everything properly, gave the correct doses, and when people woke up the worst was usually over. He still needed to learn how to communicate, Horn sometimes thought, but that was the most difficult thing of all.

"Any other business?" he asked, and closed the morning meeting by reading out a statement from the management referring to thefts in the hospital, which requested that staff lock their offices on leaving them; and also the announcement of a scientific conference on new methods for the treatment of eating disorders. Nobody wanted to attend, but that was less to do with the subject, and more to do with the fact that the conference was taking place in Innsbruck. Nobody ever wanted to go to Innsbruck – Salzburg, yes; Graz, yes; abroad, definitely; people would even travel to Linz. Perhaps it was because of the mountains: both Innsbruck and Furth had them right on their doorstep. The Viennese, Hamburgers and their Hungarian colleagues went to Innsbruck. They all thought the mountains were fantastic. Maybe I'll go myself, Horn thought. "I'll think about it too," said Lisbeth Schalk, opening her Moncler jacket. Horn was startled. Not again, he thought, I don't even notice I'm doing it. Four or five years ago Irene had first pointed out to him that he thought aloud. Like a child, she had said, or an old man, and he soon realised that it had something to do with Michael's imminent moving out, which she was longing for, but he wasn't in the least. It's always the same, he thought, when something makes me tense I think aloud, whether I know what the problem is or not. To distract himself he stared at Lisbeth Schalk's top: yellow, with a stripe of cornflower blue across the middle. He imagined what it would be like to go to Innsbruck with her and skip the talks. First they would walk hand in hand through meadows, and then shag in the hotel.

He put two fingers to his lips, just to be on the safe side.

*

Andrea Emler, the secretary, had placed a photograph on the desk of her daughter in her first communion dress. Horn was confused and wondered for a brief moment whether it was now his memory that was playing up. Andrea gave an embarrassed chuckle. She knew that the ceremony was not for six weeks and that she was a bit neurotic, but she had worried that all the nice dresses would be sold out, so she had got in there early. Her daughter hadn't minded, and to make things easier they had also photographed her straightaway. The girl looked like her mother: short, blonde and healthy, with an air of determination and a hint of mistrust in her expression. She was holding her baptismal candle in her right hand, and in her left a wicker basket with yellow and white flowers. "Very pretty!" Horn said. He thought about his own first communion, all those years ago, in the sun-drenched village church, and about how everybody said how alike he and Tobias were, tall, lanky and a little out of proportion, whereas Michael looked like Irene. Despite this the two of them had had their difficulties for years now, and he sometimes wondered whether Tobias was actually his, or maybe the son of a tenor, for example. Andrea Emler burst out laughing. Horn gave a start. She put her hand on his upper arm and pointed at the door crack from which a white toy rabbit disappeared that very instant. "It's Herbert," she said, "he's so childish." Herbert was a powerful, teddy-bear-like nurse who had once trained to be a chef. He's got a crush on her like a teenager, and she laughs like a twelve-year-old girl, Horn thought. These are the things I find comforting.

He took a look at his schedule. Visits, therapy meeting, two outpatients. Unremarkable and straightforward. Something was missing. He had no idea what it was.

*

They went to the end of the ward. Before turning right into the first room, they paused by the long corridor window and looked out over the river and the town. "'One Flew over the Cuckoo's Nest'," Raimund said. "Pardon?" Christina asked, and he said that just then it felt as if they were all in the film, a group of madmen who walk along to the end of a corridor where they stand in silence by a pane of bulletproof glass, staring at the clouds. Christina looked up at the ceiling. Raimund said she could roll her eyes as much as she liked, but it would not change the fact that in *this* film it was the ward sister who was really the evil one, and Herbert tapped his forehead.

"Are you going to cope?" Horn asked, grasping the door handle. Raimund cast him a blank look.

"With what?"

"In there's a young lady who's waiting for you to lose your cool."

Raimund attempted a smile. If he, Horn, meant that thing with the Internet, he needn't worry, he was enough of a professional. "Do you want to talk about it?" Horn asked. Raimund shook his head. "Talking is silver," he said.

Sabrina was sitting on the bed with her knees up, listening to music. "Where's your room-mate?" Horn asked. The girl turned away without saying a word. "Fine, forget it," Horn said, making to go back out again.

"I sent her to do some shopping." She pulled out one of her white earphones.

"Shopping?"

"Razor blades and painkillers."

She looks like she could be Isabelle Huppert's daughter, Horn thought, red-haired with wild freckles. "Painkillers?" he asked. "Yes. It hurts when you cut yourself, you know." She had never been given any decent painkillers by doctors and nurses, and in any case she got fed up with having to beg for them the whole time.

"What are you listening to?" Horn asked. "My music," she said, stretching out on the bed and closing her eyes. Horn could see Christina clenching her fist beside him. "Any responses to your photos yet?" he asked. Sabrina did not reply. "Some of them are out of focus," Raimund said. The girl's arm twitched briefly.

"And the composition's poor."

He's losing it, Horn thought, but before he could react Wittmann had grabbed Raimund's shirt and dragged him out of the room. Sabrina lay there, straight-faced. Horn asked whether she could tolerate the antipsychotic she had been prescribed a few days ago, and whether she still didn't want her parents to visit. There was no answer. "You look like you could be Isabelle Huppert's daughter," he said. Then he left the room.

Leonie Wittmann was leaning against the wall and tapping her head with her fingertips. "What did you do with Raimund?" Horn asked. "Sent him out for a smoke," she said. "We've got to watch out."

"Watch out? For what?"

In her opinion it was a classic key–lock situation. Raimund hated Sabrina, but at the same time he had fallen head over heels in love with her, and the girl could sense this in every pore. "We've got to keep him away from her," she said. "He loses it in seconds." Horn nodded and thought about how Raimund had been full of both rage and lust when insisting he was a professional. It's true what that little cow put up on the web, he thought, it's one hundred per cent true. And he reflected that there were some things which turned you on, whether you wanted them to or not. This was true for Raimund, for Lisbeth Schalk, for himself and, who knows, even for Wittmann.

"Who's doing her therapy?" Horn asked. "I am," said Wittmann with a crooked smile. "Who else?"

"Indeed, who else? But why you?"

"She leaves me cold. That's why."

Monday, Tuesday, Thursday, Friday. Horn thought. Four times a week she picks up all the rage, despair and malice that this wreck of a creature offloads, a sort of acid-resistant dustbin. On Wednesdays she drives along Waschstraße and, for a while, she is back to her usual self: pale, blonde and clean. There are times when I'd like to hug her, Horn thought, very tight, to find out what she smells like, and sometimes I'd like to run the palm of my hand down her back and over her bum. Leonie Wittmann looked at him with her usual hint of scepticism, but this time he had not been thinking aloud.

The sunshine made no difference – there were moments when Horn knew exactly why he couldn't stand junkies. Fehring was sitting beside a packed bag on his bed, beaming. He'd done it this time, he said, he just knew it. He felt like a brand-new person. His girlfriend had picked up on it yesterday. He was suddenly giving off this strength that had never been there before, she'd said, something really powerful, a sort of godlike energy. Life was a series of episodes, he said, good and bad, and this time he was putting a bad one behind him. I'll get a mirror so he can see the godlike power he gives off, Horn thought, from his spidery fingers, from his grim set of teeth and from those sad eyes that dart around in their sockets like a pair of tadpoles.

"We too," Herbert said from right behind him. "We're putting a bad episode behind us, too."

Fehring paused and smiled sheepishly. "What do you mean?"

"You know precisely what I mean," Herbert said. "You've been dealing your stuff in here, haven't you?"

Fehring leaped up and eyeballed Herbert. "Who says?"

"Your clients. Several of them."

"Prove it!"

Herbert pointed to Fehring's bag. "Can't. The vendor's tray is bound to be empty." "Exactly," Fehring hissed. "You can't prove anything,

71

you Nazi!" "For you, I'd happily be one. Goodbye, Herr Fehring," Herbert said, leaving the room. Horn suddenly remembered what Sabrina had said about painkillers, and he wondered just how much he was kept abreast of what went on in the department.

Fehring was standing with his arms raised. Let them search him, his luggage, his clothes, he had nothing on him, not a speck, and he was absolutely furious about the allegation that nurse had just made. They knew damn well that he had never brought anything in, and when he said *never*, he meant it. "Is someone collecting you?" Horn asked. Yes, Fehring said, his girlfriend would be there any minute. Horn offered him his hand. I'd be delighted if I never saw him again, he thought, and when I say *never*, I mean it.

Friedrich Helm, the manic–depressive court usher was visibly recovering from his lithium overdose and, if the latest laboratory tests were to be trusted, he would not suffer any damage to his kidneys. Frau Hrstic and Frau Steininger were accusing each other of stealing the newspaper, as they did every day. Frau Hrstic called Frau Steininger "Anna", which was correct. The latter denied it was her name. A new development in their relationship. Christina was wearing her fierce ward-sister's expression during the rounds, so nobody dared crack any Alzheimer's jokes. Erika Ressel, the socio-phobic florist with a proclivity for esotericism, said she was making amazing progress with her programme of exposure to the outside world. Recently she had even been to *La Piccola Cucina*, had sat in the company of strangers, and eaten a cassata. A cassata? Horn asked, and Frau Ressel said yes, a cassata. Frau Schalk had ordered a lemon ice cream with prosecco and mint, to celebrate the first warm day of spring. Lisbeth Schalk turned red, and luckily nobody came out with any comments about drinking prosecco on duty, not even Herbert.

"Do you want to take a look at Marcus, even though he's asleep?" Wittmann asked by the door that led to the secure area.

Horn nodded. There are few things more comforting than seeing someone sleeping who's tried to commit suicide, he said, and Hrachovec said he thought so too.

The young man was lying in bed, slim, dark-haired, and with a sparse, soft beard. Rope marks were visible as purple, finger-width stripes across the front of his neck. "He looks like a young Dustin Hoffmann," Raimund said softly. Horn ran it over in his mind, but could not think of a single film with the young Dustin Hoffmann. "'The Graduate'," Raimund said, grinning. Nerd, Horn thought, the key thing is that he doesn't look like Tobias, the key thing is that someone who tries to hang himself doesn't look like either of my sons. "Who's the woman?" Hrachovec asked. Horn did not grasp it straight away. "Which woman?" "Anne Bancroft," Raimund said, "the seductress with the wide mouth." Leonie Witt-mann cast him a poisonous look. He did not appear to notice.

A black leather jacket with a studded collar was hanging over the chair, a guitar case leaning up against it. "Did he have this when he was admitted?" Horn asked. No, Christina said, a friend of his delivered it to the ward early this morning. The boy turned up out of the blue, uncombed hair, bright-green tracksuit top, put down the case and said it should be with Marcus, end of story; he, by the way, was the drummer. "The what?" Hrachovec asked. "They play in a band," Herbert said. He was trying to open the case and having trouble with the clasps. After a while the lid flipped open, offering a view of a gleaming, reddish-brown electric guitar. Awestruck, Herbert took a step back. A Dark Fire, he said, the latest Gibson model, a piece of electric magic and, as everyone could see, just beautiful. Raimund plucked one of the strings. "So would you please explain to me why someone who almost killed himself has a guitar next to his bed?" he asked. "Because it's all he's got," Herbert said, grabbing Raimund's forearm. "All he's got – do you understand?" He must play himself, Horn thought, or he used to play, in

73

a band maybe, when he was twenty-one. This powerful, awkward man who mucks around with toy rabbits was suddenly fired with a passion he had never exhibited before. Horn thought of how Irene sometimes talked about her cello, with an affection and intimacy that was never evident elsewhere. It always made him feel an outsider and terribly distant, as if her dark Neapolitan instrument was her sole possession, as if there were nothing else in the world, not him, not Tobias, and certainly not Michael.

*

Two hours later Herbert had assumed the care of the young guitarist, Leonie Wittmann had talked to Raimund about aggression as a projective phenomenon, and more specifically about the need to keep his distance from Sabrina, and in an instant Hrachovec had prepared a discharge letter for Fehring, which stated quite categorically that the patient had yet again brought his stay to a premature end against all medical advice. Horn had first gone to the café with the therapy team, then listened to a tax officer with bacteriophobia talk about how nasty human beings were, increased the man's dose of anxiolytic, and now he was sitting opposite Dorothea Müllner, a chubby, retired lingerie saleswoman who, as a result of her paraphrenic syndrome, kept hallucinating about men in uniform. There had been two of them this time, she said, one with mutton chops like Emperor Franz Joseph, and a slightly younger one, who had been wearing a black eyepatch. "Like Moshe Dayan," Horn said. This surprised Frau Müllner. "How did you know that?" Horn shrugged. "Just guessed," he said. "Wotan wouldn't have been right."

"Which Wotan?"

"Exactly."

They were historical figures, he thought, an emperor and an Israeli defence minister, maybe that was significant. Dorothea Müllner's husband had run a works canteen and had died some years ago of a haemorrhage of the aorta. He had been a passionate entomologist and had left behind thousands of beetles, all in glass boxes, and all beautifully mounted neatly. There had been days when he had not uttered a single word. Horn was mulling over the fact that he knew nothing else about Dorothea Müllner's personal history, not even whether she had children. At that moment the telephone rang. Linda, the casualty sister, apologised, she hated to disturb him, but Kurt Frühwald had now called for a third time. He was highly agitated, saying how his wife had had an epileptic fit and that her personality had very suddenly changed, she was completely distraught. For the first time in years he felt unable to cope. He had begged for somebody to call him back immediately. Apart from that, there were a couple of people who had turned up to see him; he knew about it, apparently. Something had eluded him just now, Horn thought, he couldn't put his finger on it. Two women, one spoke only Hungarian, the other was from the police. A slightly queasy feeling welled in Horn's stomach. That same instant he was certain that Dorothea Müllner's father had been a policeman. The two women had a child with them, Linda said. A hot flush suddenly came over him.

*

A warrior with a dragon water bottle, Horn thought when he saw the confused and wary boy. It also occurred to him that he was now forgetting meetings and thinking aloud, and that soon people would be making Alzheimer's jokes about him. A young woman with chestnut-brown hair politely offered him her hand. She said her name was Sabine Wieck, she was from the criminal police and he needn't apologise, she could well imagine that he was up to his ears in work. As he hadn't turned up the previous day they thought it might be better to do it the other way round, so she'd driven here straight away. His secretary had said on the telephone that he was here at the hospital. The boy had enjoyed the drive in the police car, and after all it wasn't a capital crime they were dealing with here.

A child is beaten by something black, Horn thought, that's what this is about. I do remember some things.

Ilona was the nanny, the policewoman said, she had only arrived from Budapest the previous evening, because of what had happened. Ilona was short, sturdy and probably in her mid-twenties. "How do they communicate?" Horn asked. "They don't yet," the policewoman said, but as Felix had been brought up bilingual, Hungarian should work.

"Do you like her?" Horn asked. "No," the boy said.

Horn tried using gestures to make the nanny understand that she should go and sit in the casualty waiting room. The young woman smiled. "You want me to wait here?" she said in English. What a fool I am! Horn thought.

On the way to his room he snatched several sideways glances at the policewoman. He became increasingly certain that she was not the woman he had spoken to on the phone. He stopped at the door. "Who's going to ask the questions?" "You," she said, "this is your realm. If I think there's something we haven't covered at the end I can always say so."

He began as he always did when dealing with children. He explained what the role of a psychiatrist was, that some things were real and others not, and that people were normally able to separate the two, children as much as adults. He talked about how thought was logical, about the fact that counting was linked to the human body, to the fingers for example, even if teachers didn't like it, about feelings and the importance of having friends. Finally he talked about injuries, physical and emotional, about fear and threats and about what it was like when somebody couldn't stop feeling sad. The boy sat opposite him, looking over his left shoulder at the wall behind, and rolling the silver water bottle with the dragon on it back and forth. When Horn asked him if he

76

had understood everything, he nodded. "I've got lots of friends," he said.

"Lots?" Horn asked. "What are their names?"

The boy shrugged.

"They have names, don't they?"

"Andreas."

"Who else?"

Nothing. I'd like there to be an Iris, for instance, Horn thought, and a Maximilian, and for Andreas to have a new PlayStation and play "World of Warcraft" with his brother sometimes, even though the parents might not be so keen. I'd like him to tell me all this and yet what I see is him sitting there with the stubbornness of a seven-year-old, and I know that he's not going to say a lot.

"What's black?" he asked. For a second the boy looked slightly confused. After a while he tapped the dragon with his fingertip. "That."

"That?"

"Yes."

With a barb-tailed dragon at their side, every seven-year-old becomes invincible, Horn thought. He imagined telling this to Leonie Wittmann and how she would laugh, briefly revealing her large incisors. When he was asked what else was black, the boy thought for a while and then said: Batman, night-time and the Maybach. "The what?" Horn asked.

"The Maybach, it's huge, with calf's leather, real wood and two tellies, one in the front and one in the back."

"With tellies?"

"Yes. The one in the back comes out of the floor when you press a button."

"And what do you watch on this telly?"

Nothing, the boy said, nothing at all, although you can even watch D.V.D.s on it. Nothing? The Maybach was only for the business. Only for the business! The boy stressed every word. A car, Horn thought, a make I've never heard of. And you could eat and drink in it, there were fold-out tables, bottle holders and a little cutlery drawer. In my Volvo there are four handles for winding down the windows, Horn thought, and if you go for a while without airing it, it smells of sweaty feet.

"You were beaten up by something black, is that right?" he asked. "Yes," the boy said, looking him in the eye.

"And were you scared?"

"No."

"No? Was it big?"

"A bit."

"What do you mean by 'a bit'?"

"Not as big as Batman."

"As tall as me?"

"Not saying."

"Why not?" The boy lowered his gaze and knocked the bottom of his water bottle against the tabletop. Horn looked at the policewoman. She was sitting on a chair by the window, writing in a notebook on her lap. She's in the right job, Horn thought, she's got the necessary concentration, and when the situation demands it, she lets someone else take over. Most people knew they were in the right job; this policewoman did, Hrachovec and Lisbeth Schalk did, Leonie Wittmann probably did, too, and Irene, his wife, did especially. But he didn't. He never talked to anyone about it.

"Are you scared of it now?" Horn asked. "Scared that it might suddenly turn up and hit you on the head again?" The boy raised his eyes. "And shoulders and back," he said.

"There, too?"

"Yes, that's how it is."

"Who says that?"

The boy took the top off his water bottle. "Who says that's how it is – on the head, on the shoulders and on the back?"

The boy raised the bottle to his face, closed his right eye and looked into the neck of the bottle with his left. "It's black in there, too," he said.

"Why won't you answer me?" Horn said.

"If I talk the same will happen to me."

"What do you mean the same will happen to you?"

The boy clicked the top back on the bottle and stood up. "It says if I talk, exactly the same will happen to me, the bad stuff that I can't talk about. Can I go now?" Horn turned to the policewoman. She raised her eyebrows and shrugged. Yes, he could go, Horn said.

When he got to the door, the boy turned around. Satan was also black, he'd forgotten to say that, he was more cunning than any human being and had a white patch on his chest. He knew all the commands, including the secret ones you didn't learn about on the course.

The policewoman snapped shut her notebook and stood up. The boy had talked about Satan the whole way there, she said, about how he ate only a handful of flakes a day, and if need be could go without food altogether, and also about how he was the best finder of missing people in the world. So the boy thought that he could go missing and he wouldn't have to worry about it.

"Are you saying we can't be sure that Satan is a normal dog?" Horn asked. "Precisely," the policewoman said with a smile. The light from behind cast a golden glimmer on her hair. For a brief moment Horn was seized by the desire to run his fingers through it.

The astonishing thing, he said, was that the boy didn't appear in the least traumatised, but it was as if he'd made a promise, like a sort of vow. A vow tied up with a huge threat, the policewoman said, almost as if this threat were hell itself. She gets involved and she has imagination, Horn thought. Then he thought that the whole story was fairly straightforward and, to be honest, a little exaggerated. As far as he was concerned there was only one un-answered question – why the boy had talked about an *it* at the end.

"That's easy," the policewoman said. "It. The black owl. We heard that this morning."

SEVEN

"A criminal's weapon or the tooth of a wild animal?" Lefti asked, pointing to Ludwig Kovacs' right forearm. "Going beyond my remit plus senile dementia," Kovacs said. There was no way he could be considered old, Lefti said, and Kovacs muttered that he could do without the Maghreb smarminess.

Lefti threw a white-and-blue striped linen tablecloth over the round table on the terrace and put a glazed clay bottle of olive oil in its centre. "The usual, I assume, Herr Commissar? And the bandage looks a bit like a dog's breakfast, if you don't mind my saying," he said. No reason for him to turn rude all of a sudden, Kovacs replied. What's more, Lefti was very welcome to show him how he was supposed to deal with it, being right-handed. He wouldn't deal with it at all, Lefti said; he'd leave the wounded area to the care of those hands to which he generally preferred to entrust his body. "You talk so beautifully about your wife that sometimes I'd like to smack you one, just like that," Kovacs said. Lefti looked at him in horror. "Don't worry, I wouldn't actually do it," Kovacs said. Lefti bowed politely.

A painful injury plus an oversensitive partner plus a daughter who was after his money – not a good combination. Added to this was a group of noisy Carinthians sitting to his left, and to the right a young family with a baby who was whining, even though the mother was forcibly ramming a bottle into its mouth. There were times when Kovacs did not like people. His gaze wandered along the shore, from the wildlife observation centre, past the area of reeds by the river outlet, the hotel roofs, the marina, to the jagged edges of the Kammwand which towered straight above the heads of the Carinthians. Marlene had kept trying to drag him into the mountains. He had put her off with the argument that his star sign was Cancer, the crab, an animal which on land moved in reverse gear at best, which was not really much use to him or her. Then, almost exactly a year ago, she managed to get him, just once, with the night-sky trick. Picture the total darkness and the clarity – no haze, no urban light pollution, no headlights. After a three-and-a-half hour walk they had sat, frozen, outside the Paul Preuß hut, two thousand metres up, staring at an overcast night sky. Time and again she had said that these things were unpredictable, sadly, and he had sunk one schnapps after another. What is more, the May sky would have been a treasure trove of riches. Arcturus in Boötes, that impressive red giant, Coma Berenices, or Gamma Leonis, the binary star which made up the shoulder of Leo. The bedroom in the mountain hut had stunk of mouse piss – he remembered that.

"What's this supposed to be? Are you punishing me now?" Kovacs asked when Lefti placed a pot of peppermint tea and three narrow glasses with handles beside him. He was long over his crisis, he said, he had the booze under control, and it was well known that too much peppermint tea gave you tummy bugs, worms or helicobacter as they were called these days. He was sorry if he'd been fierce a moment ago, but he'd really like a beer now, please. Lefti poured tea into the glasses. Then he stepped aside.

Although he had known Szarah for fourteen years, Kovacs still shuddered whenever he bumped into her. Maybe it was to do with her figure, which was like a juvenile poplar, or a cypress, maybe it was her narrow face, like a bird of prey, or perhaps her hair, which she always wore tied up, its bluish-black lustre now interwoven here and there with strands of grey. Perhaps it was for quite different reasons, but whatever they were, Kovacs regularly lost the power of speech whenever she appeared in her silent, sleek way. "*Salam aleikum*, Commissar," she said, carefully pushing a dark wooden tray with silver handles between the tea glasses. It held several white porcelain bowls – one filled with yellow and red powder, the others empty – a small, curved horn spoon and a pile of folded cotton cloths. "Hello Szarah." Kovacs felt the need to stand, bow and tell her that she looked like a princess. He also knew, however, that it would be stupid and that he was too cowardly.

Lefti handed him a glass of tea. "Drink, Commissar," he said. Kovacs pointed to the tray. So it was right what they said, a Moroccan restaurant was nothing more than a front for dealing drugs, and what he saw in front of his eyes had to be this trendy new drug. "Cinn," Lefti said. "Cinn in the Tin, everybody's saying it, so it must be right, Commissar."

"Cinn in the Tin. And are you taking a commission?"

"Fifteen per cent, like any agent, plus a further fifteen risk premium."

"Because of the danger of gang warfare?"

"No. Because of the police presence." Lefti sipped his tea. Now and then he would smoke half a cigar, and after a large meal might drink an aniseed schnapps, but otherwise he had no interest in addictive substances. Kovacs was aware of this and he had instructed the Sheriff to ensure that the Tin remained clean. In return the Sheriff would get the occasional lamb tagine and a friendly glance from Lejla, Lefti's eldest daughter.

Szarah placed a chair to the right of Kovacs, sat down, and carefully started to unwind the bandage on his forearm. "It's because of that Florian Weghaupt," Kovacs said. He could not remember the last time somebody had bandaged him. Maybe it had been Yvonne, his wife, he thought, but he could not be sure. "They ate koftas

83

and drank ajran," Lefti said. "What do you mean *they*?" Kovacs asked. Young Weghaupt and his friends, Lefti said. They had been extremely polite and had talked about music. Kovacs said that at a certain age music was what people did talk about mainly, and Lefti said that it had been slightly different on this occasion.

The inside layers of the bandage were stuck fast to Kovacs' skin. Szarah poured peppermint tea into a bowl, checked the temperature, dampened one of the cotton cloths, and pressed it onto the scabs. After a while the bandage came away fairly easily. "I reckon a few stitches might have helped there," Lefti said. Kovacs tried to pull together the edges of the gash with the thumb and index finger of his left hand. "Yes, roughly like that," Lefti said. "Stitches don't work the next day, then?" Kovacs asked.

"At least that's what the doctors say."

Szarah squeezed drops of peppermint tea into the wound. "Doctors should be trusted, Commissar," she said. No, Kovacs thought, doctors should not be trusted. Then he thought of Patrizia Fleurin, the forensic pathologist in charge of the district. He trusted her from time to time – when she said something about dead people at least. A yellowy-green lake had formed in the narrow, perhaps ten-centimetre-long fissure in his skin. Kovacs imagined a boat on it and, at the bottom of the lake, a chub stalking its prey. Some days there's nothing in my world but thieves and crooks, he thought. It was Demski's fault, he said, Demski with his crazy child-abuse obsession, and Mauritz's, who ought to lose a few kilos for a change. Strictly speaking it was his daughter's fault, too, which might sound a bit strange now, but he'd been thinking about her the whole time before the accident. "And these were not good thoughts?" Szarah asked. Kovacs did not answer. He took a sideways glance along the elegant curve of her eyelashes to the tiny scar on the bridge of her nose, and wondered whether there were other people who were not particularly happy when they thought about their children. Mauritz was the best forensics officer he had come across in his career, with a love of detail that bordered on the pathological, but also calm when everything else around him was in freefall. In even the most barren situations he was always able to conjure a creative idea from his mind. In private he was the husband of a pale, thin social worker who coordinated the town's mobile care service for the elderly, father of nine-month-old baby Nikolaus, and a formidable table tennis player to boot. "An out-and-out attacking player," Kovacs said, something you would not imagine at all if you looked at him. If Demski had not attended this meeting of pederast detectors, but gone about his work as usual, Mauritz would not have had to expose his neurosis, and he, Kovacs, would not have had to clamber up that scaffolding. Yes indeed, scaffolding, he said in reaction to Lefti's enquiring look, steel tubing joined with sleeve couplers, boards of wood and aluminium sheet, the whole thing six storeys high, on one of those faceless constructions north of the river. "Neptun Insurance?" Lefti asked.

"How did you know?"

"We do the odd catering job for them."

"Is there anywhere in this town where you haven't got your fingers in the pie?" Kovacs asked. Lefti bowed his head. "We are given eyes to see with and ears to hear with."

"And a mouth to spread the word of the Prophet amongst the people."

"Do you not wish to convert, Commissar?"

"What good would it do?" Anyway, he had stepped over the police tape and climbed the vertical steel ladders, annoyed by the camera swinging heavily back and forth, and even more annoyed by the fact that his daughter was coming to screw him for money. When he reached the fourth storey he was utterly wound up and glad that nobody had come with him. The place where the boy had fallen was properly marked, so he had found it straight away – a jumble of footprints in an area demarcated by spray paint. One look told him that they were not going to get anything from forensic technology, but he got down on his knees anyway, to take a few photographs. At that moment the camera slipped from his shoulder. He instinctively grabbed for it with his left hand, and for the nearest hold – the transverse strut on the scaffolding – with his right, in the process failing to notice a metal pin which had been stuck through a hole in one of the sleeve couplers. The sharp end of the pin had easily perforated his sweater and shirt and cut through his skin like a knife. "A knife? My my," Lefti said. "Like a badly sharpened knife, whatever," Kovacs muttered. At first he was just irritated by the tears in his clothes, and in fact he had taken a few photographs, but then he had seen the drops of blood on the plank he was standing on. "Then everything became clear," Lefti said.

"Yes, everything became clear. I was the murderer and I had no other choice but to give myself up to the police."

Meanwhile, Szarah had put some spoonfuls of the red and yellow powders into a bowl and added a little olive oil from the clay bottle. With tiny circular movements she stirred it all into an ochre-coloured paste. Then she carefully dipped the edge of one of the cotton cloths into Kovacs' wound and waited until the liquid was soaked up. Using the tips of her fingers she dabbed the paste across the length of the gash in his skin. All the while Kovacs just watched without saying a word. She's giving you the sort of attention which knocks you sideways, he thought. Lefti poured some tea. "In our country all our wives are also qualified nurses," he said. "You're absolutely right, we are very lucky."

"But I didn't say anything."

"I know, Commissar."

It's bizarre, Kovacs thought, I don't begrudge him his wife. I do begrudge most other men their wives; I even begrudge someone Yvonne. He asked what was in the paste and Szarah said everything you could put in a spice mix with healing properties. "Chilli too?" he asked, and she said, "Yes, chilli too." She trimmed one of the cloths, wrapped it twice around the wound, and stuck it with an adhesive gauze bandage which she took from her jacket pocket. "How come you've got something like that to hand?" Kovacs asked. "Anybody with children has gauze to hand, too," Lefti said.

While waiting for his food and taking the occasional gulp of his beer Ludwig Kovacs thought about the friendship that bound him and Lefti, the type of sarcasm they shared, the fact that they could not stop talking in each other's presence, and that this Moroccan landlord was the only person apart from Marlene to whom he sent the odd text message. Lefti enjoyed his pleasures in moderation, and Kovacs admired this. He himself was a picture of self-indulgence and Lefti did not despise him for it. Lefti's relations with other people were generally based on a respect which Kovacs for the most part admired, and sometimes could not understand. When, for example, the son of Martin Fürst, a nationalist deputy in the regional parliament, had yet again called his classmate Lejla a "harem lady" or a "stinking camel driver", Lefti told his daughter that she should try to imagine how shameful it must be to have a father like that, instead of giving the boy a sound thrashing in some dark corner. Lefti's daughters loved their father even though he was a wimp. Kovacs most definitely was not a wimp and Charlotte hated him for certain. He did not love her either. At least this made the situation black and white.

The southerly Föhn wind was now blowing. A veil of mist lay over the lake, sparing only the foot of the Kammwand. The Carinthians had left and the young family's baby was fast asleep. There were days around Easter time when it felt like summer.

"Here you are – koftas and ajran. Normally you have the tagine

87

of the day, Commissar," Lefti said. "Normally I don't go pointlessly climbing up scaffolding," Kovacs replied, tucking into one of the fried meatballs. I'm trying to get on the trail of this young man by eating the same thing as him, he thought – that's how far I've come.

"They talked about music," Lefti said.

"Who?"

"The Weghaupt boy and his friends."

"How do you always know what I'm thinking?"

"Koftas and ajran – wasn't hard." No, he couldn't remember the kind of music, but the youngsters had been wrapped in a mantle of seriousness. A mantle of seriousness, Kovacs thought, no Austrian would ever come up with that. He thought about Demski's report which told of a young man who, in spite of having performed brilliantly at school, left early and started training as a builder, who lived at home with his younger brother and parents, and who had never had a girlfriend. Demski had also described the devastated parents, a group of distraught colleagues and a neighbourhood that was entirely at a loss. "Who would kill a person who hasn't got a quarrel with anybody?" Kovacs wanted to know. Lefti plucked at his beard. "Someone who's got the same problem," he said finally.

*

Ludwig Kovacs walked in the direction of the lake, past the Kingdom Hall of the Jehovah's Witnesses, the old chocolate factory and the town library. He could smell spring, could feel the beer in his head, and was waiting for the pain. Chilli, she had said, cinnamon, turmeric, cumin, paprika, fenugreek and black onion seeds, besides hundreds of other ingredients that nobody knew. There was no way it was not going to hurt. He recalled the moment as a six-year-old boy when, after leaping over a pile of rubble he stood gazing at the cut across his knee, waiting anxiously for the pain and the blood. Half an hour later he was sitting on a surgery couch, watching the white-haired doctor take one of those curved needles from a metal holder with his fat fingers. He had felt a little pain and no fear at all, he remembered this very well, and also that the needle holder had looked like a sardine tin. His mother had said to him that, if he went on like that, sooner or later he would end up in a wheelchair or in his grave, but even back then he was aware that his mother sometimes said crass things. On the whole Kovacs had been spared injury in his life. As a teenager he had been operated on after tearing his meniscus, and once when he was searching a garage a concrete slab had tipped over and broken two of his metatarsals. That had happened on the case of the stolen television sets, he remembered.

Konrad Seihs, the brand new Business Party deputy in the regional parliament, leered at him from an electronic advertising screen at the corner of the Fernkorns' garden. Kovacs turned away. There were some people he did not want to see, not even on advertising hoardings. Demski sometimes asked him why that shitface got him so worked up, and he would say that he was thinking of his fellow inhabitants on the Walzwerk estate, of the women who took off their headscarves before going shopping, and of old Yiledi, who was still afraid of being deported even though his application for asylum had been accepted a long time ago. In any case, he inherently loathed people who felt the need to have fighting dogs at their heels. Eleonore Bitterle said that people who kept fighting dogs were like people who carried guns: men plagued by a fear of castration, most of them hopelessly impotent, and Kovacs replied that she was in the right job with the police. He did not like people who only felt strong when others felt weak, irrespective of whether they were impotent.

He walked for a while along the promenade. Just before the lido he sat down on the jetty and looked out across the lake. The wind was now blowing strongly and the mist had dispersed. Further in the distance the crests of the waves were starting to foam white. Kovacs thought of his boat, of Marlene's hydrophobia and this morning's chub. He looked at the bandage on his forearm. His mind was filled with images of Szarah's hands, the fine trickle of that pale-yellow olive oil, and koftas and ajran. He reached for his mobile.

The Sheriff always answered, even when he was having lunch at his mother's house. "Bismillah, Monsieur Erdoyan," Kovacs said.

"Hello, Commissar. What have I done now?"

"The usual. You know I write everything down in my notebook. I'll cross out two black marks next to your name if you tell me what comes to mind when I say a group of young people who regularly go to the Tin for koftas and ajran."

"Only koftas and ajran? You want some grilled aubergines with that."

As he was neither a chef nor a doctor of internal medicine, Kovacs said, he had no intention of discussing the finer points of particular diets. If a name might help, the young man he was interested in was called Florian Weghaupt.

"Weghaupt? But he's dead."

"You don't say."

"If you cross out three black marks . . ."

"Watch it, sonny!"

Florian Weghaupt had bought amphetamines from time to time, the Sheriff said after pausing briefly to reflect, small amounts as a rule, never any opiates. He could not say anything about cannabinoids, but this was practically impossible now, as home-growing had totally ruined the market. All in all, his consumption pattern was what you would expect from a young creative type. "Consumption pattern – you're talking like a drug therapist," Kovacs said. "Narcotics consultant," the Sheriff said. "Narcotics consultant for the soft- and low-dose sector."

"Yeah, right, as low-dose as you're slim."

"Exactly. By the way, I'm below one hundred and fifty kilos now, Commissar."

"Your coronary arteries must be delighted," Kovacs said.

Erdoyan laughed. What, in his opinion, did Florian Weghaupt have to do with young creative types? Kovacs asked. He didn't know for sure, the Sheriff said, but he got the impression they were a group of musicians, at any rate they didn't speak about anything else but music. I know that already, Kovacs said and hung up.

*

He took the path which curved along the river outlet. In spite of the wind it smelled of brackish water and slightly of oil. It always did in this place. A grey-haired jogger in a black-and-silver striped shirt came towards him. He did not recognise the man. When the hospital and the hills above Mühlau came into view behind a stand of goat willow on the northern shore, Kovacs turned off towards the town centre. There was a trace of mint in his mouth. His arm would not hurt again, he was now sure of it.

The Weghaupt case must have been an accident. Maybe some substances had played their part, but nobody had pushed him. People had accidents: they swerved off the road, drove into the pillars of bridges, or fell from scaffolding. Accidents were common, murders were not.

Kovacs found himself looking into the window of Guys & Dolls, searching for the price tag of a woman's yellow belt studded with rhinestones. When a young man stopped next to him, he felt a combination of anger and shame well up inside him, and went quickly on his way.

There was a strange mood in the office. Sabine Wieck was stomping up and down the corridor, Eleonore Bitterle had closed the door, and Christine Strobl, the secretary, was spooning yoghurt out of a carton without looking up. "What's up?" Kovacs asked, "communal pre-menstrual syndrome?" "I'm not going to answer that," Frau Strobl said, and carried on eating. Kovacs went into his room. Sometimes this was precisely what he wished for: a team that acted up and refused to do their duty, which would give him no other option but to pack up his things and go home.

"George rang." Eleonore Bitterle was standing in the doorway, her arms folded. "And?" Kovacs asked. He would be staying on there for two or three more days, she said.

"Holiday, or what?"

No, she said, in light of recent events the pornographers' meeting had been extended. "In light of recent events?" That's how Demski had put it. He had also said that his work could happily wait, nobody need bother about it. "And an idiot like me goes climbing up scaffolding for him." Kovacs stretched out his arm. "Nice bandage," she said. Demski was a good detective, they all knew that. He was passionate, erudite and, when it mattered, precise to the point of pedantry. On the other hand he was defi- nitely not a team player. "The truth is, he hasn't thought for a moment about whether his work here can actually wait," Bitterle said. "And then he's giving us new tasks."

"What's that? He's giving you tasks?"

They were on the trail of a number of networks, he had said. The hub of one of these was in Italy and, as there was clear evidence of Austrian involvement, he had asked her to examine again all cases in the last few years that had anything to do with sex and children. "Sex and children," Kovacs said. "I can't listen to any more." He pictured Demski and his colleagues in Berlin sitting in an old brick building in front of a row of computer screens, exchanging I.P. addresses and setting up caller identification facili- ties. In the evenings they would gather in one of the Unter den Linden cafés and compare notes. Demski would drink two or three Pernods, smoke a cigarillo, and be delighted if there was a high proportion of academics on the list. For some reason he had it in for the doctors, teachers and priests amongst the kiddie fiddlers. If you asked him why he was pushing on with his studies so single-mindedly, he would say that he wanted to know how these arse-holes operated. Demski had an eight-year-old son he protected like gold, a probable anorexic physiotherapist for a partner, and an old tin duck which he chatted to from time to time. Bitterle loved Demski only as far as she could allow herself to love after the death of her husband, and Demski benefited from her intellectual bril-liance. Nobody knew whether he loved her a little as well. But the two of them would work together whenever possible.

"And?" Kovacs said.

"What do you mean 'and'?"

"What do you think I mean?"

A hint of a smile crept across her face. Over the past decade, she said, Furth police had intervened in one hundred and seventeen cases dealing with sex attacks on children. Seventy-one of these had resulted in a criminal investigation, forty-three in a court case, and eleven in a conviction. There had been nineteen acquittals and thirteen trials had collapsed. "You've memorised all those figures?" Kovacs asked. "Thirty-two offenders who've got away with it," she said.

"Or thirty-two people who were wrongly accused."

Bitterle ignored his comment. Talking of sex attacks, the station incident had been resolved. What station incident, he asked, and she said, the green-rimmed spectacles. The culprit was an assistant at the Graz municipal gardening office who spent his free after-noons travelling around chatting up girls. Their colleagues in Wiener Neustadt had picked him up as he was getting off a train. A number of schoolgirls had pointed the finger at him without any prompting. "That's really dumb," Kovacs said. "If I were a paedo I wouldn't wear green glasses."

"But you aren't one."

"True. But even if I were, I wouldn't wear them."

"There you go. The municipal gardening assistant probably isn't one either."

"What then?"

It was more likely to be a case of a repressed neurotic, she said, for whom getting caught and being punished was all part of the unconscious performance. "Someone who masturbates in the loo and then spends half a day washing his hands," Kovacs said.

"How do you know that?"

"I've got a mother, too," he said. The way she bandied around terms like *neurotic* and *unconscious performance*, he added, he couldn't understand why she hadn't gone straight on to study psychology. She had, she said – law, philosophy and psychology, all in Salzburg, none of it completed.

"Why not?"

"You've got your mother and I've got my father. But you know the story, don't you?"

Kovacs nodded. There were some things you asked about even though you already knew the answer. Either they were extremely hard to believe, or they were simply not right. Only things that were concluded were right for Mrs Brain, nothing else.

Kovacs enquired about cases on her list where there had been violations of the child pornography law, and Bitterle said that until Demski had hooked up with the Interpol group they had been very thin on the ground. In other words, nothing except an accusation made against a retired forest supervisor a year ago, which had almost certainly been a case of revenge and was without any substance at all. Demski would find something, Kovacs said, a V.P.N. or L.F.T.

"V.P.N.?" Eleonore Bitterle asked.

"Virtual Private Network," said Sabine Wieck, who had appeared behind her.

"And L.F.T.?"

"No idea," Kovacs said. "Just made it up. Maybe a disease of the liver."

Bitterle raised one eyebrow disapprovingly. The person who had filed the accusation had been the neighbour, and it was all to do with rights of use of a farm track, she said, nothing virtual; all this had emerged when the two men were questioned. Demski could uncover a sex crime even in a dispute over a right of way, Kovacs said.

Let him get on with it then, in Berlin or wherever else, Sabine Wieck said. She was resting one arm on Eleonore Bitterle's shoulder and casually brandishing a piece of paper with the other. "What's that?" Kovacs asked. "A problem," she said.

Evidently, the launching of the police investigation had not been enough to satisfy Stephan Szigeti. He had turned up the day before at his son's school and threatened the headmaster that if he didn't find out who'd beaten up his boy soon, he'd set the regional school board onto him, as well as everything else he'd surely rather do without. The headmaster had replied that he, Szigeti, ought to calm down, after all his son was not the only child this had happened to. Kovacs pinched his temples. "Exactly," Wieck said. Szigeti had written a woefully long e-mail to Eyltz, the chief of police, Steinböck, the mayor, and Jelusitz, the district governor. After the incident with his son, now another child from the first year had become the victim of an unspeakable attack, and the authorities had not lifted a finger. On the contrary, his son had been examined by a psychiatrist, as if it were the boy they actually thought was mad rather than the perverse and violent criminal wreaking terror around the place. As all too often, the police were failing in their duty, so he felt it necessary to call for the establishment of a private security service that would guarantee the children's safety.

"A *Schutzstaffel*," Kovacs said. "A what?" Wieck asked. "Forget it," he said.

The three recipients of the e-mail were fuming, she continued. Eyltz was demanding results and insisted on being given regular progress updates, Steinböck was worried about the possible effect on tourism, and Jelusitz was already assuming that the Turks were to blame. "Because they whack their children as a matter of course, we all know that don't we? And I can deal with Eyltz," Kovacs said.

"I don't know," Sabine Wieck said. "There's something else."

"Besides the second child, you mean?"

"Yes. A c.c."

"A what?"

Szigeti had copied his letter to the editors of relevant newspapers and every radio and television broadcaster he could find, as well as posting it in various places on the Internet.

"So everybody's to know, are they?" Kovacs asked. He realised just how much he hated those c.c.ing and forwarding psychopaths, the kinds of individuals who took a wicked pleasure in putting pressure on other people under the pretext of information disclosure. "We've already had a call from the *Kurier*," Wieck said. "What should we tell them?" "Anybody who smacks their children is a suspect," Kovacs said. "That's what we'll tell them."

*

Britta Kern was said to be a shy and independent girl, typical of a child with younger siblings, Sabine Wieck said when the three of them were sitting in the meeting room. In her case, all the mother's attention was taken up by her little sister. Britta liked to spend her time making bracelets and playing with her Abyssinian guinea pigs. She seemed to be interested at school, and was less easily distracted than most of the other children. Her mother worked in an auditor's office, and her father ran a D.I.Y. store. The two had met at commercial college, Wieck added.

"And they all lived happily ever after . . ." Kovacs said. Wieck put up her hand in protest. She couldn't bear such fairytale nonsense, and anyway, the parents had separated two years ago. The father now lived in Zeltweg, in Upper Styria.

"Commercial college graduates with back gardens and guinea pigs hit their children too, by the way," Bitterle said.

Kovacs looked out of the window. Two wagtails were chasing each other on the roof opposite. A garden, guinea pigs and children – these were the things most people wanted in life. Then some plummet to their deaths, while others row out to the middle of lakes on their own. He thought of Marlene, her penchant for patterned fabrics and candles on the table, and the fact that she looked at her happiest when arranging wild flowers in a vase. He thought of his brother, who drank himself stupid and kept on finding women who would stay with him even though he beat them up. Finally he thought of the yellow belt studded with rhinestones and how he had walked away before finding the price tag. The price did not matter to him.

EIGHT

The bright-red line runs along the doorframes, always four centimetres from the edge, up over the top and down, then runs parallel to the floor until the next door, then up over the top and down
again. The windows have been spared; nobody knows why. The
painters did what they were asked to do. Three doors lead off
the room. Two are escape routes, the third leads to the kitchen. It's
a dead-end. Between the door to the kitchen and the cupboard
with the glasses there's a small grey mark on the wall. It's from a
meal moth. It was squashed by the man I now call Bill. Almost
every creature on earth is useful in one way or another. But I'm
not so sure about meal moths.

She's sitting on her chair and not eating anything. She always
behaves like this when it's over. She juts her chin out and, with her
eyes closed, presses her lips together until it goes white around
her mouth. The mad woman tries to make the roast chicken and
potatoes sound appetising. There's something songlike in her
voice when she says how lovely the food is. But it doesn't make any
difference. When the mad woman gets furious her skin turns
yellow. Everyone else probably sees it differently, but for me it's the
yellow of rape. Not lemon yellow or egg-yolk yellow, but oilseed
rape. The mad woman spears pieces of chicken and chunks of
potato on a fork and pushes it towards Switi's face. First Switi turns
her head left and right, this way and that. When that doesn't help,
she starts thrashing around. The mad woman starts thrashing

around, too. The fork moves along Switi's lower lip, from one corner of her mouth to the other. The mad woman screams that she can't do it on her own. The man I call Bill has already eaten his chicken. He gets up, walks behind Switi's chair, and says very calmly: A child has to eat. From behind he clasps Switi's shoulders and upper arms with his left arm, and with his right hand grips her jaw as if he were using a pair of tongs. He presses only very gently and Switi's mouth opens like a nutcracker. "It's pure skill," he says. The fork goes in and out. Switi swallows like a good girl. Sometimes she has to retch. When the plate's empty, the man I call Bill says, "Now then. That wasn't so bad, was it?" The mad woman doesn't say anything. Her skin is rosy again.

When I come into the room Switi is lying curled up on the floor by her bed, asleep. It's something you learn over time, to be able to go to sleep just like that, when you need it. I sit next to her and look at the fine hairs on her chin and the tiny nobble on the edge of her ear. There's something on the floor by her mouth. It's bright green and about the size of a sweet. I pick the thing up carefully and take a look at it. It's a sort of pebble, flat and smooth. Switi opens her eyes. "Manka," she says, taking it out of my hand and putting it back in her mouth.

I help her into her quilted jacket with the penguins on it and tie her shoelaces. I know all that stuff about fresh air is what old people go on about, but sometimes you really do need it. We do our usual walk: towards the lake until the turn-off to the gorge, up to the viewpoint above the waterfall, back, then past the owl rock and on to the marina. There's frost on the jetty. But we go to the end anyway. I look back at our footprints and tell her the story of a little pelican kept in captivity by humans, who one day starts collecting objects in his mouth: a knife, a pair of pliers, a few lighters, a pack of cigarettes, a file and a tiny camera. By using these things he eventually manages to escape. "How do you catch

99

pelicans?" Switi asks. She draws a wavy line in the frost with the tip of her foot. "In the normal way," I say, because I can't think of a better answer.

The marina is almost empty. People have put their boats in large sheds to keep them dry, in Waiern, for instance, like us. They get washed and scrubbed there, and the joins are resealed. Out on the lake there's a lone electric boat heading slowly for Sankt Christoph, probably someone from the wildlife place observing families of ducks or water fleas. Switi's staring at her fingers. "Should we have brought gloves for you?" I ask. She shakes her head and says nothing.

I think they're doing all the things to her that they did to me. At some point it gets less regular, and then it's someone else's turn. That's what happened to me. The visions don't begin until later. They never stop.

I stand on tiptoes and look through the window. Neither of the cars is there. That means she's on one of her trips and he's at the office or with a client. Nobody knows where her trips take her. When she says she's off, he gets nervous and tries to take the car keys away from her. She says he should have a good think about it, and he lets her go. The way out through the garage is escape route number four. It's really easy and it works because the garage door can be opened by a button from the inside. From the outside either you need the remote control or you know the code. Two letters, three numbers.

Tyre prints from the X6 are visible on the garage floor, wide and clayey. The man I call Bill sometimes drives into the countryside with his clients, to the meadow between Waiern and Moosheim, for example, where they used to cut peat. They shoot deer there, or otters if they've been released. There's no trace of the mad woman's Mini.

Switi sits in her red pedal car and snakes around the garage, shrieking loudly the whole time. When she starts deliberately grazing the walls on the turns I stop her and lift her from the car. "You're too big for that," I say. "You've got to learn to ride a bike." She shakes her head.

We go into the house and look in all the rooms on the ground floor. I always do that when they're not there. I turn the page of the calendar in the hall. A Dalmatian with two children. In the kitchen dirty plates are piled next to the sink. I put them into the dishwasher even though I know Marika's coming tomorrow. I really hate seeing dishes lying around.

I fetch the key I need from the old sugar jar behind the water glasses. A stupid hiding place; any old fool could find it there. "Come on," I tell Switi, "let's go and practise." She shakes her head again. "You have to," I say, taking her hand.

We go up the stairs, turn left and go into their bedroom. I hold my breath and look over to the window and up to the ceiling. We go to the back of the dressing room, to the little door between the cupboards that you can only see if you know it's there. I take the picture of the hedgehog and the owl off the wall. Behind it is the keyhole.

There are three rooms: the white one, the stripy one and the flower room. I named them after the mattresses lying in them. To be precise, there are two white mattresses and one with bright-blue dots in the white room; in the stripy room there's a huge double mattress with wide blue and yellow narrow stripes; and in the flower room are four mattresses piled on top of each other, all covered with pastel-coloured blossom. The two tripods with the cameras are always in a different place. This time they're in the white room.

"Which one do you want today?" I ask her. She stays silent. I say, "Stripy."

She lies on her tummy and I tell her about the film I discovered in the red and yellow sleeve, about all the things that can happen to you, and about the five-point palm stroke that stops your heart. Now and then I press her face into the stripy mattress, telling her she's got to keep her eyes open. Every time I grab her neck she whines like a dog.

NINE

The classroom smells of children, of Julia's curly hair, Stefan's boiled-wool cardigan, Lara's dog, and Manuel's sweaty feet. The aroma of the lilac bunch, which she put on her desk yesterday, is drowned out by the competition. The board has not been properly wiped clean, which is always the case when Sükrü is class monitor. On the right-hand section are the words: THE SUN MAKES THE MOON SHINE. Because Easter is linked to the full moon she has been trying to teach the children a little astronomy. What is a fixed star, what is a planet, why does the moon shine? Because it's got a really strong electrical connection, was Leonard's guess, and Katrin said: When the moon shines criminals don't dare go into the streets.

She can feel her throat tighten. It is partly the sentence on the board, but also the image of a huge black man in front of her, beating somebody up. She doesn't want it, she doesn't want it at all, she is certain of this.

She strolls the length of the wall to the back of the classroom. Somebody has put stickers of Diddl, the cartoon mouse, and a hen with three chicks on the door of the craft cupboard. Julia and Sophie are sitting right next to it. Both of them love stickers. Knowing things like that gives her security. She goes to the window and looks out into the courtyard. Fine threads of rain are falling, even though the sky is mainly blue and the sun is shining on the roof of the library block. She rummages in her handbag, pulls out a file, and begins tidying her fingernails. She always does this when she is waiting for somebody, and sometimes when she is in the car, too. Things like that get on some people's nerves.

Elke Bayer appears first and walks to her left across the white gravel surface towards the car park. She is wearing anthracite-coloured pumps, a light-grey suit and a dark-red velvet bow in her blonde hair. She is almost running. It is remarkable that she is here at all. She never usually comes to extraordinary meetings. Maybe it is because she is the form teacher of the other first-year class and worried that the business might affect her soon, too. To begin with she had deliberately ignored the headmaster's instruction to discuss it with the children. Then she discovered that Michael Richter from her class had been going around for a couple of days already, bragging that he would stick his father's taser into the black owl's stomach until it had an electric fit. This put paid to her argument of "What I don't know can't hurt me". Everybody had a good laugh about the electric fit, although they were only too aware of Michael's father and his gun licence, collection of steel truncheons and re-enactments of World War Two battles.

Trude Lassnig and Veronika Derkic leave together, one a special-needs teacher, the other the form teacher of 4B. They both live in Sankt Christoph and do a car share. Then come Reinhard Gelich, 2A's form teacher, and Dienbacher, the headmaster. From the outset Gelich has behaved as if none of this has anything to do with him: No-one in my class has ever been battered. He is living proof that arseholes become primary school teachers too. The key thing about him is that he drives a Corvette. Sometimes he takes his favourite pupils for a quick spin, the others are allowed to watch.

When Bauer trots in from the other direction in his grey cotton uniform, she throws the nail file back into her bag. She used to keep a Stanley knife with a yellow handle in her manicure set. It has been a while since she last needed it.

Bauer is waiting for her in the cloakroom. He jabs her nose with his index finger. "Where were you?" he asks. "In the classroom," she says, opening her locker.

"You mean you spoke to the children?" he says, laughing.

"Sort of," she says.

He does laps of the room while she gets changed, listening as ever to music on his iPod. After a while she stops him, even though she's wearing nothing but her bra and has one leg in her tracksuit bottoms, and pulls his earphones out. "That's driving me potty," she says. "Great," he says.

"What did you think of the meeting?"

"Unnecessary," he says, jogging on the spot and murmuring. *When you are near / It's just as plain as it can be / I'm wild about you, gal / You ought to be a fool about me.* By now she knows the lyrics by heart. The zip on her sweater has stuck. He notices this, goes up to her, carefully jiggles it about to free it, and gives her a kiss on the lips. "Why are you laughing," he says.

"I just thought of something."

"What?"

"A sentence."

"What sentence?"

"I wrote it on the board today: *The sun makes the moon shine.*"

*

They run his standard route. Diagonally across the first courtyard, through the ground floor of the senior school block, across the courtyard with the fountain, through the utility corridor into the rear garden, through the gate in the railings by the tall plane trees, along the northern wall of the abbey grounds, right into Abt-Reginald-Straße, past the tax advisor's office, the kindergarten and the tiny esoteric shop with the brightly painted facade, before taking a short cut though the municipal lorry park to reach the promenade by the riverbank.

The rain stopped a while back. Beneath the willows and alders it has stayed dry. He increases his pace on the springy ground. Like a Masai running after his cattle, she thinks, lean and lanky, all he's missing is the long stick. She knows that he will stop and wait for her after a few hundred metres, she keeps her pace and tries to take in everything around her, the smell of freshly cut grass and elder-flower blossom, the bright green flickering in the trees, and the birds who are even loud in the afternoons at this time of year. She thinks of Michaela Klum and the folder printed with different types of tits that she had in front of her during the meeting: great tit, crested tit, coal tit. She said nothing throughout, and after-wards, when it was all over: It's absolutely ridiculous. I gave my daughter a slap only yesterday. She'd called me a *bloody cow*.

She watches him disappear around the next bend. He'll wait under one of the prominent trees, under the lime above the first cataract or under the oak where the path branches off to Hohen-wart cavern. On the opposite bank of the river, someone is using a high-pressure hose on the landing jetty of the rafting centre. Business usually gets going in the last weekend of April, if the weather is settled.

Nobody on the staff can establish a connection between Felix and Britta. Gelich sits there, pulling a soppy face, and says he is convinced that the over-spiced Hungarian beat up his son himself. Britta's mother wouldn't do a thing like that, Trude Lassnig says, her husband left her and she's got nobody except her daughters. That's exactly why, Gelich says. Do you hit your children? Lassnig asks, and he taps his forehead at her.

The surging and fading of the high-pressure hose sounds like a strange song. The rushing of the river joins in. *Spirit on the water / Darkness on the face of the deep.* There's something biblical about it, she thinks, I'll have to ask him. She listens as she quickens her pace. She can no longer hear his footfall. A great spotted woodpecker flies over her head with a loud clamour. So as not to have to turn around she pictures the native species of woodpeckers: black woodpecker, green woodpecker, great spotted woodpecker, white-backed woodpecker, wryneck. Who had ever seen a wryneck? She thinks of Dienbacher, how he had slammed the table with the palm of his hand and insisted, "Dear colleagues, this is a serious situation, a really serious situation," and how she had thought that he had probably never experienced a really serious situation in his life.

If you do not stop before the first cataract, you have to go through it. Some years ago the river rescue service winched up a kayaker wedged between two boulders and laid him out on the sandbank below the rapids. They said his face had been completely obliterated, as if someone had taken him by the legs and dashed him against the rocks hundreds of times, as they do to octopuses in Greece. Apparently the man was a tourist from the Czech Republic.

She meets a walker, an elderly man in a straw hat with a dog dancing at his heels. As she runs towards him the man keeps his eyes fixed on her breasts. He gives her a smile as they are about to pass each other. She imagines herself stopping, walking right up to him and asking, "Do you think it's a good thing that women have breasts?"

She makes herself run on her heels. You move quicker that way, and it protects your joints; at least that is what people who do a lot of running claim. She pushes her chin out and tries to shake off the vague feeling lingering at the back of her mind. In five days it is Palm Sunday. Most of the children will come to the procession, each with a bunch of pussy willow, box and thuja. All of them will be smiling and some will be wearing new clothes. That is what it is like in a Catholic primary school.

He has disappeared from view. Past the first rapids you have a view of a long right-hand bend, it must be at least three hundred metres long. Mister L.D.R., she thinks, my inconsiderate, asocial Mister L.D.R. She thinks of the period after last Christmas when he was not once able to put his iPod away, not even in bed, when he occasionally talked in one of his voices about how the only way was to be fired into the cosmos in a space capsule and fly solo to Jupiter, Uranus and beyond. Yet he gave her a sense of security that she had hardly ever felt before.

Each breath burns inside her chest. She cannot go any faster. He is chasing after her. He will catch her up. He always catches up with her. She will stumble and fall. He will loom over her like a giant and laugh, a little bit muddy and a little bit embarrassed. Then he will bend over and help her up by her arm.

Suddenly something brushes her elbow. She spins round and stumbles. In two swift paces from behind the elder bush he catches her. Now she is screaming out loud. He beams at her. She thrashes at him wildly.

TEN

Sometimes he suspects that she is just pretending to be freezing cold. It's the sort of thing people do to make others feel guilty. She was sitting in one of her oversize roll-neck sweaters, wrapped in a blanket, and shivering. Her face registered a look of laboured disinterest. Sometimes he would go and fetch some gloves, and if he said he might find it easier to believe her if she left out the hysterics, she would reply that, professionally, she couldn't afford to have frostbitten fingers. He would laugh at this and she would get livid.

"Yes, yes, Mister Eskimo," she said, spooning out her egg. "It's at least sixteen degrees," he said. "Too hot for an Eskimo." Fourteen degrees was the threshold. When it was warmer than fourteen degrees he took his breakfast outside, if his schedule allowed it. On those Wednesdays when the child protection group met in the afternoons, he always gave himself extra time in the mornings and would leave home an hour later. He would set the table on the terrace behind the house, make soft-boiled eggs or scrambled eggs with tomatoes, and look forward to her company. Usually she came of her own accord, with rosy cheeks and glowing ears, and carrying a sheet of music. Occasionally he would tiptoe into the former cowshed and stable, now a music room, to listen to her before they had breakfast. But today he had not. "What were you playing?" he asked. "Opus five, number one," she said. "It's warming." "Of course. Opus five, number one." He hated it when she tested him. "Beethoven, my dear. Mister Psychiatrist needs to concentrate more on his music," she said. He took the egg in his left hand, rolled it in his palm, and sliced through it with his knife. He carefully removed the top. A tiny brown and white feather stuck to the shell. I fail to concentrate on most things, he thought, on music, books, my house, my wife. Maybe people became psychiatrists to cling onto the illusion that they were concentrating on everything, and in reality they were concentrating on nothing. He sprinkled some chives on his egg and mixed them into the yolk with his spoon. "Why don't you say something?" Irene asked. "Right at this moment I'm concentrating on the whole world," he said. She gave a short laugh. She supposed he meant the question of the perfect egg. No, he meant the question of what anaesthetisation and self-harm had in common, he meant young men who tried unsuccessfully to hang themselves from the ceiling, and mothers who couldn't give a damn about it, more important was that they had the opportunity to be in the spotlight. She looked directly at him. "What have you got against me at the moment?" she asked. "Nothing," Horn said, he was merely thinking too much about tenors.

They had not bargained on Tobias. All of a sudden he was standing right beside them, supporting himself on the tabletop with one hand, pointing the other at his father, and saying, "You've got to do something." Horn noticed that his hair had not been brushed, he was not wearing any socks and he looked pale. "Are you ill?" he asked.

"No. But you're a head doctor, aren't you?"

"If you're not ill, by my reckoning you ought to be in school in half an hour." Horn felt himself getting angry.

"Well, aren't you?"

"Aren't I what?"

"A head doctor? A nerve doctor?"

"Yes. And?"

"Mimi's falling over."

"What do you mean Mimi's falling over?"

Tobias explained that the cat had followed him into the bathroom, and as usual jumped straight on the sink to steal the top of the toothpaste tube. After patting it around for a while, she had taken it into her mouth and was about to leap onto the rim of the bathtub. At that instant she froze, tipped over like a block of wood, and lay there still. His first thought was that she was dead, but then he noticed her whiskers twitching and he poked her side. She tried to bite him, and all of this had happened in slow motion. "So where is she now?" Horn asked. "On the greengage tree," Tobias replied.

"What's she doing up there in her near-death state?"

"You're not taking me seriously."

"I mean, did she climb the tree in slow motion, too?"

Tobias went red in the face and rapped his knuckles on the table. "You're such an arsehole!" he shouted. He explained how the cat had soon started behaving normally again, doing her normal thing of chasing after a blue tit, and the blue tit its normal thing of being faster.

"Cats do tip over," Horn said, "just like that. It's common knowledge and it's got nothing to do with being ill." There was a glint in Tobias's eye. "Do you know what? I really pity your patients."

"You mind what you say!"

"Raffael!" Horn noticed too late that he had raised his arm. "What? Are you going to hit me?" Tobias asked. "It seems to be all the rage at the moment." Horn took a deep breath. "I've never hit you," he said, "you know that." Tobias grinned, then acted very cold. There were three occasions he could remember, he said, and surely a psychiatrist didn't need telling about the times he couldn't remember. "Once only," Horn said, "if ever."

"Three times," Tobias said, bending over the table. "Do you want to know what it felt like?" Horn leaned back and eyed his son. In his mind he saw Tobias lying asleep on the bed, a dribble of saliva by his mouth, and he recalled the word his son had used to describe the cat's condition. Then it just came out, without his being able to stop himself. "Are you stoned again?" he asked.

Irene sat there, rigid, her hands flat on her lap. The blanket had slipped from her shoulders. A wasp was hovering at her plate, carving tiny pieces from the remains of a slice of ham. A look of confusion spread across Tobias's face, then he seemed to withdraw inside himself completely. His gaze was fixed half a metre away when he stretched out his arm, lifted Horn's egg from the eggcup, closed his hand around it and squeezed. A yellow sludge seeped through his fingers. He took a napkin from the table, wiped his hand thoroughly, scrunched it up and placed it in front of Horn. Then he turned around and went into the house.

Like a painting, Horn thought as his gaze drifted over the table: the jug with the orange juice, the white loaf that had been cut open, the scrunched-up napkin with an Easter bunny on it, and the wasp flying off with a morsel of ham between its front legs. In the background the field with hazelnut bushes, and beyond that the woods. In the air, the perfume of meadowsweet which grew to the right of the corner of the house, the chirruping of a male redstart, and the rattling of a motor mower. Behind him he could hear Irene's footsteps heading back towards the house. At that moment it occurred to him that wasps were incredibly rare at this time of year.

After the fourth year of primary school Tobias had been ten and full of energy. He drew Ferraris, saved baby hedgehogs and scored his first goals for the under-12 football team. It had seemed a perfectly logical idea to send him to holiday camp in the Waldviertel with his best friends, Jakob and Benny. They had bought him a sleeping bag, a food container and a headlamp, and in the end they had decided to leave Mike the teddy bear at home after all. He had lain down to sleep next to his packed rucksack, and nobody had entertained even the slightest idea that anything might go wrong. Horn got up from the table.

She was sitting with her head lowered on her stark bentwood chair, playing a wild melody he did not recognise, alternating rapidly between bowed and pizzicato passages. He liked it. He stood by the wall next to the door and listened.

"He's not taking drugs," she said suddenly, letting her arm fall, "I'm absolutely sure he's not taking drugs." Play on, Horn thought, don't talk, just play on. She leaned back and looked at him. What did he think he was doing, accusing Tobias like that, she asked, she wasn't born yesterday and she'd never noticed anything, no funny smells or anything like that. Horn thought of the parents of anorexic girls who didn't notice a thing right up to their daughters' deaths. He did not answer. She played a low note. "And what was all that hitting stuff he was talking about?" she asked. "Children are being beaten," he said.

"Aren't they always?"

"No, this is different. More systematic. And it's happening here."

"What's it got to do with you?"

"Nothing. Nothing at all, actually," he said. She took hold of her bow again. Opus five, number one came into his head, but what he had just been listening to definitely wasn't Beethoven.

"What's your tenor up to, by the way?" he asked as he was about to leave the room. She gave him a baffled look. "He's protecting his voice," she said at last.

*

Horn sat in his car and mulled it over. The holiday camp business was clear-cut. That morning Tobias was lying on his side in bed, his mouth tightly shut and fists clenched. Both of them had stood there shaking him, struggling with the notion that nothing in the world could have stirred him. When he got up at half-past eight, five minutes after the coach had left, sat down at the kitchen table and asked, "Where's my breakfast?" Horn blew a fuse. He had grabbed Tobias's hair with his left hand, twisted the boy's head around, and slapped him with his right hand, left, right, palm on the left cheek, back of the hand on the right. Once again he could feel the uncontrollable fury from back then, and in his mind he saw his son's face which had registered barely any surprise or fear, only contempt and triumph. They had not spoken about it afterwards, not a word. The rucksack had remained on the floor of the children's room, unopened, for eight weeks. Eventually Irene found it too ridiculous and unpacked the thing. Horn had never apologised.

He started the car, reversed a few metres along the country lane where it had been standing, and manoeuvred the Volvo back onto the road. The first marguerites were flowering by the roadside. The sun lit up the young leaves on the trees, making them appear yellow. The town lay before him, rolled out as if the distances between individual points had become increased. The helicopter landing pad on the hospital roof towered above the river like a diving board. It's spring, he thought, I'm fighting with my son, and I'm not talking to my wife enough.

On one occasion she had pulled Tobias's hair. He was perhaps twelve at the time, and had tipped the beef stroganoff she had cooked, together with the rice and salad, from his plate back into the pan, complaining that he'd asked for ravioli. He did not know whether she had ever hit him. It was different with Michael. Maybe this is a kind of role distribution, too, he thought, one of you hits one child but not the other, and with your partner it's vice-versa. He recalled an episode when Irene had given full vent to her anger at Michael's dyslexia. He can't read, she had said, he can't write, and if you try to help him he puts on a face like a frog. He doesn't know a single note, either, she had added quietly, and for the first time he pictured her hitting Michael when he was not there.

*

Frühwald was waiting for him in the hospital car park under a sky dotted with fleecy clouds. He was leaning against his minivan, smoking. "I'm sorry, I didn't ring you back," Horn said. "You're a busy man," Frühwald replied, pushing himself off the van. He was as tanned as if it were high summer. "Do you fill up on sun before the swimming season?" Horn asked. "The swimming season has already begun," Frühwald said, "a good week ago." As a medical man, Horn said, he found that terribly alarming, the lake couldn't be more than twelve degrees. "Thirteen point two at one twenty deep. That's what the biologists say." A year ago they had installed an electronic monitoring station at the wildlife observation centre, which measured the temperature and oxygen content of the lake as well as the concentration of nitrates in it. The locals had been fairly sceptical at first, but tourists had begun to make pilgrimages to the lake, as if they all had gills. How did he tolerate the cold? Horn asked, seeing that he was definitely not a penguin. "A walrus, perhaps," Frühwald said. "I've always been fascinated by walruses, by elephant seals, too. On the one hand they're soft giants you'd love to sink your fists into, like foam rubber, but then they've got jaws they could bite you in two with." He was a friend of Frank Holderegger, the owner of the water sports shop, he said, and Frank always lent him the right kind of wetsuit. That was the secret, not some sort of hidden layer of fat around the vulnerable organs. From Easter onwards, as long as it didn't fall in mid-March, a four-millimetre shorty was usually sufficient, and at the beginning of June the lake was eighteen degrees, which meant trunks only. "What about now?" Horn asked.

"Now? Now, you can forget it." In theory it should be six-millimetre

115

conditions at the moment, Frühwald said, with arms and legs covered that would be enough to keep him warm for the entire three and a half kilometres. But, as Horn well knew, this was purely theoretical as far as he was concerned. His wife's current condition meant he couldn't leave her alone for longer than a few minutes, so swimming was out of the question. "It makes me imbalanced," he said, "very imbalanced." He flicked away his cigarette. He was sleeping badly, being unfriendly to those around him and had started smoking again. Horn looked around. "And where's your wife now?" he asked. "At home," Frühwald said, looking at his watch. "It's only twenty minutes. Shall we go?"

"What do you mean?"

"I want you to see her." He opened the passenger door. Horn put up his hand in protest. "You know it's not that simple for a hospital doctor," he said. "Where there's a will, there's a way," Frühwald said, grabbing Horn by the arm. Horn reached into his jacket pocket and pulled out his mobile. "Are you calling security?" Frühwald asked. Horn shook his head. "I may not swim as much as you, but I shovel cow muck on a daily basis," he said, "and because I've got a bigger reach I reckon I could deal with you on my own." Frühwald grinned and let him go.

Herbert picked up the telephone. No, there were no dramas on the ward. In a fit of night-time confusion, Frau Hrstic had clambered over her bed guard, tumbled onto the floor, broken her upper arm and been transferred to casualty for the time being. Her room-mate, Frau Steininger, was annoyed by her absence and kept on looking for her. There had also been a raft of phone calls: several newspapers, Sabrina's father and the police. No, he didn't know what the police wanted. The policewoman had said it wasn't urgent. What else? The usual.

"Let's go," Horn said. Frühwald took a deep breath. "Thanks," he said.

They drove along a stretch of the riverbank and took the exit for

Furth north at the roundabout by Severin bridge. A milk lorry slowed them down for a while. Frühwald shifted endlessly between third and fourth gear, not saying a word. He only opened his mouth when they turned east into a side street just by the blocks of flats. "Do you know why I admire you?" he said, without turning towards Horn. "I admire you because you're able to deal with children." Horn did not ask, and Frühwald explained that he had read about it in the paper.

The house, hidden away on the crest of a hill behind a horn-beam hedge, was an unspectacular 1960s bungalow: L-shaped layout, pitched tiled roof, adjoining garage. As if built for a wheel-chair user, Horn thought. "We don't need a stairlift," Frühwald said, "but that's about the only advantage." The internal doors, for example, were only seventy-five centimetres wide and so they'd all had to be changed, and then there were the loo and bathroom conversions and the re-laying of the driveway. Frühwald pointed to the concrete path that snaked up the slope in two shallow curves. A few metres from the front door he stopped and said just what a mess it had made widening eleven doorways by fifteen centimetres, quite apart from the cost. At that moment something flashed across his face. "You're a doctor, right?" he asked. "Yes, I am a doctor," Horn said. "You know that."

"So you're bound by confidentiality?"

Of course he was bound by confidentiality, Horn said, why the question? Frühwald turned the key in the lock. She's dead, Horn thought, he's strangled her and wants me to certify a natural death, like a protracted epileptic fit or a pulmonary embolism. Frühwald turned his head. Horn put his hand to his mouth. Not again, he thought. "I can't hear anything," Frühwald said. "She must be sleeping."

Margot Frühwald was lying on her back in bed, her eyes wide open, staring straight at the ceiling. All that was visible was her face, surrounded by dark-blue bedclothes with a silver peacock-feather pattern. What they were witnessing was simply one variant of her behaviour at the moment, her husband said. At other times she would bellow incoherently or whimper to herself for hours on end. And then there were the fits. Oh yes, fits plural. Over the last three days she must have had ten epileptic fits, some only a few seconds long, others three or four minutes, with cramps, going blue in the face and incontinence, just as you imagine it. He had given her diazepam, both in drops and rectal tubes, but nothing had worked. Horn walked up to the bed. "What are you doing?" Frühwald asked, grabbing his arm again. "I'd like to examine her," Horn said, pulling the covers back.

The straps were white, about eight centimetres wide and attached to the bed frame on her right and left. They were fixed around her wrists with magnetic catches. "I'm sorry, I had no other choice," Frühwald said, looking over to the window. Beads of sweat were closely packed on his wife's forehead. Now Horn understood what Frühwald had meant by confidentiality. "Undo them," he said.

Half an hour later, Horn and Frühwald were sitting at the kitchen table drinking schnapps. Margot Frühwald was on her way to hospital in an ambulance. *Confused state after cerebral attack*, Horn had written on the ambulance form, and had allocated her to his own department. His people knew what to do, and he himself would pop over there shortly.

Somehow he had been able to accept the paralysis caused by the accident, Frühwald said, "We all have our crosses to bear," but now that he was no longer able to have a meaningful conversation with her, it had become intolerable. She would talk about railways, her sister Hedwig, with whom she had not been in touch for decades, and a man called Sylvester who he didn't know. He found it most difficult when she talked about children at the kindergarten as if nothing had happened, about the trips and games, about *Who's sitting next to me?* and *Ball over the rope* and about *We're the animals of the jungle.* "She was the love of my life, you understand?" Frühwald said. "She was ruined for me." He reached for the bottle to pour more. Horn put his hand over his glass. "Do you drink every morning?" he asked. Frühwald raised an eyebrow. "Only when I've got a psychiatrist visiting," he said.

They talked about the series of examinations she might be expected to undergo, about the likelihood of developing epilepsy even a long time after an epidural haematoma, and about the various drug treatment possibilities. Gradually Frühwald seemed to regain confidence. "O.K.: all her medical notes, a few nighties, a dressing gown, slippers, magazines," he said finally. Horn thought about asking him where he had got the immobilisation straps, but let it lie.

Horn decided to return on foot. As he left he noticed that the elder in Frühwald's garden was starting to blossom, and that the first buds were opening on the juvenile broad-leafed lime growing on the bend of the drive. Normally he would be happy, Frühwald said, when things started growing early in the year, when the wild crocuses pushed through the last of the snow, or when the blue clematis threw out its stems at the end of February, but this time he was totally indifferent. Horn stopped by the garden gate and turned to him. "In your opinion, who would go around systematically hitting children?" he asked. Frühwald thought about it. "Do you mean this black owl thing?" Horn nodded. "Maybe someone like me." There was the hint of a smile on Frühwald's face when Horn held out his hand.

*

The beds lining the paved path which ran between the blocks of flats had recently been planted up with roses and box. The musty smell of fresh compost hung in the air. Ants scrabbled around for worms between the small plants. Horn thought of Irene, of her enthusiasm for the garden and her inability to deal with pests. She loathed chemical pesticides, and if the aphid infestation ever got so bad that she felt it necessary to use nettle spray or diluted vinegar, she was wracked by guilt. When, not long ago, he had gathered up the night-time snails which were devouring her sacred dwarf asters and cosmos, and drowned them in beer, she had called him a murderer. She had offered a half-hearted apology later, and suggested getting a pair of Chinese runner ducks. "They feed on snails," she had said, and when he replied, "If you do that, I'm going to feed off Chinese runner ducks," she was deeply offended. She never leaves me cold, Horn thought, she thrills me, she sets me on fire; sometimes she makes me so soft, sometimes she hurts me; but she doesn't leave me cold. And yet I've never called her *the love of my life*, he thought, never said it to anyone else and not to her either. Maybe because he never wanted to be in the situation where he would have to say it in the past tense, like Frühwald, or maybe as a psychiatrist you lost your faith in such states of emotion. "Love is first and foremost a hormonal imbalance," Cejpek, head of the department of internal medicine, had said. Christina had replied that she was pleased their senior consultant would never be threatened by this disorder, and Cejpek had said that this was not quite true; the sight of a sixteen-pointer in a forest clearing could upset his internal balance. Cejpek had leased some hunting land on the south-western slope of the Kammwand massif and he spent every free moment there. He was an expert on the local fauna and a good shot when it really mattered. He pursued women in the same way as he did small game, quickly and loudly, a strategy which had not yet brought any lasting success. Irene spoke time and again about love. Sometimes Horn took it seriously, sometimes less so, depending on whether or not a half-Italian tenor was on the horizon.

He crossed the square in front of the Protestant parish centre and took the route along Ettrichgasse. My wife freezes ostentatiously

120

when she sits at a table with me, he thought, my son crushes my breakfast egg, and my patients are strapped to their beds by their husbands. And the cat's falling over. There were days when it was better to be invisible. He tried to focus his mind on what awaited him: Frau Hrstic's daughter, who would scurry up to him at the entrance to the ward in one of her gaudy suits, and irately declare that her mother's fall could only have been the result of some foul play; Sabrina's father, who left a trail of slime behind him even on the telephone – will this skin cutting never end? I can't explain it, please tell me what I can do, Herr Doctor; and that Marcus with a "C" and the electric guitar, who he would probably be able to talk to this time, finally.

There was something reassuring about the housing development. It housed people and it had no pretensions. At most there was the odd length of showy terrace railing, or a sign at one of the garden gates warning of an alarm system. No advertising, no display windows, no brass plaques belonging to doctors' or lawyers' practices. In one of the front gardens a man was using a strimmer. A well-maintained structure of compulsive behaviour is the motor of European society, Horn thought, the trimming of lawns, the drafting of food standards and the squeezing of people into a uniform straitjacket of lifelong learning. Behind all this, nothing but greed and hatred; at best there was a slight diversity of focus: a little more infantile orality in Italy, more aggressive narcissism in France, and in Austria that friendly brand of malice, which was actually none other than a defence mechanism against the certainty of a permanent erectile dysfunction. "In this country we don't like shagging that much," his training analyst had once said. "We prefer going to church or parent–teacher evenings, and afterwards we beat the shit out of other people," she had added.

At the turn off to Linzer Straße a patrol car drove towards him. He thought of the detective who had come to see him twice recently, the first time with Felix Szigeti, then with Britta, the blonde girl whose surname he could not remember. There had been something extremely reassuring about the young woman, both in general and in the way she dealt with children. He imagined her behind the wheel, stopping, opening the window and asking him if he would like a lift. He would get in and gaze at her out of the corner of his eye. When the car passed him he noticed two uniformed policemen through the window. One of them was Töllmann, the other he did not recognise. Töllmann was known as the sniffer dog of Furth police, with an unerring instinct for finding illegal substances and relentless in his pursuit. The junkies hated him, as did his colleague Mike Dassler, head of the addiction unit. Dassler took a more moderate line; Töllmann took no notice and often got quite rough if anybody hesitated, even for a second, when emptying their pockets. Recently he had brought the thirteen-year-old Diego Veith to the department in handcuffs, because after a body search he'd said that he would not only knife his fucking parents, but Töllmann too, the moment he got the chance. Raimund had asked Töllmann whether it was really necessary to handcuff a child, and Töllmann had said he was of the old school, and anyway, a thirteen-year-old criminal was primarily a criminal rather than a child. Horn suddenly pictured Tobias being caught by Töllmann with a pot pipe in his mouth, and being led away in handcuffs. He pictured himself raising a revolver and aiming it at Töllmann. This did not make him feel bad.

✳

A few hours later they were climbing the steps to the children's department. They talked about Margot Frühwald, who had suffered a grand mal seizure during admission to P2, and who was recovering very slowly; about Marcus who, since he had woken up from his sedation, had been sitting on the bed with his eyes closed, one hand on the body of his Dark Fire, totally silent; and about Sabrina's father. The man had been stalking up and down outside the department in a patterned woollen jacket and bright-green shirt, playing the pseudo professional at the top of his voice, and trying to see his daughter. Sabrina had threatened to cut off her little finger if they let him in, nothing would stop her, not even ten thousand euros, and Leonie Wittmann had gone out to tell him the price was ten thousand euros, and even then there was a degree of uncertainty as to whether Sabrina would actually allow him to see her. Absolutely she would, the man had said, even if it meant he had to come with his lawyer, and Wittmann had told him to go ahead and do that, his daughter would probably amputate her ring finger as well. "The man stinks of aftershave and cat's piss, wears the ghastliest jacket imaginable, and is one hundred per cent sure that nobody can touch him," said Renate Mutz, the social worker. "Which is true," Christina replied. Kiddie fiddlers, Horn thought, and was surprised by the banality of the term. With some men you knew it the moment you saw them, and to a certain extent he could explain this. It was a mixture of self-love and sleaziness, a marked tendency to rush straight in on the attack, plus reaction formation as an underlying principle: threatening others with the very thing you were threatened with yourself, the judge or the police, for example. The younger the children when their torment started, the more assured were the men. An abused four-year-old was worthless in court later on. A school beginner who had had a man's thing shoved in her mouth for long enough would be guaranteed to stay silent whenever questioned. Sabrina's father was not quite so assured. "Maybe I'll bring him in myself," Horn said. "Do that," Christina said. Occasionally, if the children had sufficient protection, there would be conversations in Horn's room which had never become official. Horn did not know whether they served any purpose, but at least he felt better afterwards. If anybody asked him what he had been discussing with these gentlemen, he would say there was no discussion; he had merely been making them aware of certain things. He would always begin in the same way: "I grew up in the country, you know, in a pack of children. We were organised into gangs and I was always the strongest."

The nice thing about the conference room in the children's department was that it was in the far south-western corner of the building, right above the escarpment of the hill, so you got the impression that it was jutting over the river. Directly opposite, the remains of the old town wall extended above the eroded river-bank, and in the middle of this stood a squat round tower with slate conical roof, which without any historical justification was called The Coinmaker's House. A little to the west began the reed bed of the river outlet, and beyond that lay the dark-green lake.

I'm here because that's exactly what I want to be looking at, Horn thought, the movement of the reeds, the towers of the abbey church, the coinmaker's house, the conglomerate layers of the riverbank and the silhouette of the Kammwand. To those who talked scornfully of petty bourgeois mentality and rural idylls he would assert that people who got all puffed up about rural idylls were in fact fighting against their own longing for security, he knew this because he'd been married to a militant idyll evangelist for more than twenty years now, and that for once he was actually interested in appearances, in how things looked. Nothing in life was without consequence, he would say, especially not the things you looked at every day, sometimes even from early childhood; so somebody who had grown up in a narrow valley and had to lift their head to see a horizon would behave differently from a Greenland Inuit, for example, or a Mongol. If anybody suggested that such a notion might not be particularly popular amongst the inhabitants of narrow valleys, he would reply that popularity was not a factor in the understanding of the human psyche.

Besides Renate Mutz and Christina there was Lisbeth Schalk,

who usually conducted the psychological examinations of the children, Strasser, head of the children's department, Roman Wagner, his senior outpatient doctor, and Evelyn Heimerle, his deputy ward sister. Tamara Shafar, the paediatric gynaecologist, was the last to arrive as always, trying to rearrange her curly hair with her fingers and complaining quietly about Jarovsky, her boss, who had once again put her down for the first block of morning surgery. Even though he knew exactly when the child protection group met. Jarovsky was a hypomanic anarchist, but then so were many others in surgical disciplines.

Seeing as she was already up to full speed, would she please start the meeting off, Wagner said. It was just the sort of comment she had expected, Tamara Shafar hissed, rummaging through her notes. If she couldn't find anything she really wanted to discuss, she would leave again immediately. Wagner held up his hands apologetically and swore to dispense with the paediatric jibes. The sarcastic straw-blond Prussian had a thing for the small, surly half-Egyptian with her fiery eyes, everybody could see it. Wagner's girlfriend, who worked as a midwife in the same department as Shafar, could probably see it, too. Horn pictured the two women standing opposite each other, tense and mistrustful, eventually turning away, one to the left, the other to the right, without saying a word. Then he looked at Lisbeth Schalk, who was sitting opposite him, and tried to imagine Irene beside her. He could not.

Tamara Shafar told them about a sixteen-year-old girl she had seen in the outpatients' department seven times over the past year, each time because of a full-blown vaginal infection. They had found a variety of germs in her smear tests, gonococcus, trichomonads, fungi – whatever the zoo in question was sharing with her. This time she was pregnant too, in her tenth week, if it was possible to be certain at this stage. When asked about her sex life she had lowered her eyes and said she didn't have one and that she couldn't account

125

for the pregnancy. It was only when she had asked the girl how they were supposed to explain it to her mother that she had snapped out of it and said, "No way! You can't say anything to her, it's the law, I know that." When she was then asked, "And what if we tell her anyway?" the girl said, "I'll report you to the police." Horn thought of Sabrina, of Fehring and of all those others who insisted on their right to self-harm. Finally he thought of Tobias, how he was surely smoking dope, and how all offers of help were, without exception, rejected as unreasonable demands. When he listened to stories like that, vaginal infections and pregnancy, he was nonetheless relieved that he had two sons. Christina kicked him in the shin. Tamara Shafar jumped up and leaned over the table. "Do you really think that's helpful?" Horn recoiled. Within half a second he understood. "I know it's not a good excuse," he stammered, "but I tend to think aloud." Tamara Shafar fell back into her chair, flinging her arms out. "I could happily live with daughters, too," Roman Wagner murmured. As far as she was concerned, his promise to leave out the silly remarks was still binding, Shafar hissed, and what was more, could someone please tell her, finally, what she was to make of this brattish girl's story? "Is she voluntarily dropping her knickers for all-comers, or is someone forcing her to do it?" Those were precisely the two possibilities, Renate Mutz said, but either way they couldn't do anything against her will. She had the right to assert her sexuality freely; in this, she couldn't be safeguarded from unpleasant experiences and especially not from any peculiarities in her choice of partners. "I like 'peculiarities in her choice of partners,'" Strasser said. "Would you put it in those very same words if she were your daughter?" The social worker did not reply. Sometimes she said that she couldn't stand paediatricians who thought mothers were fundamentally illiterate, and that breastfeeding and changing nappies were medical procedures. And she especially loathed those who continuously brought their own children into play. "Give me her phone number, I'll invite her in for a chat," Lisbeth Schalk said to Shafar, and with that the tension was dispelled at a stroke. She's taking the matter in hand, Horn thought, just as she learned to do on the farm where she grew up. She knows all about wild flowers, about pregnancies, and maybe she also knows that when you're a girl there are times you shag someone you really don't want to be in bed with.

Afterwards Wagner told them about a four-year-old boy who had grabbed a pan of hot coconut fat from the cooker and given himself extensive burns on his chest, and Renate Mutz talked about a family in a state of extreme deprivation, living in a former hunter's cabin between Furth and Sankt Christoph, running water outside their door, no electricity. She was in the middle of describing the condition in which her colleague from the child welfare office had found the three children, particularly the lice infestation in the youngest – one and a half years old – when the door opened.

Leuweritz was no taller than one metre seventy and he ran marathons. It helped you stay calm when dealing with a patient who had the tip of a fence post touching their pericardium, he said, and it was good for long operations and tiresome bosses. He was the senior casualty doctor and had been at loggerheads with Lissoni from the start. Horn had liked him even before that. "What's traumatology looking for in these poor rooms?" Wagner asked. Leuweritz ignored the remark and took an outpatient form from his coat pocket. "Sen Wu," he said. "Eight-year-old son of Chinese parents, born in Furth. Mother's a carer, father's a metal worker. Someone's broken his collarbone."

ELEVEN

The *Osteogenesis imperfecta* thing was just a coincidence and thus best forgotten, Eleonore Bitterle said. Nobody could say for certain that the boy's collarbone wouldn't have snapped in two anyway. Collarbones were not exactly the titans of the human skeleton. "But I still want to understand it!" Kovacs was edgy. They were being forced to expend their every effort on this kids' stuff, all very vague and blown up by the media, and now that something of substance had turned up – Osteo whatever it was: brittle bone disease – he was supposed to forget all about it; no way!

"O.K., if that's what you want." Bitterle went over to the white-board. She would have made an excellent teacher; that was quite obvious. When she stood there in her roll-neck jumpers, explaining the world and expressing it in pictures and diagrams, she was surrounded by a bright incandescence. She told them about the genetically determined metabolic disorder which was the basis of the brittle bone disease, explained that there was no cure and outlined the various manifestations. The extremes were type two, which was associated with a life expectancy of no more than a year, and type one, the most harmless form, which was generally discovered by chance, for example if a child broke a number of bones in a relatively short period of time. In Sen Wu's case, he had broken his right upper arm, right shin and left radius within two years, which was why the boy had been given a closer medical examination. The father had come under suspicion in the past, comments had been made about the authoritarian way in which Asians brought up their children, and they recalled the case of Norbert Schmidinger, who had hurled his five-year-old daughter against a washing-line post, smashing both her legs. "Schmidinger's still inside, isn't he?" Kovacs asked. Sabine Wieck nodded vigorously.

At the time she had stood there sobbing in the interrogation, absolutely powerless and livid, he could still picture her. Immediately beforehand she had tried to question the girl in hospital, and had come up against a wall of fear and resistance. Kovacs had stormed out of the meeting, jumped into his car, and driven straight to Erdoyan. The more that people were in your debt, the greater the latitude you had as a policeman. The Sheriff had understood at once and had only asked whether he was free to choose the method. A few weeks later Schmidinger confessed at his trial, straight up and without hesitation; he even spared them his favourite plea of psychological illness. In the courtroom Kovacs had noticed two Turkish-looking men; one of them, with a grey moustache, was bald, the other, younger man had had one of those ceramic eyes hanging around his neck. Schmidinger had turned to look at them several times. Kovacs himself had not known them. He had not discussed the matter with the Sheriff afterwards.

"If he serves the whole of his sentence he's got two and a half years left," Wieck said. "We've crossed him off already."

"Crossed him off?" Kovacs was baffled. "Off our list," Bitterle said.

"What list? Why don't I know about this?"

"Because you don't like expending your effort on kids' stuff. As we were just hearing."

Kovacs muttered something under his breath. The Schmidinger affair had really upset him, too. The case they were dealing with now seemed banal by comparison. Who hit children? Everybody. Everywhere and every day. Maybe not in quite the same way that he had been hit back in his day, with belts and willow rods, but people still did it. So what was on the list, he asked eventually.

Crimes committed against minors, domestic violence, notifications from the accident ward – basically whatever they could think of, Wieck said.

"How many suspects does that make?"

"One hundred and seventeen."

"There you go."

"What does 'there you go' mean?" Wieck asked, and Kovacs said, there you go, everybody hits their children, even if they always maintain the opposite.

"Do you hit your child?" Bitterle asked, and Kovacs replied, "I'll be able to tell you that tomorrow. Maybe."

Bitterle described Sen Wu's injury, the marks on his skin from the beating, which suggested a stick, and said that the haematoma was relatively unpronounced, which meant the blows could not have been dealt with much force. The parents could probably be eliminated as suspects because they were aware of their son's illness and so would have hit him on the buttocks or in the face rather than on the collarbone. "He's a lucky boy, then, our little Chinese fellow," Kovacs said. "You're not taking it seriously," Bitterle complained. "I am!" Kovas said. "What's he himself saying?"

"Sen Wu? He looks at the floor and says nothing."

"Like the others?"

"That's right, just like the others."

Kovacs asked what the three children had in common besides their age, and Eleonore Bitterle said that he was wrong: they weren't all the same age. Sen Wu was actually in the second year of primary school rather than the first like Felix Szigeti and Britta Kern, and if you knew about children of that age you understood that they found those things very important. Apart from that Britta Kern lived with her mother and a younger sister, Sen Wu with his parents and two sisters, Felix Szigeti was an only child and his parents' marriage was solid. They'd already been notified that Sen Wu would be seeing Raffael Horn. "Like the others?" Kovacs asked.

"Yes, like the others."

"What's Horn found out so far?"

"Nothing, effectively," Sabine Wieck said.

"Why do we need him then?" Kovacs asked.

"Because it's better for a psychiatrist to find out nothing than a police officer."

In any case this was not entirely true; Horn had established that neither Felix Szigeti nor Britta Kern appeared traumatised, and yet both were very frightened, as if they felt honour-bound and threatened at the same time. Felix had said that if he told, then the same thing would happen to him, while Britta pressed her lips firmly together and just shook her head. "'If you don't keep your mouth shut, I'll beat you again, but properly this time.' That's what 'the same thing' means," Kovacs said. "I don't know," Sabine Wieck said.

"What don't you know?"

Some situations were simple, and the violence towards children was hardly one of the more complicated things in life, Kovacs said. Precisely, and because it is so simple, people don't generally just hit children on the back, shoulders and head, as Felix and Britta had stated. "People hit children all over," Kovacs said. Anyway, nobody knew if these two children were telling the truth. "It's a well-known saying that children and fools speak the truth," Bitterle said. Kovacs laughed out loud. "Nonsense," he bellowed. "Children lie – everyone knows that. I lied when I was a child, you lied, and the Felixes and Brittas of this world lie too." "A fractured collarbone doesn't lie," Bitterle said, and Kovacs had no answer to that.

Christine Strobl was standing in the doorway, looking irritable.

Since she went home yesterday evening, she said, thirty-two messages had been left on the answer phone, including one at twenty-seven minutes past midnight, one at nine minutes past two, and another at half past three exactly – evidently from people whose biggest problem was insomnia. At least half of the calls were hazy allegations about neighbours or divorced spouses. One man, for example, had said in his message that his ex-wife was owl-shaped, liked dressing in black and had a tendency towards violence against weaker individuals. Most of the other messages were racially motivated: it was common knowledge that the favourite pastime of Muslims was mistreating children – they educated their own to become suicide bombers and sacrificed foreigners' children for training purposes, and of course the Chinese, well, they were on the point of taking over the world, weren't they? In her opinion, Christine Strobl said, two of the messages were of interest. First, the nine-minutes-past-two caller, who sounded slightly bewildered and paranoid, said that he had spent his entire life looking into secret societies and there was a whole raft of them with the colour black in their name, including a lot of flowers: Black Rose, Tulip, Lily, Black Eagle, Black Wolf, even Black Hamster – which he found puerile – Black Window, Black Tower, Black Sunday, and of course Black September. On the other hand he had never come across Black Owl, but it might well be a new organisation. If the reports in the media were to be believed, he thought that these blows were not abuse, but rather an initiation rite, a sort of accolade. "Twat," Kovacs said. Frau Strobl looked offended: "Well, I thought it was interesting anyway." "It is," Wieck said. "Horn spoke of a pledge, too." As a psychiatrist he could allow himself to spout all that stuff with impunity, Kovacs said, standing up. He couldn't understand it, he said, a few children had been beaten and suddenly people were talking of pledges and secret societies, no doubt only to deflect attention from what he'd been saying before, the fact that everybody did it, hit their children, he meant. Now he was going to go away and try to be productive.

There was just one other point, Strobl said, but if he wasn't interested then he should feel free to go and she would do something unproductive with the other ladies, like synchronising their premenstrual tension. "Oh, Christ!" Kovacs sighed, raising his hands in submission. "Pardon?" Wieck asked. "I'll tell you later," the secretary said. So secondly, Eva Weinfurter, a social worker at the town's youth welfare office, had left a message just after seven o'clock, with the cautious advice that the investigation team might be interested in what the office had to say on the subject of violence towards children. If this were the case then she suggested that they return her call. Kovacs slumped back down into his chair. "And?" he asked. "What do you mean 'and'?" Wieck asked.

"I'll do it," Bitterle said, turning to Strobl. "Could I have the number, please?" The secretary rolled her eyes and gave her the slip of paper. "Why you again?" she hissed. "I love lists," Bitterle said loudly. She envisaged that the youth welfare office list might also contain a hundred or so possible culprits. Assuming a certain overlap, that meant that the two lists together would give them perhaps one hundred and fifty suspects. "When will Demski be here?" Kovacs asked. "Never, if you don't haul him back," Wieck said.

"What's Mauritz doing at the moment? And where's Lipp?"

I'm lacking all assertiveness, Kovacs thought. Instead of immediately ordering Demski back from Berlin, I'm making temporary arrangements. On the other hand, everyone knew that a frustrated Demski was nothing but a burden.

"Lipp's still on patrol. We could probably get him if you asked Eyltz nicely. But what would we do with Mauritz?" Wieck made a gesture indicating her colleague's corpulence. "Doesn't matter. Give him a section of the list. Tell him to leave his chemistry set at home and talk to people," Kovacs said. "But don't let him climb any scaffolding."

Apropos climbing scaffolding: Strobl pointed to Ludwig Kovacs' right forearm. What she could see of his bandage looked slightly rotten, if he did not mind her mentioning it.

*

Kovacs had to think for while about where he had left the Vectra the day before. I'm getting old, he thought, my tolerance is on the wane, I'm a misogynist in the eyes of my female colleagues, I think people take children too seriously, and finally, I've forgotten where I parked the car. To top it all, it's a filthy pile of junk that reeks of cigarettes, not a work car, he thought, slamming the car door. He drove towards the centre along Seestraße, turned left into Severinstraße, crossed the river and took the western exit at the roundabout. After the petrol station the road climbed for a bit so that he was suddenly on a level with the tops of the poplars that rose above the wildlife observation centre. The sky was full of tiny clouds. They seemed to be standing still, waiting for an order. It calmed him. A grey heron flew in a downwards arc towards the lake.

There had in fact been two categories of beating when he was a boy: the predictable and less predictable ones. The predictable ones were for performing poorly at school, being naughty, or saying no when this was not the answer your old man wanted to hear. Up until the fourth year in primary school they were caned with a slim willow rod, after that with the belt. Basically, all his friends had got this same sort of punishment, apart from Helmut Grimm and Walter Dorner, both of whom were teachers' sons, and who were brought up differently. What it ultimately amounted to was that your contempt for your parents grew until the point when you were able to pack your things and move out with a good conscience. Occasionally his mother had been able to give him a sign, a blink of her eyes, or a quick movement of her hand: *For God's sake, get out of here!* But mostly it had happened to him without any prior warning. People who could use a pen or a soup spoon equally competently with their left or right hand were called ambidextrous, he knew that from Marlene. Sometimes they had other unusual talents, too, like memorising tunes, artwhistling, or reciting entire telephone directories from start to finish. His father could beat him with either hand, one after the other or both at the same time, and you never knew which side the pain was coming from, even a split-second before. He could still feel the sensation of those coarse hands landing on his face, either flat or clenched into a fist, and he also remembered that the worst thing was not the pain or the fear of being beaten, but the vivid image of his father's fingers: how thick they were, how raised his knuckles were, and how unbelievably red, even redder than his face. Afterwards he would squat by the wall of the shed; he could still picture this exactly as it had been, the blood running from his nose and his horror of those fingers. He would fix his gaze on the edge of the forest beyond the ditch in the meadow in Upper Styria and wait for a deer. But none ever came.

The sheds of the poultry farm came into view on his left. Ever since Schilcher had changed to the barn system, the outside walls were no longer covered in graffiti. Kovacs had liked the slogans: FREE THE CHICKENS! DO YOU WANT EGGS LAID BY NAKED SLAVES? ASK SCHILCHER WHERE HE BUYS HIS BREAKFAST EGGS! His favourite slogan, though, had to be I'D RATHER HAVE TOHFU! TOHFU with a silent "h". Schilcher had repeatedly complained to the police about criminal damage and intimidation, and using his contacts with Eyltz had even got the police to set up a forensic crime scene. Mauritz had moved in with his special sprays and his luminescent lights, allowed himself two days, at the end of which he told Schilcher in confidence that, regrettably, he had

135

only found his, Schilcher's, fingerprints, which meant that the sole outcome could be a charge against him of attempted insurance fraud, in view of his application to the insurance firm for compensation. After that the matter was shelved with remarkable speed.

He took the turn-off for Waiern, drove through the village and straight after the church turned westwards onto the old lakeside road. The sliding door to Fred Ley's boathouse was open. As he drove past he could see the hulls of two white catamarans on stands, side by side. This is where Kovacs had left his own dinghy over the winter, and if any repairs were needed, Ley saw to them without asking much. Right next to it, the clubhouse of Waiern sailing club. Fred Ley had been its president for more than twenty years. Some things followed a simple logic. The road that gave access to the lakeside restaurant, the supermarket and the primary school. There was no black owl here, although people no doubt hit their children in Waiern, too. The agricultural machinery dealer with his excessively large showroom, then three residential roads which all led north. Kovacs took the third. The gabled houses all looked the same, even the front gardens held little to distinguish themselves from one another. Forsythia bushes, white and purple lilacs, daffodils, grape hyacinths, and the first irises dotted here and there. In front of number twelve there was a fountain with a concrete carp spouting water.

The woman who opened the door was holding a shoehorn. Kovacs stared at it, puzzled. For a moment there was a bizarre paralysis between the two of them. Then the woman said, "No, I'm not going anywhere. I'm tidying up." She took a step backwards. Tidying up was basically all she'd been doing since the accident, she said, working and tidying, there wasn't anything else. She worked in the office of the old people's home in the village and could do overtime, as much as she wanted. No-one noticed at home, because her husband came home late anyway and Leo, her younger son, didn't want to have anything to do with her at the moment. "As if I'd done it," she said. "What?" Kovacs said, even though he knew what she meant.

"What do you think?"

Did that mean that she still thought her son had been pushed from the scaffolding? Kovacs asked. She couldn't bear to contemplate the alternatives. "Could you imagine your child slipping on a pool of lubricating oil and falling to their death? Or tripping over a piece of timber that someone had left there?" Kovacs thought of the bandage hidden by the sleeve of his jacket and said nothing.

Gerlinde Weghaupt was a strong, dark-haired woman; one could imagine her quite comfortably living with three men. A woman who laughs even though they're all a bit complicated, Kovacs thought; a woman who asks her husband week after week to mow the lawn; a woman who makes sure that the fridge is full and that the council tax is paid on time. She just hadn't reckoned on this tragedy. She walked ahead of him. By the stairs that led to the upper floor she turned around. "On the television relatives always offer detectives a cup of coffee," she said. "I hope you weren't counting on one. I just can't do those sorts of things at the moment." Kovacs waved the suggestion away. For goodness sake, no, he knew that Demski had spoken to her a number of times already, and that the whole process was an imposition for her, but sometimes he needed to see things with his own eyes, and anyway, he liked looking at people's rooms.

The wall going up the stairs was hung with watercolours of flowers. She paints them herself, Kovacs thought. In autumn she turns over the soil in the vegetable patch, and in spring she paints crocuses and wood anemones. "Where does your husband work, exactly?" Kovacs asked. For Apollo, a temping agency, the woman said, climbing the stairs in front of him. It might sound like poor money and exploitation, but it wasn't. As a paper-machine engineer he was able to seek out the good jobs and organise his work in such a way that he had time to play at weekends and during Carnival. Accordion, she said when Kovacs remained silent, dance music. He played in a quartet: accordion, fiddle, clarinet and double bass. They were in demand all over Austria, sometimes in Bavaria and Switzerland, too.

The woman took a key out of her pocket and unlocked the door. Kovacs imagined her doing this on a daily basis now, locking the door again once inside the room even though there was nobody else in the house, and then sitting on the bed or at the desk.

The famous photograph of Keith Jarrett's Köln Concert hung above the bed, next to it Chick Corea with Bobby McFerrin on a huge open-air stage, and Friedrich Gulda in a photograph from the time before he wore a cap. "He wanted to follow in the footsteps of his father," Kovacs said. The woman shook her head. "He took it more seriously," she said. "It wasn't just about earning money and that." Kovacs went over to the nut-brown piano by the wall to the right of the window and lifted the lid. GEBRÜDER STINGEL, WIEN, he read, K. & K. HOF-CLAVIER-FABRIKANTEN. The woman smiled briefly. The compulsion to lift the lid of a piano, he'd had that too, she said, he'd always got himself into trouble in museums, like at Mozart's birth house in Salzburg. He was still quite small at the time, but his hand was straight on the piano lid and bang! One of those ghastly museum attendants was there in a flash, barking "Please, don't touch!" Kovacs pressed down a key, carefully so that it did not make a sound. He could feel the felt of the hammer touching the string. "It's from 1908, a Viennese action mechanism. He bought it on eBay from a junk dealer in Ljubljana. Last summer he did a course in piano restoration specially," the woman said. In a golden frame on top of the piano was a photograph of a black man at a grand piano. Thelonious Monk, the woman said – he'd been an idol, someone for whom music was everything, for whom nothing else existed. Kovacs thought that there were things he knew something about, such as freshwater fish, the way in which people dealt with loss, and the difference between a red giant and a white dwarf; but other things he was totally ignorant of, such as spring-flowering plants, what women liked to wear, or music. "The piano's a solo instrument, isn't it?" he asked. The woman gave him a wary look. "Didn't your colleague tell you?" she asked. "About the band, I mean?"

"No, well, maybe he did and I wasn't really listening." Sometimes you lie and don't know why, he thought, you obey an impulse and can't explain it. There were five of them, the woman said, guitar, bass, drums, flute and him on the keyboard. He also played piano on some numbers, but not many. "They're good," the woman said. "He composed and wrote lyrics, they mainly played their own songs." R. & B., he would say if you asked him what sort of music he played, Austro R. & B. – she didn't really know what it was herself. They'd recently been to see a production company in Vienna to discuss a recording project. Although it hadn't gone well, and the person there had sent them away after talking only about the sales they might expect and a possible deal where they'd put in some of their own money, something would come of it soon, she was absolutely sure. "What are they called?" Kovacs asked. She did not immediately understand. "Who? The label?"

"No, the band. What's the band called?"

The woman thought for a moment and then shrugged. She didn't know, she said, the band had been called many things, to begin with it was Furth Five, then names like Stille Nacht or Grobverputz; she couldn't say what the current one was. Now she's lying, Kovacs thought, he couldn't possibly say why, but she is. He thought of Weather Report, Attwenger, Manhattan Transfer, The Beatles, The

Rolling Stones and Rammstein, and all of a sudden wondered whether The Black Owl might not be a brilliant name for a band. He was close to asking her, but then let it pass.

She talked about the family crisis caused by her son's decision to leave school after the fifth year to begin a builder's apprenticeship, and how he'd been a role model for his younger brother, with his passions and his sharp critical mind which had never blunted, even though he spent every day building brick walls, cementing foundations and pouring screed. Finally she explained how her husband would occasionally stand outside their son's door, listening, and how in the beginning, when they were lying in bed at night, he used to call him an idiot whose obstinacy was doing him out of his school-leaver's certificate and a university education, but then he had started to rave about how musical he was and the power of his lyrics. "Can I see some?" Kovacs asked.

"What?"

"Lyrics."

"No," the woman said, shutting the piano lid. Had he now seen what he'd needed to see, she asked. Kovacs nodded. He thought so, he said. By the way, he wanted to tell her that her son definitely hadn't slipped in a pool of lubricating oil up on the scaffolding. Nor had there been any lengths of timber lying around that he might have tripped over. He knew because he'd been there himself. The woman looked over his shoulder towards the door. She knew something else, as well, she said: Her son had definitely not killed himself.

*

He had as little time for pharmacies as he did for doctors. The smell of them made him feel sick, and he was also repelled by the tactic of masking disease and decay, mainly by filling shelves with boiled sweets and sun creams. He could just about bear the Dromedary Pharmacy. This was because of the dromedaries and

140

Viktoria Stich. He had liked dromedaries since childhood, their ascetic lifestyle, the proud way they held their heads, their legs which were endlessly long and yet broad as they moved, and the ambling pace with which they overtook a car in the desert if they wanted to. He liked Viktoria Stich, too. The young pharmacist was small, moody, a homeopathy freak, and told police jokes the moment anyone from the force entered her premises. "No," Kovacs said when he saw her grinning, "no jokes today and none of those homeopathic pills. I'm wounded, and my bandage is a mess. At least that's what the ladies in my office say." He took off his jacket. "They're right," the pharmacist said. "Do you just want to buy the stuff, or shall we do it here?" Kovacs was briefly irritated, then he looked around. Apart from an assistant, who was processing a heap of prescriptions and arranging small boxes of medicines on the rack in front of a huge cabinet, there was nobody in the shop. Other people have affairs, Kovacs thought, I have women who bandage me. He pushed up his shirtsleeve. The pharmacist cut through the gauze and removed the bandage in one piece. "Does it hurt?" she asked. Kovacs shook his head. The cotton cloths had absorbed Szarah's secret paste and everything that had seeped from the wound, presenting a shockingly colourful picture. Beneath was the gash in Kovacs' forearm, smooth and dry with a thin crust. "What on earth did you put on it?" the pharmacist asked, frowning and chucking the old bandage into the bin with a pair of plastic tweezers. "A Moroccan spice mix," Kovacs said. "Chilli, cumin, coriander."

"Looks like it."

"But it worked."

Yes, she said, apparently it had. But to be honest she suspected that he'd been secretly taking the Aconitum C 200 that she'd given him when he had stomach cramps. "Stomach cramps?" he asked.

"Commissar!"

141

"O.K., stomach cramps. Many years ago."

While the pharmacist was applying the aluminium-coated dressing pad, a slim, grey-haired man entered the shop. She waved at him. He stayed in the background. "How is she?" she asked. "The usual," the man said, brandishing a prescription. "She's on a new antipsychotic. And she's not sleeping again." The pharmacist wrapped the dressing in a self-adhesive bandage. How did he get this injury in the first place? she asked. Kovacs noticed that something was making him tense. "You're not going to tell any jokes today, and I don't have to tell any stories," he replied, before paying and leaving.

Outside he took a deep breath. It's strange, he thought, I think I'm dealing fine with my own insomnia, but if somebody else talks about sleep disorders I feel as if I'm standing on the edge of the abyss. Apart from that he suddenly felt that he had betrayed Szarah, and at the same time had the irrepressible urge to have sex with Marlene.

There was a note on the shop door: CLOSED TODAY DUE TO HOUSE CLEARANCE. Kovacs reached for his mobile. "Who are you clearing out?" he asked. "An architect who's moving to Finland to be with her husband," Marlene replied. "Finland, oh God," Kovacs said. "Darkness, alcoholism and suicide. And saunas save only a very few of them."

"The midnight sun, a thousand kilometres of canoeing and elk calves aplenty," she said. "What do you want?"

"To get straight inside you, to tell the truth."

"That's what I thought."

"So why are you asking?"

"Because I wanted to hear it."

In fact she was quite taken by the idea of having sex right now, Marlene said, but there were more than a hundred items of clothing and all sorts of odds and ends, so he'd just have to be patient.

A hundred black roll-neck jumpers, Kovacs said, that wouldn't take long to sort out, and she replied that there was a little more variety amongst female architects. She'd still need a good hour there, then they could meet at his flat. Kovacs tried again: "I'll come and help you sort through the clothes." The architect wouldn't like that, she said. "You win," he said. "So what am I going to do for an hour?" "Go to Lefti's, or make yourself something to eat," she said, giving him a kiss down the telephone. "Animal," he said, and hung up.

He gazed at the window display for a while, at a pink suit with the sign ONLY WORN TWICE, at a raw-silk grey trouser suit with the label NEW, SMALL FLAWS IN THE WEAVE, at a row of size thirty-seven women's shoes, and at a collection of Hummel porcelain figurines with absurdly chubby cheeks. Offer of the week was a pair of Murano glass swans, one petrol-green, the other dark red, on sale for €23.50. The woman I'm sleeping with earns her living from stuff cleared out of people's houses and kitsch, he thought, and in a funny way that makes me happy.

When he turned south at Rathausplatz and drove past the abbey, he saw that the granite flagstones of the courtyard were being scoured by two tractor-like cleaning machines. He had last seen Easter-time cleaning back in his childhood, soft soap and gloss wax, taking curtains down and chamois leather for the children to wipe the windows dry with. His mother would spend a week prowling irritably through the house, and his father would disappear off somewhere. That was the only good thing about it. Yvonne had had a fundamental objection to cleaning, and Marlene did it when she felt like it. For the last two and a half years he had employed Sznezana, who lived at the eastern end of the Walzwerk estate in one of the former workers' blocks, and who came to his flat for one morning a week. He thought of Gerlinde Weghaupt, of the fact that there were other reasons for cleaning apart from dirt, of the ornate writing on the inside of the piano lid, and why he had from the very beginning ruled out the possibility that Florian Weghaupt had committed suicide. Then he thought about Marlene again, about her brash humour, about the fact that she could never be angry for long, and about how she went completely silent if sex was particularly good.

*

As always at this time of day, children on their way home from school were loitering around the fountain. In the very middle of them were Hakan, the Sheriff's youngest brother, who was the most promising young talent in the field of shady deals, despite being wheelchair-bound because of a congenital spine deformity and Isabella Neulinger, the school ghost. Nobody could remember who had first given her this name. Although she was almost permanently absent from class, somehow she always managed to submit good-quality work and gave legendary talks on drugs and child prostitution, thereby splitting the teaching staff at the secondary school right down the middle. Ever since the time that Töllmann had handled her more roughly than usual, her only way of communicating with the police was with her middle finger. She simply ignored Kovacs. He took that as a tribute.

Slightly apart from the group, a girl with a signal-green mohican was kneeling on the ground, throwing bottle tops at a black-and-white cat. Kovacs did not know the girl. The cat belonged to Alexander Koesten, the architect who lived directly below him. Its name was Koolhaas, and roughly every other day it would leap from the balcony into the juniper bush below. Each time Koesten would get into a flap and suspect his neighbours of kidnapping the thing.

As he was rummaging around for his key, Kovacs narrowed down his choices to an omelette or a ham and cheese toastie. His preference was for an omelette, but there was a slight uncertainty over the egg situation. In the past he would have been able to list the contents of his fridge off the top of his head. But this was no longer the case. I'm getting old, he thought.

"Hello." Kovacs was startled. The girl with the green mohican was standing behind him, smiling awkwardly. She was wearing a black, studded leather jacket with a ripped shoulder seam, several rings through her nose, and a silver skull in her left ear. "Hello," Kovacs said. "Can I help you?" "Dad!" the girl said.

There were moments when life chucks a spanner in the works, so abruptly that you can no longer move your arms and you fall flat on your face. It takes a while to get to your feet again. "Dad?" the girl said again. Kovacs stared in turn at the key, which was still in his hand, and at the girl. "What have you done to yourself?" he asked, finally. "I've lost a bit of weight," she said, "and I've got older." Kovacs pressed his fingers onto his eyes, before putting the key in the lock. "Where's the cat?" he asked. The girl pointed at the fountain: "With the others."

They went up the stairs in silence, Kovacs first. When he reached his front door, he turned to the girl. "Eighteen months ago you were a sack of potatoes," he said. "What are you now?"

"A sort of punk."

"I know nothing about punks. How long are you staying?"

The girl smiled awkwardly again and shrugged. "As long as I'm allowed," she said. "It's the Easter holidays."

"Have you got any stuff?"

The girl nodded and gestured with her thumb to a silver-coloured plastic bag with a red volcano on it that hung over her shoulder. "Is that all?" he asked.

"I don't need anything else."

Girls generally had endless amounts of gear, Kovacs said. She didn't think she was like other girls, his daughter said.

Kovacs took off his jacket and threw it onto the chair in the hall.

Then he untied his shoelaces. The girl just stood there, watching him.

"I'd like to ask you something," he said. "And think carefully before you answer. Have I ever hit you?"

Kovacs could see tears slowly welling up in the girl's eyes. "You say such stupid things," she said eventually.

TWELVE

The soul is three finger-widths below the navel. In a single motion you thrust the tant vertically into that point, until its tip is touching your spinal column, push the blade to the right, then upwards in an arc, and when you can hear your insides gurgling, you lay your chin on your chest for the kaishakunin's strike. The whole thing is a fluid movement, and your face shows neither fear, nor anger, nor humility, nor doubt, but the world as it is, nothing and everything.

Some days I just sit here looking at things on the Internet. When Frau Steinmetz comes into the classroom and points to her watch inquiringly, I just say please, please, and she laughs and lets me. I read about India, about Mumbai and Delhi, about the beaches in the west and the town which I think is mine. I print out some things and put them in a plastic sleeve. I read about Gatka, the Sikh martial art, the clothes they wear, the moves and the weapons. Since I've had the film with the red and yellow cover I've also been reading about Japan and the samurai, about the katana, the wakizashi and the tant. I'm not a Sikh and I'm not Japanese so it's all the same to me. I read about seppuku, about the correct posture, about the duty of the friend, and about the final poem. They play it safe, I like that. Seppuku knows when you're dead. Others don't.

I come home and the mad woman has a go at me, asking me where I've been again. I tell her that there's not always a P.C. for everybody, not even in I.T. classes, and as my parents haven't bought me a notebook yet, sadly, I'm sometimes second and have to wait longer. She says I'm a lying toad and she doesn't believe a word I say, and I clasp my hands in front of my chest and bow. She leaps up, slams the door and runs off.

There's a funny smell in the room. I know what that means and take a look around. Switi's not lying where she usually does, by the bed. The wardrobe door is slightly ajar. I open it wide. She's curled up on the bottom shelf, like a cat. She darts a look at me then shuts her eyes again. I kneel down, reach into the cupboard and pull her out. She's wet and stinky.

When I come out of the bathroom with two towels, one wet and one dry, the mad woman is on the landing. "Has she shat herself again?" she asks. I say yes, I'll deal with. She says, "She's a little pig!"

She does everything I tell her. She sits by the bed, she puts her arms up so I can take her dress off, she stands up. She keeps her eyes closed the whole time. There's a ring of white around her lips, it looks funny. I take off her knickers. Down below there's a mixture of red and brown. I wipe it all away for her. Under that she's slightly bluey-black. That's from before. She stays perfectly still when I clean her up round there. I tell her, I've bought you some ointment, a magic ointment, it's in my desk drawer.

While I rub in the ointment I tell her that I was in the Dromedary Pharmacy and that I said to the lady there that my sister's skin is so thin in places that she bruises easily, and she gave me this ointment in the blue and white tube. She listens. She keeps perfectly still. I tell her she has to stay like that for a few minutes so that the ointment can be absorbed. She stands there, lifting her arms from time to time as if I were trying to take her dress off again. I tickle her under her arms and try to laugh. She tries to laugh, too. Then she lies down.

I tell her, you're lying there like a dormouse. She doesn't say

148

anything, but how would she know what a dormouse was? "I know what they do," I say, and tell her about the orange rubber tube that they shove into you from behind so that you're totally clean inside, and that after a certain time nothing helps any more because they do it to you for longer. I tell her how they sometimes blindfold you and how they wear a stocking over their heads, and how only the man I call Bill is never masked because he stands behind the camera and you don't need one there. By the time I start talking about who prefers which room, she's fallen asleep. That drives me a bit mad. I grab her by the hair and say that it's bad to be sleeping all the time. Her green Manka thing is on the carpet by her mouth. I push it right up to her lips.

Later we go for a ride on our bikes. I try to teach her the different makes of cars. I've got the feeling that cars might be important, but I don't know why. She plays pretty dumb and calls all cars Volvo. I don't like that because I think Volvos are a bit ugly. We cycle towards the river and then along the embankment until she's complaining too much about the gravel and wants to go back. We sit there for a while and look at the foaming water, the bikes by our feet. "Tell me a pelican story," she says eventually. Sometimes I get a bit cheesed off with pelican stories, but I don't tell her that. I tell her about a pelican who heads for the South Pole because he wants to have a penguin for a friend. All his friends advise him against it because it's dark and cold there, but he won't be put off. He flies via Borneo and Australia, and meets a porcupine and a wombat. When he gets to the South Pole it really is dark and cold. The penguins warm him up between their folds of fat, and from time to time they put a fish into his bill. His new friend is all fluffy and doesn't have a clue about pelicans, but that doesn't matter. When, a few months later, it gets light and warmer, the pelican has had enough and flies back home. "No," Switi says. "What do you mean *No*?" I ask.

"Again – with the proper ending!"

"What is the proper ending?"

The friend has to fly back with the pelican, she says, and when I say that penguins can't fly, she says: "The pelican takes him on his shoulders then." "Or in his throat," I say. "Does that work?" she asks, and I say that the most unbelievable things can fit into a throat like that.

On the way back a grey Chevrolet stops dead in front of us and we almost smash into the driver's door. A man gets out and starts shouting at us. Switi pedals furiously and screams loudly, "Volvo!"

Before our house comes into view I say, "Escape route number one. I'll show you something." She knows what to do and turns into the cul-de-sac by the florist's. I overtake her and we cycle past the housing development to the yellow factory building. Above the gate you can see some old-fashioned, dark-red writing: WIRE FACTORY. SCYTHE PRODUCTION. GALVANISING PLANT. I once looked up what galvanising means, but I can't remember exactly. I do know that it's got something to do with electricity and acid. We push the bikes along the side wall of the shed for a bit, then lie them under an elder bush. Here, nobody can see us from the street.

At the corner of the shed there's a rusty tin barrel standing on a row of wooden boards. I push the barrel aside and lift up three of the boards. A narrow set of stairs leads down. "Don't be scared. It's light inside," I say.

Inside, the factory is divided by brick walls and wooden planks into a number of areas. My room is directly below one of the paned windows. "This is my workshop," I say. In a strip of wood on the wall are thirty-four scythe blades, all of them completely rusted. On the workbench that runs the length of the room, there's one which isn't so rusty any more. "I'm making a Hattori Hanz sword," I say. "It's hard work, but I've got time." I hold the scythe blade in front of her and try to get her to touch it, but she doesn't dare. "It's not dangerous yet," I say. She puts her arms behind her back and shakes her head. "The curve is wrong," I say. "That's the challenge. Where it's blunt there at the end it's supposed to be sharp." I show her my tools, a hammer and file, both of them from our shed at the house. "The file is too fine," I say, "I need a coarse file, tons of sandpaper and something I can make it red hot with." Switi is only half listening to me. She runs her finger through the dust on the workbench and then puts both her hands into it, leaving two prints.

When we get back to the elder bush there's a grey dog sniffing around our bikes. I know him, he belongs to the second house after the florist's and his name is Findus. Switi points her finger at him and starts to laugh. "He's a wombat," she says. "I say he's a wombat."

Escape route number four, opposite direction. I know the code for the garage door. The mad woman has a problem remembering things and writes them down on pieces of paper; one of these is tacked onto the calendar in the hall. Two letters and three numbers.

The X6 is not there, but the Mini is. We lean the bikes against the wall and go quietly into the house. You never know what will come into her head. I pause in the hallway and listen. Nothing. Eventually we find her in the sitting room. She's snoring. A spit bubble is swelling in the right-hand corner of her mouth. There's a packet of pills on the coffee table in front of her. "We can go upstairs," I say to Switi. She looks at the floor and shakes her head. "You have to," I tell her.

The man I call Bill used to sell mattresses. That's where the supply comes from. Then he switched fields. He says this a lot: "I switched fields." "I don't have obligations any more," he says that a lot too, and "I only do things that are worth my while." I think that's what he says most often.

We start in the flower room. I drag the top mattress from the pile of four and lie it on the ground. It's full of pale pink flowers. We kneel on it, push our fists into it, lie on it. "This is a soft foam mattress," I say, "easy to clean, but if you sleep on it for a long time you get pains in your spine." The big mattress in the stripy room is a sprung mattress, and you can feel the wires if you fall down heavily on top of it. The mattress with the bright-blue spots in the white room is also a foam mattress, only thicker and firmer than the flowery one. The two white ones are natural latex mattresses with coconut fibres inside and a cotton cover. They're the most comfortable to lie on and they smell nice, too. I show Switi the labels sewn onto all these things. If you want to escape you have to be well informed, I say, and then I say she should choose the white mattresses if she can.

THIRTEEN

Eleven. It has not changed. It is the fourth time she has counted, but there are no more, eleven children from the first year, seven from her class and four from Elke Bayer's. Julia and Sophie, inseparable as always, Leonard, Stefan, Oliver, Günseli, even though she is a Muslim, and Lara with Longbottom, her Labrador. All of them are dutifully holding their palm bushes made out of pussy willow branches, thuja, box and juniper, except Günseli, who has a bunch of forsythia and lilac, but she cannot know about these things. Julia is wearing a new dress, white with turquoise stripes, and Stefan's felt jacket looks new, too. Some other children from her class are standing with their parents in the group of adults, their hands firmly grasped so they cannot get away: Kevin, with his outrageous streaks of green hair; Jacqueline and Magdalena, the twins; Therese, wearing an eco-dress with large checks, like her mother; Philipp, whose elder brother keeps punching him in the side; fat Vanessa; Britta Kern. People are being careful, she thinks.

The sky is as blue as it can only be in April and October. Cumulus clouds pass overhead, and beyond them the vapour trails of aeroplanes linger. All of a sudden she pictures a path in the Lungau she once walked along years ago from alp to alp in springtime. In her mind the sky is exactly the same as today, tufts of bright-green needles are growing on the larches, and the purple snowbells are just coming into flower. She is standing there, watching the marmots slide down the snowy fields like children, and wondering whether everyone has good moments in their lives.

Into the first courtyard from the arched passageway emerges a delegation from the town's wind ensemble, in loose formation and out of step. They line up on the church steps, directly beneath the rose window, and play "O When the Saints". Michaele Klum is in the first row, blowing on her clarinet, possibly annoyed that she had forgotten to give her daughter a good hiding that morning.

The crowd applauds, and then the processional cross appears in the main portal, followed by the entire throng of servers and padres, and at the rear, Clemens, the abbot. Bauer says he hovers: he has no contact with the ground when he moves. He is a few centimetres closer to Eternal Bliss than the others, and therefore must be the right person for the job. Bauer himself is two rows in front of the abbot. A white lead runs from his left ear into the neckline of his chasuble. With each step he bends slightly at the knee, as if ready to jump at any moment. She has come to expect that now. When the long yellow-and-white flag hanging out of the top window of the left-hand tower cracks above their heads he is startled. The musicians are playing "Komm, holder Lenz". Her cue. She starts to organise her children.

She recalls her job interview, Dienbacher sitting behind his desk, drumming incessantly with his fingertips and insisting that, although this was a state primary school, it had a very close rela-tionship with the abbey, and so the teaching staff were expected to take part in church festivals: Christmas, Corpus Christi, Palm Sunday. She stands there, thinking everybody can see I can't do anything and can't cope with anything and I've got no imagination and I'm only concerned with myself and my crappy little life, and she says yes, of course, no problem. He asks whether she has any relationship to religion, and she lies through her teeth: Average, she says, like most people in this country. She goes to church occasion-ally and has a crucifix on the wall at home. Dienbacher nods and

154

notes something on the personnel form. She leaves his office, runs down the stairs, across the courtyard towards the car park, gets into the car, tears open her handbag, takes the Stanley knife from her manicure set and cuts herself in the forearm, one lengthways incision. She has not done it since.

If the weather is nice the procession will be extended and become more like a walk, Bauer said yesterday evening, she should wear comfortable shoes and maybe bring a snack. This appetite for rituals lasting several hours was typically Benedictine, he said, you only had to think of the Latin choral masses that went on and on. She had no experience of those, she said, laughing. They drank wine, joked about the black owl as a motif for Easter egg painting, and she had felt a little unwell. In bed they listened to "Modern Times", "Workingman's Blues No. 11", "Beyond the Horizon" and finally "Spirit on the Water" on a permanent loop. There's nothing more Easter-like, Bauer said.

The convoy wheels round to the west as it proceeds across the Rathausplatz, moves northwards along Severinstraße as far as the bridge, follows the river eastwards, and back towards the abbey along Abt-Reginaldstraße. The band plays "Ol' Man River" and "Stars and Stripes" and "Oh, What a Beautiful Morning", which creates an atmosphere quite conducive to walking. Now the people are relaxing, laughing, gossiping and breaking rank, and Oliver starts sweeping the ground with his palm bush. "Stop it!" she says, and he flinches. Lara stops all of a sudden, sticks out her arm and feels for her hand. "I'm sad," she says.

"Why are you sad?"

"Because Susi's not here."

"Susi? Was she your friend?"

"Yes, and Longbottom's too."

The dog is named after Neville Longbottom in *Harry Potter*, the gawky boy who all of a sudden can dance like nothing else and in the end becomes a hero. Most blind people use sticks and do not have a dog. It is different with Lara. Longbottom was around when she was only a few months old; he was small and she was even smaller. Since then he has completed his guide dog training, but the truth is that they are like brother and sister. If you ask Lara why she is blind, she says, "Too much goodness." These are her parents' words. She was a premature baby and because of a lung maturity problem had to be on a ventilator for quite a long time. The oxygen destroyed her eyes. These things happen, even nowadays. Lara says she has no idea of what sight is, and nor does she miss it. If someone says *round* or *large* or *pointed* she knows exactly what they mean, and she also has an idea of *red* or *blonde* or *sky*. The children treat her normally, although Kevin sometimes says, "You're disabled." Anybody who knows Kevin's parents can guess where that comes from.

In truth it is less down to her lies about being averagely religious, and far more because of Lara and the fact that she herself completed a few courses in Braille that she ended up in Furth. "Did Longbottom like Susi?" she asks. "Yes," Lara says, "and he protected her, too." "Protected?" she asks. "From whom?"

"Everybody."

No, she doesn't know Susi from kindergarten, Susi wasn't in kindergarten. Where she's gone there aren't any kindergartens. She asks Lara if she knows exactly where Susi has gone, and Lara says she only knows that she's gone to India, to her real parents. "'Collect', she always said, 'collect'. And she laughed."

To the end of Abt-Reginaldstraße, then right into Weyrer Strasse, all the way along the library block, left and across the newly polished granite flagstones of the church courtyard. As they climb the steps something catches her eye. It takes her a while to work out what it is: police.

The organ, Bach to start with, or at least that is what she thinks, then "Praise the Lord". Various readings about exultation and hosanna and green twigs in people's hands, which is nonsense, taken literally, because the willow twigs with their catkins are anything but green. They move down to the third row. Their seats are on the right. Dienbacher is standing in the aisle, wearing a sort of benevolent headmaster's expression and making sure that everything is going to plan.

The abbot addresses the children. He says that the story of Jesus' suffering is very long, but also very exciting, and that normal things happen, too, such as having supper with friends or a cockerel crowing. He says that the story is also brutal and deals with treachery, with torture and murder, and then ends very sadly, so sadly that every laugh goes silent and all music, even the organ, stops playing and, according to popular belief, the bells of every church fly away to Rome, only to return on Easter night to celebrate the Resurrection. She listens and thinks that the abbot really is hovering, the entire congregation is hanging onto his every word; it is just as you would want a good school lesson to be. She imagines the crowing cockerel, a sad organ, and the traffic of bells in the air above St Peter's Square, all landing, one bell after the other, forming rows, the congestion and the sound when they knock into each other. "Why are you laughing," asks Lara, who is sitting beside her. She says, "You can't see that," and Lara says, "Yes I can." She nudges her gently with her hip. Longbottom, sitting on the other side, feels it and protests.

Just so you know, I'm the Evangelist, he said. Now he really is standing by the microphone, reading the text from St Matthew's Gospel. Wilhelm with his Marlboro voice reads the words of the Lord, and Thomas, who still looks like a schoolboy, but has a degree in theology and history, reads all the other parts.

Julia and Sophie whisper throughout, and Günseli says out loud, "That's really horrible," when the ear of the high priest's servant is cut off. Longbottom starts singing quietly.

Wilhelm does not have many lines, and it seems as if he is trying to compensate for this by reading in a particularly dramatic tone of voice. For instance, when the traitor Judas says to him, "Hail, master," he replies, "Friend, wherefore art thou come?" and it sounds as though he wants to thrust a hammer and some nails into Thomas's hands straightaway.

She is aware that these pathetic tales of men – with nothing but high priests and elders and that cowardly arse Pilate – are making her feel increasingly tense. Her knees are twitching and something is compelling her to keep opening and closing her handbag. "Elisabeth Vock from 2A is sitting behind you," Lara says when she turns round for the third time. "Thanks," she whispers into Lara's ear, "but I think I've got to go to the loo soon." She tried to distract herself by picturing the flying bells, but it does not work. Something is breathing down her neck.

Bauer reads the "Eli, Eli, lema sabachthani" quite beautifully, his delivery a touch casual and yet poignant, she can still hear this from the periphery. When Jesus finally dies and there is a short silence, she is already below the organ loft, and when the rocks are split apart and the curtain in the Temple of Jerusalem is torn in two, from top to bottom, she rushes out into the light, covered from head to toe in sweat. A young, uniformed policeman comes up to her in concern and asks whether he can help. She shakes her head. "Thank you," she says, "it's just the incense – it's making me feel sick."

She is sitting on the steps when Bauer comes out a little later in his chasuble, holding a chalice. "Are you crazy?" she says. "Yes," he says, "you know I am." He sits down next to her and asks whether her blood-sugar is a bit low; he could help her out with a couple of hundred grams of communion wafers. He's mad, she thinks, but he looks after me. "Aren't you going to be missed?" she asks. No, he says, communion's just started, nobody will notice if he's not there for a few minutes. He puts down the chalice, leans back, and sings softly: *I'm pale as a ghost / Holding a blossom on a stem / You ever seen a ghost? No / But you have heard of them.*

"Sometimes the old things come back again, just like that," she says. "There's nothing I can do to stop them." He strokes her neck. "Right there," she says, "I feel them right there, blowing cold at me". "I know," he says.

They are silent for a while, then she asks him whether church bells have landing flaps. He lets out a loud laugh and helps her to her feet. He stops just before he gets to the portal. He had a sort of déjà-vu in there, too, he says, much more harmless than hers. On the right-hand side, in the rearmost third of the congregation, he saw somebody who was in the monastery with him briefly. The man was soon booted out because he kept stealing things.

Great, she thinks, as she pushed herself past people in the aisle, one of them hears voices, another steals, and somewhere at the front there's a dog singing.

FOURTEEN

In the staffroom the coffee machine was gurgling, there was the scent of vanilla, and Vessy was laughing. On the table was a bunch of bellflowers, yarrow and wild oats. It was strange how some things went together. "What is it?" Herbert asked. Vessy could not stop laughing. A Russian psychiatric nurse, usually as grumpy as a bear, is sitting there cackling with laughter. Horn thought, it looks as if it's going to be a good morning. He sniffed and asked where the vanilla smell was coming from. Herbert sniffed too, and grinned: "What vanilla smell?" Frau Steininger's daughter had just brought in a load of fresh puff pastry cream slices, as a thank you for having looked after her mother so well, but in actual fact it was probably just to compete with Frau Hrstic's daughter, who was clearly not as talented at producing homemade cakes. "And?" Horn asked, looking around. Herbert patted his stomach and said he was sorry, but there had been eight of them at shift handover, Doctor Hrachovec was always hungry, and he himself usually left home in the mornings without having breakfast. "My department doesn't give me anything to eat," Horn moaned. "A psychiatrist demanding parentification, that's not on," said Leonie Wittmann, who had just come through the door. What did she mean? Horn asked, and she replied that parents should be looking after their children and not the other way round.

"It's because of Frau Müllner," said Vessy, who had now calmed down and was wiping her eyes. "But she's not here," Horn said.

"Yes, she is," Vessy said. "She's always here." Dorothea Müllner not only came dutifully to her outpatient appointments, she would also turn up again and again, silent and unnoticed, on the pretext of visiting one of the old ladies with dementia, but would then seek out the nursing staff, more specifically the men, Herbert, Raimund and Günther. "This morning she gave Günther a medal," Vessy said.

"A *what*?"

"A medal." She waited until after handover, then went up to him and asked where he had served. He clicked his heels and said, Leoben nursing home, wheelchair pushing, shit wiping, and she then opened her handbag, took out a medal, pinned it to his chest and said, "You're my soldier now, Herr Günther." Günther saluted, thanked her and then tried to give her the medal back, but at once she started weeping bitterly. "She was utterly serious," Vessy said. Wittmann said, of course she was serious, what did she expect? and Vessy asked whether she ought to have a bad conscience about having laughed so much. "It's your conscience and yours alone, Sister Vesselina," Wittmann said, and Horn thought that it was probably only the deeply serious things that were truly funny.

He imagined this small, round woman trying as hard as she could after the death of her husband to venerate his memory, dusting the show cases with the butterflies and carefully storing the chemicals, and none of this worked; instead her overpowering father was resurrected, the soldier, and he took her by the hand, saying: Now look, wasn't that ridiculous?

"Does this mean Günther's now parading up and down the ward with a medal?" Horn asked, and Herbert said, yes, and whistling the Italian national anthem as he goes. It was pretty annoying.

"What's he whistling?"

"The Italian national anthem," repeated Herbert, "Fratelli d'Italia", the only song he knew that sounded a bit martial. He also supported Juventus Torino which was an elderly lady, too, so everything came full circle.

Horn poured himself some coffee, to avoid any accusations of parentification, he said. Herbert said that Marcus was playing his guitar again occasionally, unplugged, even when he was there with him in the room. He had been talking about his training in timber construction, about how much theory was taught and how little sawing, cutting and planing, and once he said something about his mother: "I don't know where she lives." His care seemed to be working well, and yet Herbert had the feeling that something else was still to come out. "It's always what remains unsaid that's significant," Wittmann said, stirring sugar into her coffee.

The day before, Friedrich Helm had been discharged with normal kidney values, Johanna Seidler, a depressive farmer from Sankt Christoph, was feeling less guilty about her mother's cancer, and Leo Schaupp, a retired school caretaker from Furth had for the first time in ages gone to sleep without being convinced that he would suffer a night-time heart attack. Margot Frühwald's attacks were now far less frequent, and Sabrina had refrained from bloodbaths for more than forty-eight hours. "What are you doing with her?" Horn asked. "We're working on the structure," Leonie Wittmann said.

"What does that mean?"

"I sit there for the sessions and she doesn't turn up."

"Do you get annoyed?"

Yes, she did, but that wasn't important. So what was important? he asked.

"Merely that I'm there and that there's a place she can be, both for real and in me, that's what's important," Wittmann said. Some people have a lot of room inside them, Horn thought, and others none at all, some you can enter, find yourself a corner and lie down, and with some it already looks such a crush from the outside that you decide it's better to do an immediate U-turn. He was about to ask how she thought about her daughter when she spoke to someone like Sabrina, but then he remembered the rumours about the sculptures out of waste packaging and he let it drop. She interests me and she doesn't give anything away; I'd love to know what she eats for breakfast, whether she's got a cat or a tortoise, and she tells me nothing. Actually I'd like to know what it would feel like to kiss a mouth with teeth like that, he thought, putting a finger to his lips for safety. She grinned all the same.

They're all there, Andrea Emler said, and if they had cameras around their necks you could easily mistake them for a party of Japanese tourists. Chinese, Horn said, these were Chinese people, and Emler said, Chinese, Japanese, Koreans – they were all the same to her, and pretty unbearable in groups of more than five. That's exactly what I think, Horn thought, but I don't say it. There were five exactly, no more, waiting in the outpatients' area, and as a bonus a powerful-looking man he did not know, but he was definitely not Chinese.

She thought he might want to speak to the whole family, said the woman who approached him first, by now her son had sort of got used to dealing with doctors and hospitals, but he didn't really know what to expect from a psychiatrist and, if she were to be honest, neither did she. "Psychiatrists are peculiar," Horn said. "They don't wear white coats, which means you can't recognise them, they want to know everything and if you ask them something they either say nothing, or 'I fear you will have to learn to live with this uncertainty'." The two girls whispered while the man came and stood hesitantly beside his wife. He essayed a smile and offered Horn his hand. The boy remained seated, looking out of the window. His left arm was wrapped in a Gilchrist bandage. There's very little of the tourist group about this lot, that's a good sign, Horn thought, no loudness and only a minor tendency to knock people out of the way. The man at the back got up. He was even more of a giant than he had seemed at first. "You're taller than me," Horn said, "and I'm almost one ninety." "Sorry," the man said. His name was Mauritz, and he was the head and only permanent member of the local forensics team. Today he was standing in for his colleague, Frau Wieck, who was completely tied up with the black owl business. He knew a little bit about children, even if his own son wasn't yet a year old. He had promised Sen that he would show him his Aladdin's Cave of forensic equipment, and Sen had seemed to be very taken by the idea. "I've already met the inspector's little son, because the inspector's wife is my boss," Frau Wu said, beaming. The large inspector shrugged. It's true, I'm afraid, he said. His wife ran the town's mobile care for the elderly service and Frau Wu worked there as a nurse. Frau Elisabeth is a fantastic boss, Frau Wu said, and Nikolaus a delightful little boy, but you can't yet tell who he looks like. "My wife, thank God!" the inspector interrupted. "These people are so polite." An idyll is born from the most bizarre situations, Horn thought: his wife is her boss, she thinks his son is sweet, and both men have the same hedgehog haircut. All of a sudden even the size difference between the inspector and Herr and Frau Wu seemed insignificant.

While Horn took the inspector and the boy to his room, a saying came to mind he loathed because of its revolting imagery: *It's a dog's breakfast.* "That's what I think, too," the inspector said. His belly quivered as he laughed.

*

Horn caught himself staring into the boy's eyes. "Do you want to take a closer look?" the boy asked, bringing his chair nearer to the desk. "No," Horn said, "no, I'm sorry." "Everybody wants to look at my eyes," the boy said. "They all say it's not so common with type one." He held open the lids of his right eye with thumb and fore-

164

finger. "Thanks, I've already seen it," Horn said, leaning back. It's like in the textbook, he thought, he really does have blue sclera, the dark-brown iris that you'd expect, and sky-blue conjunctivae all over, as if it were a manufacturing defect. "He showed me it, too," the inspector said. "I think it looks great, like an alien."

"Does it actually hurt?" Horn asked, pointing to Sen Wu's shoulder. The boy shook his head. It had never hurt, apart from the very first night when he turned over in his sleep.

"And is the bandage now helping?"

"Yes," the boy said, nodding keenly. The doctor had said that it was very important to keep the strap in place. "Do you understand why?" Horn asked. "Because of the collagen triple helix," the boy said, looking at him trustingly. He's an eight-year-old clever clogs, Horn thought, understands the basics of his illness, and yet does what any child with a Gilchrist bandage would do – when it suits him he slips the strap off. He asks the boy whether he's good at school and what he's interested in, and the boy says, one, yes, he thinks he is, and two, geography. Yes, he'd been abroad twice already, to Croatia and Hungary, he especially liked Lake Balaton, where he went out on a pedalo when it was choppy. He might go to China next year, maybe the year after, to see his grandparents and his father's sister, his mother didn't have any brothers or sisters. They hadn't been able to do this trip yet as it costs a fortune for five people. "What's the capital of Denmark?" the inspector asked from behind the boy. "Copenhagen," Sen Wa said.

"Portugal?"

"Lisbon."

"The longest river in the world?"

"The Amazon."

"The highest mountain in North America?"

He wasn't that interested in mountains, the boy said, did that matter? No, on the contrary, the inspector said, the fewer mountains the better. What was the deepest point in the world's oceans? "The Mariana Trench," the boy said, although this was not definite, as they were forever measuring the depths of the oceans. The city with the most inhabitants? Mexico City. The longest river in Africa? The Nile. The largest city in Asia? Easy – Shanghai. And a difficult capital city question, what was Australia's? Also easy – Canberra. O.K., the most difficult capital city question of them all – Florida's. The boy thought about it. The real capital in this case was Washington, he said, but he surely wasn't thinking of that. "No," the inspector said, "the capital of the of Florida state." Miami, Orlando, Tampa, Horn thought. He pictured this enormous man as an eight-year-old, poring over the atlas and encyclopaedia and learning capital cities by heart, and the following day he'd be called names at school like swot and creep, and would be the last boy chosen for the football team. "Tallahassee," the boy said. "Good grief!" The inspector slumped back into his chair. He couldn't believe it, this rascal had scarcely learned how to read but he already knew Tallahassee. The boy looked at the table, embarrassed. Horn was certain that he had been reading for some time.

He wondered, Horn said, whether a boy who knew about Tallahassee and Canberra and the Amazon, i.e. a boy who was up to third-year standard at least, knew first-year children such as Felix Szigeti and Britta Kern. Yes, the boy said, and Felix lived nearby, too, and not long ago the two of them had saved Hermine, the tame but rather stupid guinea fowl belonging to Hrdlicka the junk dealer, from a stray dog. "Did he want to eat it?" Horn asked. "Maybe," the boy said. He, Sen, must also know that something similar had happened to Felix and Britta as had happened to him, it was not as serious, of course, because the other two hadn't broken any bones. The boy nodded. Had he ever spoken to them about it? No, not yet, the boy said. "What do you mean by *not yet*?" Horn asked.

"I might."

166

Horn pointed to himself and the fat inspector. "And how about us?"

The boy closed his eyes and shook his head. "No."

"Why not?"

"Because the same thing will happen to me."

"The same thing? What same thing?"

"The thing I saw."

"What did you see?"

He mustn't tell.

"Because otherwise it will happen to you?"

"Exactly."

And if he spoke to Felix and Britta about it, it wouldn't happen?

"I don't think so."

"Why not?"

"Because they're part of it."

"What are they part of?"

The boy swallowed and said nothing. He's not as cool as Felix Szigeti and not as stubborn as Britta Kern, Horn thought, with him the fear is most palpable. Horn stood up and fetched a pad of paper and coloured pencils from the therapy materials cupboard. These sorts of conversations were like gym lessons, he explained, sometimes you needed a bit of free time. The inspector raised his hand. "Have you got a pencil for me too, my biro's given up the ghost," he said. Horn tossed him a felt tip.

"Do you like drawing?" he asked.

"It's alright," the boy said.

"A tree, maybe?"

"Maybe an aquarium?" The boy gave Horn a testing look. "Is this a trick?" he said. No, it wasn't a trick, an aquarium would be great. Horn sat down again at the table and pushed the paper and pencils towards the boy. The boy opened the box of pencils and turned the pad around once. Then he sat there stiffly. "Do you need anything else?" Horn asked. The boy shook his head. It didn't have to be an aquarium, Horn said, he could also draw a house, a dinosaur or a tiger. "Or maybe a tree after all," the inspector said. The boy started lining up the coloured pencils next to one another. "That's not the problem," he said.

"So . . .?"

It was because of his O.I. one, because of the collagen triple helix. Horn said he didn't understand. The boy looked down at his bandage. "I need to take it out of the strap," he said after a while.

There are moments when life becomes a freeze frame, Horn thought, it's to do with recognition, mostly. Spring light poured into the room, three of the four steel chimneys of the woodworking factory sparkled in the bottom right-hand corner of the window, by the wall a two-metre-tall police inspector sat drawing spirals on a piece of paper, and right in front of him an eight-year-old boy with blue conjunctivae and a well-developed conscience was trying to make them understand that he was left-handed. "Can you not do anything with your right hand?" he asked. "I can eat with a fork," the boy said.

"Write?"

It all goes jaggedy and horribly wrong, the boy said, which is why school had let him off writing for the moment, but in all honesty he found it a bit silly. Horn bent over and undid the Velcro on the strap on his forearm. "I won't tell anybody and the police haven't seen anything," he said. The boy looked around. The fat inspector was deliberately looking at the ceiling, saying that as far as the police were concerned, taking one's arm out of a shoulder strap did not constitute a particularly grave misdemeanour.

The boy drew an aquarium that took up almost all of the piece of paper, platyfish and cleaner wrasses, snails, crabs, lots of plants, and underneath on the bottom a grim-looking catfish. He was evidently displeased with the size of the circulating pump and his attempt at perspective. Horn praised the picture and said he thought it remarkable that a boy of his age could draw with perspective at all.

"What were you hit with?" he said straight out. "A stick," the boy said. "You're allowed to say that?" Horn asked. The boy shrugged.

"What did the stick look like? Normal? Long, short, thick, thin?" The boy thought for a few seconds, then shook his head. "Not normal," he said. "What does 'not normal' mean?" Horn asked. The boy reached for a blank piece of paper and in no time had sketched a stick, a double line diagonally across the paper, the width of a thumb, and joined up properly at the top and bottom. Then he painstakingly drew dark knobbles at regular intervals from one end to the other. "I've forgotten what those sticks are called," he said. Horn held up the sheet of paper. "But that's easy," the inspector said, "much easier than Tallahassee, especially for someone whose family comes from China . . . Come on! Pandas eat it." The boy grasped his forehead. "I'm so stupid," he said. "Bamboo."

Why bamboo? Horn asked, and the boy said he had no idea, but maybe he would get his own bamboo stick soon, and all the others who were involved. Why did he think that? Horn asked. Because that's what it said, the boy asked.

"And who are all the others – Felix? Britta? Anyone else?"

Horn saw the irritation in the boy's face, but also a hint that he was prepared to give them some information, he saw the inspector bending forward so he could hear the answer better, and right in front of him he saw the bamboo stick and the catfish at the bottom of the aquarium with its barbels and large mouth.

Andrea Emler was a confident secretary who was rarely stressed by anything, not even by Horn. She was sorry, she said, she knew she was only to disturb him with urgent calls, but his wife was on the telephone and she sounded very worried. Horn groaned and went to the door.

Irene Horn never usually screamed. The last time she had done so was just before Michael had moved out, in the weeks when mother and son had made a pretty catastrophic attempt to clear the air between them: I've bent over backwards for you and I've never had a single word of thanks! You're a nasty woman and you've never liked me! All that was five years ago, and since then the two of them had learned to give each other a wide berth.

"Tobias!" she shrieked into the telephone. "It was Tobias!" What was Tobias? he asked. "In the car, he was in the car!" she screamed. He walked into the corridor. He hated it when worry about someone in the family suddenly brewed up inside him.

"In which car?" he asked.

"In the Volvo! In your Volvo!"

The Volvo's in the garage, he said, I'm sure it is. He'd gone by bike that morning, she'd seen him leave with her own eyes. "Exactly!" she shouted.

"What do you mean *exactly*?"

It was still in the garage when she got into the Suzuki at half past eight. She had done her three hours of teaching at the music school, gone to the supermarket, and then driven home again. About a hundred metres after the turn-off from the main road she met the Volvo coming the other way. She did not register it until she recognised Tobias at the wheel as the cars passed each other. The car had already reached the main road before she had time to react, and in her rear-view mirror she was unable to see whether it had turned left or right. Irene seemed to calm down a little as she told him all this. Sometimes she can be mistaken, he thought, but not this time. I mean, nobody would steal that car if it were parked unlocked on the street, let alone from a garage that only hamsters would stumble upon, or hikers if they're lost. "I'll call the police," she said. Save yourself the bother, Horn said, he already had the police to hand, literally. She should wait until he got home. "When will that be?" she asked.

"As soon as I can. It's quiet here."

170

"I'm scared," she said. Me too, he thought, but did not say so.

Inspector Mauritz was sitting next to Sen Wu at Horn's desk, helping him draw a criminal. "A real one," the inspector said, grinning. Because Sen had told him that the person who had beaten him was not a real criminal. Horn looked at the picture. Evil eyes, a handkerchief tied around the nose and mouth, a gun in his hand and another in his belt. The inspector was adding boots to the man; the boy was drawing a checked pattern on the handkerchief over his face. "Your son's going to be a lucky boy," Horn said. "Why?" the inspector asked. "Because he's got a father who knows what a criminal looks like." The inspector laughed. "Knowledge is always relative," he said. When the two had finished, Horn asked whether he might keep the drawings. The boy put the sheets of paper side by side and looked at them. Not the stick, he said finally, he wanted to keep the stick.

At the door he could smell lunch. Horn almost collided with Hrachovec, who was racing past. "What's up?" he said. "Nothing, just Margot Frühwald," Hrachovec said. "One should never celebrate too soon."

*

The fat inspector and Horn walked together to the exit and discussed Sen Wu's caution, his intelligence, his thirst for knowledge, and what he was so afraid of. They did not come up with anything new about the culprit's personality or possible motive. If you really wanted to injure someone, though, the inspector said, a bamboo stick was not terribly efficient, unless you sharpened the end to stab with. Bamboo spears – he had read about them as a boy, Horn said, in Thor Heyerdahl's books. "Who?" the inspector asked. "A man who crossed the sea on a raft and caught fish with a bam-boo spear," Horn said. He was probably a little too young. The inspector laughed. One day he might take his son fishing with a bamboo spear, preferably in the reeds just down from the hospital, but just then it was not a priority. Talking of fish, while Horn was on the phone Sen Wu had said that the catfish in his picture was a Siamese rock catfish, which needed a three-hundred-litre tank at least and liked hiding in cavities. One night it had eaten all the neons. His father had been so angry that he'd almost flushed the fish down the loo, but the boy had intervened and said he'd give his father all his anthias if he liked. His father said O.K., and now the catfish was allowed to grow old. Apart from that the boy had given an odd answer to Horn's question about who else would get a bamboo stick. He said, the wild eighty-eight, maybe it was the crazy eighty-eight – something that sounded like a children's fantasy, like the *Famous Five*, *SpongeBob* or *Harry Potter*. Horn stopped him and stuck out his right hand as if he were trying to catch something. He failed.

They said goodbye and he watched the giant puffing and panting as he squeezed himself into an old silver Renault. He enjoys being a father, he thought, and his son will enjoy being a son. He'll eat toasted marshmallows and know that Popocatepetl is a volcano.

Horn pressed his thumb against the side of his front tyre. The pressure was O.K. The nose of a dark-blue Lexus was jutting into the bicycle park. Horn got annoyed and kicked the front tyre.

As he was cycling westwards along Achenallee, he thought of Tobias, his lethargy, the contempt he showed for adults, and how he'd even gone so far as to crush an egg. He imagined him sitting in the Volvo, bombing along a country road, putting his foot down whenever he could, and the fruit trees whizzing past to the left and right. He pictured triumph and anger in his face. Who taught him how to drive? he wondered, but no answer came. *He* hadn't, and Irene certainly hadn't. Probably one of the dopeheads he hung out with. Maybe he's got debts and he's using the Volvo as security, he thought, maybe he's just doing the decent thing and taking the car to a dealer. Then the phrase "A stinking young man is sitting in a stinking old car" came into his head, just like that, and this made him laugh so much that he careered into the pavement for a second. A lady in a grey felt hat jerked on the lead of her poodle and threw him a filthy look.

Irene came to meet him outside the house. "Have they got him yet?" she asked. "Has who got who?" he said, steering for the garage. "The police," she cried, running after him. "Have they got him yet?" The police first had to pass on the information, he said, before any sort of manhunt could get underway.

"God knows where he'll have got to by then!"

Horn got off his bike and locked it away. He wouldn't get far in that car, he said, the last time he looked the tank was only just half full, and knowing his son, he wouldn't have any money on him. He went up to her. She recoiled. She could not stand his cynical composure, she said. In this case, he replied, he was responsible for the composure and she for the panic, it was similar to the division of labour in their relationship between rationality and idyll. "Have you at least called him?" she asked. "He's driving," he said, "think about it." She stood there on the gravel path, looking at him and started to cry. I'm playing games with her, I'm letting her deal with her fear on her own, I'm making her feel guilty and this doesn't make me feel bad, he thought, I love my wife and yet at the same time I need to punish her. He walked towards the house. "What are you doing?" she shouted. "I'm going to get changed and give the climbing hydrangea a prune," he said. "It'll give me the chance to think." He could hear that she had not moved from where she was standing behind him. He did not turn round.

While he was on the ladder with secateurs and garden wire he recalled the day when he had taught Tobias how to ride a bike, the boy's stubbornness, his tendency to fall to the left the moment he let go of him, and the triumph that both of them felt when he was pedalling but did not realise for some time that Horn was no longer holding onto him. He recalled that December in Tobias's third year of primary school when for no apparent reason he had refused to go on a school trip, the birthday party a few months later when he had encouraged all his friends to throw sandwiches and cake at each other, and the miserable state he had been in the previous year when he tore his meniscus in a football match. Horn had packed his knee in ice, prescribed him a can of Coke and two diclofenac pills, and told him about the operation he would have to have. Only after that did he put him into the car.

He climbed down from the ladder, gathered up the hydrangea prunings in a basket, and took them to where they had their bonfires behind the barn. The air was damp and smelled of grass. A sombre, greenish lustre hovered above the lake, like a pane of frosted glass. It was like that when the elevation of the sun was at a particular point. The Kammwand had a fringe of whitish-yellow clouds. He wondered what sort of a city Tallahassee was, and where. Perhaps beside a lake. Then he remembered the trip to the Limestone Alps in Upper Austria, when his father's brother had opened the door to his light-blue Opel Kadett and said, "You drive." He had been sixteen.

All was quiet in the kitchen. The fridge motor clicked in from time to time. He called the cat, but she did not appear. Easter's almost upon us, he thought, and yet I'm barely aware of it. He thought of Easter egg hunts and how Tobias used to bite the ears off the Easter bunny. He's older than I was then, he thought, and obviously he knows how to drive.

Black with a few molecules of sugar, that's how she liked it. Horn put both cups on the tray and headed for the barn. She was playing long, deep notes, first descending, then going up again. "Sounds like a didgeridoo," he said, putting her coffee down. She lowered her bow and said nothing.

He'd been thinking, he said, and he had now remembered the

second time that he'd hit Tobias. It had been on his birthday, she must remember it. He'd booked a table in *La Piccola Cucina*, especially for the boys and the restaurant's *pizza diavolo*. Tobias was sitting in the living room, he said that "Mr Bean" was on and that Horn could go and stuff his birthday dinner. Then Horn asked him again whether that meant he would rather watch "Mr Bean" than celebrate his father's birthday, and Tobias said, yes, exactly.

She drained her coffee, put the cup on the floor and set a sheet of music on the stand. Horn sat on one of the chairs by the wall and listened. Sometimes it was comforting to feel that you didn't have to behave like an arsehole all the time.

The call came half an hour later. Horn fished his mobile out of his trouser pocket. Irene, who had been practising again and again a short, wild piece Horn did not know, broke off in mid-flow. It was Michael. Tobias had just turned up at his work, with the Volvo and the cat. He didn't want to come home for the time being, so Michael would take him back to his flat. "With the cat?" Horn asked. Yes, with the cat, but that was a long story. Anyway, he was fine, and Gabriele would be back from work soon to look after him.

"Look after? Tobias?"

Yes, he obviously needed a bit of looking after and, no, he hadn't had an accident, nor had he been brought in by the police. Eighty, he had driven about eighty kilometres in all. Yes, a small stretch of motorway, too. No, he didn't want to talk to his parents just yet.

"Is he stoned?" Horn asked. "What, are you mad?" Michael said. Horn looked at Irene, as if Michael's answer were her responsibility. She sat there crying. Two brothers, Horn thought, just those two words. "Do you mind if I ask just one more question?" Horn said. "Did you teach him how to drive?"

"What do you think?" Michael said.

175

FIFTEEN

At two o'clock in the morning the April sky was like summer. Ludwig Kovacs was standing on the flat roof, his head back. Corona Borealis was at the zenith, directly to the west was red Arcturus, to the east the Summer Triangle: Deneb in Cygnus, Vega in Lyra and Altair in Aquila. The sky's reliable, he thought, everything's in its right place at the right time. He looked through the eyepiece of his telescope and swivelled round to Albireo, the head of Cygnus, a double star in which one partner shone orange, the other blue. To the north of Daneb he found Lacerta, the little lizard, a constellation one could only see if the conditions were really good. He was delighted and freezing cold. In summer he would sometimes bring his mattress and duvet up to the roof and spend the night outside. He had not yet been able to persuade Marlene to do the same. Now she was probably fast asleep on that strange futon in her flat. Charlotte ought to spend the first evening alone with him, she had said, with nobody resembling a stepmother anywhere nearby. But she wasn't a stepmother, he had said, and she had replied that, yes, she *was* one, of sorts. "But I'd still love you to be here," he had begged her, and she had said, "You're such a cowardly father." Now he was indeed alone in the flat with his daughter, he felt insecure and hassled and was gazing at the stars. Sleep was out of the question.

He thought of Marlene, of the double crown at the back of her head, right by his nose when he lay behind her, of her passion for old things and the flights of jealousy that sometimes overcame him. The truth is that I'd like to have her as my mother and not as my daughter's stepmother, he thought, but that's almost as kitsch as those chubby-faced porcelain dolls in her shop. He thought of the things she had told him about her marriage, about her husband's gambling addiction, his infidelity, and his fits of despair. She had shown understanding, acted as his guarantor and paid up; in the afternoons he had gone to addiction counselling, and in the evenings to the casino. In the end they had got divorced; she was left with forty thousand euros of debts, and he had vanished from one day to the next, just like that, no forwarding address: *The number you have dialled has not been recognised.* She swore never to let a man near her again, and kept this up for two years. Then came the break-in.

There was no sign that the shop door had been forced, not even a scrape. The burglars had taken a Renaissance cupboard with alabaster inlay, and had chiselled out a safe which had been built into the wall behind the desk in her office. It had contained a few watches and pieces of jewellery from people's personal estates, which beneficiaries had given to Marlene to sell on commission. She ran around the shop in circles, again and again – he remembered it well – saying, "I'm going to kill him. I'm going to kill him." He spent some time taking photographs and making notes, notified Mauritz, and finally brought her a large mocha with whipped cream from the café across the road. She looked at him with wide eyes and he said, "Strong coffee's good when someone's done you over, and whipped cream's always good." She gave a sudden laugh and sat down to go through the details with him. Two days later he already knew that she liked wearing brightly coloured underwear and what it felt like when she grabbed him between the legs.

A hand's width above the hills to the north, and shining bright yellow, was Capella, the goat's head on the shoulder of Auriga,

177

the charioteer. The flashing light of a plane slid slowly between the breasts of Cassiopeia. Further to the west, the night lights of the woodworking factory diminished the view. Kovacs put the lens cap back on the eyepiece.

Eyltz had given him an earful when he went to request Lipp: What sort of a team was it if they needed back-up for such a trifling matter? And was Demski just doing university work again? Demski was busy joining international networks that dealt with sex offenders, Kovacs said, and the fact that this matter was trifling was what made it so difficult – nobody took it seriously and yet everybody was getting worked up about it. Get Demski back from Berlin, Eyltz ordered, a day or so wouldn't make any difference, and anyway, Furth was hardly a hotbed of child pornography. Michaela Moor, that's all I'll say, was Kovacs' reply, and Eyltz said, yes, but that was now nine years ago, the perpetrator was a tax officer from Wels and there had been nothing international about that case, no Internet deals or any stuff like that. He didn't really know much about the Internet and that sort of stuff, Kovacs said, standing up, but he knew it wasn't good. Eyltz shouted after him that he could have Lipp if he promised to nail the culprit by Easter. "Which year?" Kovacs asked, but Eyltz must already have been out of earshot. He's wearing a new jacket, Kovacs thought as he left, brown tweed with leather buttons, and he pictured Eyltz shooting ducks or wild goats on one of those Hebridean islands, and then having himself measured up for the jacket.

He folded up the tripod, put it on his shoulder and went down the iron spiral staircase to his flat. He leaned the telescope against the wall of his bedroom and did not even attempt to go back to sleep. He stood in the living room and cocked an ear to the gallery, where Charlotte was sleeping. Nothing. "How do punks sleep?" he had asked her, and she had said, "Standing up – so you don't ruin your mohican." He had believed her at first. They had eaten olives and cheese and drank lemonade. He told her about the black owl, described how her grandfather's hands had felt on his face, and admitted that he still found the issue confusing. She looked at him sceptically and said hitting children was sick, irrespective of whether it was with bamboo sticks, belts or hands. "And?" he asked. She knew what he meant straight away. "Yes, once," she said.

"When?"

"You were drunk."

"You're mistaken. I only started drinking after you left."

"No, *you're* mistaken." He'd come home one evening, muttering that old Strack was a Nazi who didn't have a clue about investigative work, but could drink like a bloody fish. Kovacs had staggered through the flat, reeling from one wall to another, and she had been absolutely terrified. When he'd gone to take a pee and left the door open, she'd told him, "That's not on," and he'd slapped her immediately, once on her left cheek, she remembered it clearly, and she also remembered that shortly afterwards at school she'd learned about the effects of alcohol and nicotine, and she'd felt very ashamed. It was in the first year, you learn about these things in the first year, she said, and he thought it was obviously a good age to be smacked, too. He did not say he was sorry. He would have thought it ridiculous after such a long time.

He switched on the kettle, put a few dried mint leaves into a glass and poured the water. The mohican had nothing to do with neglect, Charlotte had said, on the contrary, it had to be groomed and stiffened every day, which you could sort of manage yourself so long as it was not taller than a hand's width. No, she didn't get any help from her mother on that score, nor in buying clothes; her mother didn't see the point of black leather with studs. Kovacs was absolutely certain that Yvonne still wore beige suits from April onwards, and grey trouser suits from October, but he kept quiet.

Who beats seven-year-old children? he thought. Fathers who leave the door open when having a pee. He took his first sip of peppermint tea and scalded the tip of his tongue. As usual.

*

"You should put something more comfortable in your office." I'm being woken by a grey-haired angel, Kovacs thought, making sure he did not move – anthracite-coloured roll-neck sweater, a narrow face full of intelligence and goodness, and a hand resting on my shoulder, which will relieve the pain that's coming. "I can't bear to look," Eleonore Bitterle said, "the way you're sitting there." "Don't look, then," Kovacs said, pushing on the armrests of his swivel chair and slowly manoeuvring himself into an upright position. "Are you the first?" he asked.

"Yes, but the others will be here soon. What's that? Evidence?" She pointed to the desk.

"Yes, of my cluelessness." It was a present he had decided not to give after all. "For Marlene? I'm sorry. I mean, it's none of my business . . ." Bitterle said.

"That's O.K. It's not for Marlene anyway."

"Who then?"

"Charlotte."

"Your sack-of-potatoes daughter?"

Just so. The point was that his sack-of-potatoes daughter had recently got herself a bright-green mohican, and with the best will in the world a sun-yellow belt was not going to go with that, rhinestones or no rhinestones. He was right, she said. "Did she send you a photo?"

"Yes, she did."

"Have you got it on you?"

"No," Kovacs said. Why am I lying? he wondered.

Sabine Wieck and Florian Lipp arrived together, followed soon afterwards by Mauritz with the breakfast pastries. He could not

180

stop humming. "Good sex, then?" Wieck asked. "No," he said, "I mean, that anyway, but Nikolaus said his first word: 'Papa.'" "At ten months? – Yeah, right!" Wieck tapped the side of her head. Mauritz looked hurt. Lipp knocked him on the shoulder. "They just don't understand us – have you noticed? And that starts at ten months." "Ask Elisabeth," Mauritz said. Wieck grinned. "About the sex or 'Papa'?" Mauritz took off one of his shoes and threw it at her.

They began with a situation report while they drank coffee and ate pastries with hazelnut filling. Lipp was visibly enjoying himself. There were no hazelnut pastries for breakfast when he was with the uniformed officers, nor did he get the chance to sit next to Sabine Wieck. Like an adolescent, Kovacs thought, the roughly cropped black hair, the zit scars, and the way he beams and looks around nervously when he talks to her. Lipp was twenty-four, played badminton and, contrary to what Kovacs had concluded the previous year, was apparently not gay after all.

What have we got? Kovacs wrote on the whiteboard and sat down. "A Siamese catfish," Mauritz said with his mouth full. "A what?" Wieck asked. Mauritz gave her a dismissive wave of the hand. "Later," he said.

Panic in the community, Bitterle said, media hysteria and politicians working out their tactics, but most importantly three children who have all been beaten in the same way, two seven-year-olds, one eight-year-old, one girl, two boys. They all go to the same school, the two seven-year-olds are in the same class. It happened to the first one, Felix Szigeti, mid-morning, between 10.40 and 11.25, to be more precise, during the Catholic catechism class he didn't take part in. Britta Kern and Sen Wu were attacked after class, Britta on a Friday between 11.30 and 12.30, Sen Wu the following Tuesday between 12.30 and 1.30, both of these incidents most likely taking place on the way home from school.

181

Why was she talking about an attack? Lipp interrupted. How else to describe it? Bitterle said. After all nothing was taken from the children, Lipp said, and Bitterle replied that she saw it differently.

The pattern of the beatings was the same – back, shoulder, head – and a hand and bamboo stick were used to administer them. The blows did not appear to have been particularly forceful. The injuries to Sen Wu had probably not been intentional; only his family, his doctors and the school had known about his condition. It was Britta Kern who had described the perpetrator as a "black owl", both verbally and in a crayon drawing. The other two had basically confirmed the name. What did "basically" mean? Lipp wanted to know and Bitterle said, "They're not saying anything." The psychiatrist who had conducted the interviews with the children had said that it was not a post-traumatic reaction, nor selective mutism, but unwillingness to give information because of a concrete fear. "If I say anything the same thing will happen to me," she said. "What same thing?" Lipp asked. "Great question," Mauritz said.

While he was listening to Bitterle, Kovacs caught himself contemplating the two techniques of eating hazelnut pastries. He and Sabine Wieck worked along the spiral, eating the pastry from its end to the middle. The others just took bites out of it, Mauritz only a few. Wieck poked him in the ribs: "Excuse me, boss, do tell us where your thoughts are wandering." Kovacs looked around the room. From the edge to the middle, that is what he had just been thinking, he said. "Great image," Mauritz said.

Wieck and Bitterle were talking about the results of their meetings with the social workers from the child welfare office, the surprisingly high proportion of overlapping data, the differences between impulsive fathers and overworked mothers, the reasons why some violence against children was deliberately not reported, and the fact that the easiest way to recognise a true psychopath was that after meeting him you felt the urge to wash your hands. At that moment Christine Strobl came into the room with a telephone message. "First: George rang. He's completely off his rocker, blabbering on about something huge and saying we should sit tight if at all possible. He'll tell us what to do and when. Second: A father from Sankt Christoph, Peter Ludwig, rang to say eight-year-old daughter, Julia, was attacked yesterday, can't go to school today, says it was the black owl." Mauritz had a coughing fit. Lipp slapped him between the shoulderblades. "Yes, it's still going on," he said. But that wasn't why he was choking.

"Why then?"

Demski was seriously getting on his nerves, Mauritz said, first of all it was his fault that he had almost had to scale scaffolding, and now he was issuing orders from Berlin, instructing them to sit tight. He reached for a second pastry. Three bites, Kovacs thought, four at most. "I'll call him," he said, "and you can shut up about the scaffolding." Kovacs got up. "What are you doing?" Wieck said. "I'm going to Sankt Christoph," Kovacs said.

"On your own?"

"No, with you."

Florian Lipp raised an arm in protest. Wait, there was something about a fish, he said. "A Siamese catfish," Mauritz said, wiping the corner of his mouth.

"And?"

The biggest threat to Siamese catfish is being flushed down the loo, Sen Wu had said.

*

He needed to talk to Eyltz about getting a new work car, Kovacs said as they drove south along Grazer Straße, the Vectra was not at all suitable, and meanwhile Eyltz was hogging the Puch G all to himself. Wieck shrugged. "The main thing is it goes," she said.

There was a queue of cars tailing back from the entrance to the Kammwand tunnel. Cleaning work, twenty minutes' wait. Kovacs switched on the blue light and Wieck held out her I.D. to the man holding a sign where the lane was closed off. "Everything's urgent," Kovacs said when she gave him a rather odd look.

The hairpin bends that wound down to Sankt Christoph were bathed in sunlight. Kovacs liked this stretch of the journey, the cliffs beside the road, the view of the roofs and the lake, and the screeching of his tyres as he accelerated out of the final bend. The car park at the entrance to the village was half full. The tourists came at Easter. He asked Wieck whether she had ever been part of a gang when she was sixteen, hooligans or anything like that. She laughed. She had been a girl guide for a while, she said, but had soon found it a bit too stuffy. "What did you want most of all when you were sixteen?" he asked. "A prince and a horse," she said. No, he meant for Christmas or her birthday. "Money," she said, "as much money as possible."

"For what?"

"A horse."

"And what would you give to a girl punk?"

"Money," she said. Also for a horse? he asked, and she said, no, just like that, money was always good.

The drive through the village was pretty clear, they only had to overtake the Pony Express which started operating in Holy Week. There was an elderly couple sitting in the last of the three carriages, but otherwise it was empty. They drove along the embankment towards Mooshim until they reached a copse of willows. Beyond it a narrow cul-de-sac led up a hill to a small plateau. "Lovely view," Wieck said as they got out of the car.

The house, one of those woodcutter's cottages typical of the area, had evidently just been renovated. The stone walls had been completely taken down, they had re-plastered around the windows, and a generously sized conservatory had been added to the narrow side of the house. Someone who likes having no neighbours, Kovacs thought, and someone who likes being at home. "Nice front garden," Kovacs said.

"Sort of," Wieck said.

"What do you mean 'sort of'?"

Too neat, she said, the edged lawn, the layout of the roses, the paved path to the biotope – more maths than nature. He didn't understand a thing about gardening, Kovacs said, on the flat roof above where he lived there was an olive tree growing in a wooden tub, and that was it. A friend had given it to him when he got divorced – so that he would still have something to look after. "Olive trees are sensitive to frost," she said, pressing the doorbell. She knows what she's talking about and she thinks I would let let it freeze, Kovacs thought.

The man was wearing a freshly ironed shirt. He was short and thin, mid-thirties, with a scratch above his left eyebrow which had only just formed a scab. "Pruning fruit trees," he said, noticing Kovacs' stare. He led them into the conservatory. They sat down in brand-new armchairs. "It's good you're here," the man said. "Where's your daughter?" Wieck asked. Julia was in her bedroom with his wife. When she heard about the police investigation, she was immediately in bits again. What did he mean by "in bits"? Wieck asked. The man gave her a hard stare. Howling, screaming, panic, he said, they had to remember that she'd just been given a severe beating.

The day before, Julia had visited a school friend who lived in the village, he said, he'd brought her there himself shortly after two o'clock. To begin with they had painted Easter eggs with her friend's mother, then played Pokémon on the PlayStation for an hour. At half past four Julia had said she wanted to go home, and as she was absolutely sure of the way along the upper lakeside path, which took ten minutes at most, they let her go. Then she'd turned up at home at half past five in a desperate state, filthy, clothes torn, swollen face. He thought he'd go berserk, he kept on asking her: Who was it? Of course he'd harried her, it seemed the natural thing to do; he'd grabbed her by the shoulders and shaken her, but what father wouldn't in such a situation? Eventually he got it out of her: "the black owl". And she'd repeated it when his wife asked her the same question. He'd driven her to the family doctor in the village right away. The doctor hadn't found any serious physical injuries, just a haematoma on the left cheek and one on the chest. Mentally, on the other hand, she was all over the place. "Would you go and get her, please?" Wieck said. He would try, the man said, and stood up uncertainly.

"With some people you want to wash your hands before they open their mouths," Wieck said with a shudder. Her vehemence astounded Kovacs, and then it struck him that the man had left him cold, too. I'm not even moved when I hear him telling the story about his daughter, he thought. "Do you know what's odd?" he said, unexpectedly. "I don't think I've ever painted an Easter egg in my life."

The girl being pushed into the room by her mother had her hands over her face. The father came in ahead of them and sat back down in his chair. "This is Julia," the mother said. She was at most a head taller than her daughter, dark blonde, round face and wearing denim dungarees. "We've still got the storage room to paint," she said apologetically. "I've been filling cracks."

"Were you helping your mother?" Wieck asked. The girl shook her head.

"What then?"

"She was playing with her Pokémon cards," the woman said. Wieck said she knew nothing about Pokémon. "But I do," Kovacs said. The others looked surprised. To be more precise he knew about one single Pokémon, did she want to know which one? Julia nodded. Snorlax, Kovacs said, a school class he had chatted to about police work had given him a toy Snorlax as a present. From what he could make out, Snorlax did nothing but sleep.

"Not true." For a second, the girl put her hands on her hips. The left side of her face was aubergine coloured, the finger marks were visible even a few metres away. "Not true, he's got lots of psycho attacks." "Does it hurt?" Kovacs asked, pointing to the haematoma. The girl tried to put her hands up again. Her mother stopped her. Her father had said that she'd been mistreated, Kovacs said, was that right? The girl stood absolutely still. "Tell him," the man said. The woman looked at him and then outside at the garden. There were some people who took pleasure in hitting children and frightening them, Kovacs said, it was the police's job to stop this happening. "Do you understand?" The girl nodded. "What did the black owl look like?" Wieck asked. The man got up, took a piece of paper from the shelf and passed it to the two of them. A single dark wave with a round head on top. "Was it big?" Wieck asked. The girl nodded.

"Very big?" The girl nodded again.

"Bigger than Snorlax?" Kovacs asked. Julia looked at her mother for help. The woman shrugged.

Kovacs stood up abruptly. "Would you please tell your daughter again what the police are there for?" he said to the woman.

"For our protection," she said.

"Should you be frightened of the police?"

"No, you shouldn't."

Kovacs walked over to Julia. Now he was going to say something in her ear which was for nobody else to hear, he said, and he wanted her to listen. The mother gave the child a nudge. Kovacs took her hand and went with her to the corner of the room. "What are you doing?" the man asked. Wieck waved her hand at him to be quiet.

Kovacs squatted down and whispered something in the girl's ear. The girl whispered back. "We're just going to pop to the car," he said. "We've got to fetch something." The girl looked expectant as the two of them left the room. The woman stayed where she was, motionless. The man sat in his rattan chair, tapping his toes. "I hope she can cope with this," he said. "Children can cope with quite a lot," Wieck said.

"Were you beaten as a child?" Kovacs asked when the two of them returned. The man slowly got out of his chair. "What are you talking about?" he asked. "We know the story," Kovacs said. "People get beaten repeatedly throughout their childhood, they swear they won't do it to their own children, but it happens nonetheless." "What are you talking about?" the man said again. His face had turned ashen. His wife took tiny steps backwards; they were barely noticeable. Frau Weinfurter from the child welfare office was already on her way, Kovacs said. She would organise the counselling the family needed. He would file a report on their visit under the heading "Interrogation following self-denunciation", to ensure that the matter was settled out of court and that the man wouldn't receive a sentence. Did that seem fair to him? The man said nothing. To begin with the girl just stood there for a few moments, uncertain what to do, then she went over to her mother and said softly, "I'm going upstairs now." The woman nodded.

*

Just after the child welfare lady had arrived she'd needed to wash her hands, Wieck said on the drive back, even though the loo in that house somehow seemed contaminated, too. Nothing could change how she felt, neither the man's compliance, nor her sympathy with the mother and daughter, nor the fact that the social worker appeared to be an extremely sensible woman. And anyway, he had been wearing a crappy shirt. But it was ironed, Kovacs said. In his view the man was one of those neurotics whose actions were principally though unconsciously aimed at self-punishment. Wieck looked at him in astonishment. He'd been doing his psycho lessons over the years, too, he said.

"By the way," she said, "how big is this Snorlax?" In the booklet that came with the cuddly toy it says two metres tall and almost five hundred kilos, Kovacs said. He'd been fascinated by that, more than by the descriptions of the attacks he could perform: Headbutt, Body Slam and Amnesia.

"And that's how you got the little girl to talk?" she said.

"What do you mean?"

"With Body Slam and Amnesia."

"Not directly." It had been far simpler.

"What then?"

"Money."

She spun around. "You're not serious?!"

"Yes, I am." Kovacs said, "Five euros for Pokémon cards and she couldn't stop talking." After all it was Sabine who'd told him that money always worked. She shook her head and turned away. "You can be terrible sometimes," she said.

This time there was no hold-up at the Kammwand tunnel. Two point two kilometres into the tunnel, the overhead lighting flickered for fifty metres or so. The cleaning vehicles had vanished. "It's just as filthy as it was before," Kovacs said.

At first the girl had seemed terrified, her eyes darting all over the place. When he explained about the digital camera and dictaphone, she calmed down a little, and as soon as he started talking about his own daughter she relaxed. He had told her about what Charlotte used to like playing with, about her dolls' houses, Lego and her mother's old dresses which she would wear for days on end. Julia had listened, picking at her thumbnail. She had been especially interested in the thing about the old dresses, and had wanted to know whether one of them had been light blue with

189

white stripes. He could not remember. At one point he asked her whether there were blue marks anywhere else on her body similar to the ones on her face, and what he had hit her with. She pulled up her sweater and vest and said, "Only with his hand." Then he asked her straight out whether her father often got like that, and she said, "No, never." He had tried to draw a Relaxo in his notebook – a pretty poor effort – and then he had given her the five euros. When he asked her why her father had beaten her, she said, "Because I was cheeky." "What did you say?" he asked her, and she said, "You can't even earn money."

Wieck sat beside him saying nothing, her face still turned towards the window. He briefly felt the urge to reach across and touch her, but resisted. "Should I be feeling bad?" he asked when they turned into Seestraße after the Abbey. "You've never asked me anything like that before," she said.

Kovacs noticed the squat woman with short hair before he got out of the car. She was leaning against the wall by the entrance to the police station, holding up her face to the sun, and she looked familiar. Images of flowers came into his mind, a strange fountain, a shoehorn. Then he remembered: a nut-brown piano, with a photograph of Thelonious Monk on it. He approached her. "Did you want to see me, Frau Weghaupt?" She nodded, and started rummaging through her handbag.

Wieck said goodbye and went inside. She had said something to him as she walked past. It hung on the very edge of his consciousness.

Gerlinde Weghaupt pulled out a piece of paper, unfolded it and gave it to him. "I printed it out," she said. "Song lyrics?" he asked. She shook her head. He mustn't think badly of her, she said, but when your child dies you do strange things: you lie on his bed, you smell his clothes, and you keep the contact lenses that used to float in his eyes every day. So she had gone through the list of calls on his mobile as well as stuff on his computer, particularly his e-mails. She had decided either to keep them to herself or delete them. Whatever happened, she wouldn't show them to anyone else, it was just this one she couldn't keep secret. Kovacs glanced at it. What did she mean she couldn't? "I think it's a sort of farewell letter," she said.

"From your son?"

"No, *to* him," she said. Then she started crying.

Kovacs read the letter twice. "I understand it all apart from the sender's address," he said when Gerlinde Weghaupt had calmed down a bit. "Dark Fire," she said. "That's the name of his guitar. It's all he's got."

They talked about the other members of her son's band, their expectations, their vulnerabilities and their families, and finally about how shy the five had been whenever you said you wanted to listen to one of their rehearsals. It's strange, Kovacs thought, one wants to die and he doesn't manage it; the other plummets to his death, even though he doesn't want to die, and the farewell letter that the first one writes doesn't fulfil its promise, nor does it arrive in time.

"He's in hospital," Gerlinde Weghaupt said. Sometimes he had behaved so weirdly, as if he wanted to have nothing to do with anyone else. She did think, however, that Florian had been his best friend.

He watched the woman leave. She walked slowly, her knees rubbing together. He remembered how she had leaned against the wall, her face to the sun. When she had gone, it came to him what Wieck had said as she passed him: "The answer's 'yes.'"

191

SIXTEEN

Switi's gone. I'm back from this rubbishy language trip, I go into the sitting room and say, "Switi's gone." The mad woman looks at me and asks, "What do you call her?" I say, "Switi," and she says, "But that's not her name." I say she's my sister and I'll call her what I like. She says, "She's not your sister," and I say of course she's my sister. She leaps up to pounce on me, but I'm quicker than she is.

Everything has gone from her room: the doll's house, the big and little unicorns, Betty, the stuffed chicken, the elephant that has to be within reaching distance of her bed, the box with the Playmobil figures, the pinboard with drawings. The bed has been stripped. I can see hundreds of spit stains all over the pillow. The mattress is made out of foam, with white and brown diagonal stripes. I can't see anything on that. There was always a rubber cover over it. I open the cupboard. It's empty. The clothes have gone, the blue sweater with silver stitching, the checked trousers that look like they belong to a clown, the green raincoat, the quilted jacket with polar bears. Even her swimming things are gone, and her knickers. I reach my arm into the shelf where she sometimes lies curled up. Nothing.

I sit beside the bed, on the spot where she always lies. "Just be glad you weren't on the language trip," I say. I talk about the couple I stayed with who walk hunched over, the smell of celery in the house, the dog which has to wear a frilly dress, and about the fact that they kept on calling me "our little brown girl". I talk about Selina, who says my skin's like the surface of the moon, that I smell funny, and that I speak more Indian than English, and about Verena Steinmetz who gazed at Cedric, the long-haired bloke from the language school, as if he were God. Finally I tell her about the morning when the lady gave me a telling off because she said my hair had blocked the shower. That lunchtime one of my delightful classmates stole the manicure set from my bag, and on the coach trip to Canterbury that afternoon, Philip Denck got his thing out next to me – I think it was for a bet. I imagine Switi repeating her phrase, "One time I'll bite it, so hard that it'll come off," and laughing a little while scowling like an old woman. Anyway, that was the best day of my wonderful language trip.

When I come back downstairs, the man I call Bill is there. I say, "Switi's gone," and again, I shout it: "Switi's gone." He asks, "What do you call her?" I say I can call my sister what I like, and he says, "We've sent her back. It wasn't working out any more." He drinks water from a glass which has a slice of lemon swimming in it, and suddenly it seems as if those two things go together: sending Switi back and having a slice of lemon in his glass. I listen to the two of them talk in strange voices, high-pitched and as if they were speaking through cotton wool. For a moment I think I'm going to laugh out loud, then I have to compose myself so I don't fall over.

I walk slowly to my room. I lie on my bed and try to go to sleep. It doesn't work.

After a while I hear the front door being locked. He's got important clients, she's going for a drive. I lie there quite still for a few more minutes, staring at the ceiling. Then I get the key from the sugar jar.

The picture with the hedgehog and the owl is still there, the keyhole too. The mattresses are still in the rooms. I count them, they're all there. They're stacked a little differently from usual, the flowery ones two on top of two, but sometimes it's like that. The cameras are in the stripy room, pointing to the wall. It looks a bit funny. I take a sniff. The air smells very fresh, as if taken and blown in from the waterfall. Occasionally you see small birds sitting on branches there, with black heads and yellow and red spots on their wings. I think about them.

Out of habit I hold my breath when I go into their bedroom. I can't do it for long. I lie on my stomach and look under the bed. The dusty fluff in front of my face reminds me of the balls of tumbleweed in the film about American landscapes. Under the small red rug at the end of the bed I find a fifty cent coin. I leave it there.

The right side of the walk-in cupboard belongs to him, the left to her. The dresses in her hanging space are yellow, black or grey; one is brightly coloured with a large flower pattern, another is purple with metal bits sewn into it. A moth flies from a grey woollen jacket with black specks when I push it to one side. All her tights are tied in knots, which is stupid. He's got lots of pairs of jeans and jackets and shirts with button-down collars. Switi isn't anywhere, not on the right side and not on the left.

I find the cuculla between his two pinstripe suits. I remembered the name because I think it sounds like a nest full of baby hedge-hogs. He showed it to us years ago. It's the gown monks wear on feast days. He said he was once a member of one of those societies for a short while. He just took it with him because he liked it. "I take what I like" – he still says this sometimes. And now I'm taking it. I like it, too, because of all the folds.

I go down into the basement, into the garage, into the shed, then I do another tour of the ground floor. I look behind every door, in every chest, on every shelf, as if she'd suddenly shrunk and was now lying hidden somewhere, behind the teacups, for example, or between the rolls of wrapping paper.

In the study I open the cabinet and take out the hanging files. Nothing but application letters. Photographs of people who all look the same. The desk drawers are locked apart from the middle one, but all I find in it are stamps, paperclips, rubbers, things like that. I push back the swivel chair and crawl under the desk as far as the wall. That's where the safe is. Two letters and three numbers – it's so primitive I'm almost embarrassed. She's not in the safe either, ha ha. A file with documents I don't understand, bank and legal stuff, deeds, a casket with a pearl necklace, several rings and two small gold bars, an envelope with fifteen thousand euros in notes, and two bank books. Forty-three thousand euros on one of them, on the other one hundred and twelve thousand. A slim folder with only four sheets of paper; on each of these are some names, addresses and telephone numbers. A pile of D.V.D. covers, eight in all, the same words on each one: "Eating Sweet Brownie". I think about England, the porridge for breakfast, the dog with the frilly dress and the smell of celery. I'm getting that cotton wool feeling again. Things are beginning to spin.

Escape route number four, the opposite direction. Out through the garage, on Fürstenaustraße towards the Walzwerk estate, Hakan and the school ghost are sitting by Block B, she calls out to me me, I look at the ground, she leaves me alone. Down to the railway line, under the barriers and across the tracks, someone shouts "That's dangerous" from a Fiat, right into Stiftsallee, over to the other side, along past the visitors' car park to the garden entrance, between the pruned conifers, past the fountain with the pseudo-Greek statues, behind the greenhouse. The double door to the utility corridor, you just have to push the fixed side slightly inwards, it's best to walk in your socks along the corridor because it echoes so loudly, the narrow staircase beside the stationery store, up to the first floor.

It's dark in the classroom. If I turn sideways in my seat and look at the map of Europe hanging on the wall, I can still make out a few words: Gibraltar, Ceuta, Tangier, Rabat, everything at the bottom. On the board are the equations that Altmann put up in the last maths lesson before our language trip. No-one's wiped them off. It feels strange.

I take the double D.V.D. box from my rucksack. One disc is red, the other yellow. There is another D.V.D. under the red one. I boot up the computer and put in the disc. I know immediately where we are. Broad blue stripes and narrow yellow ones. 160 x 200. Someone's breathing.

SEVENTEEN

Skis, sticks, rucksack and shoes – she takes the things into the hallway and puts them by the front door. At the same time she ticks off items from her mental checklist: sun cream, apple juice, gloves, cap, sunglasses, avalanche transceiver. She goes into the bathroom, stands by the mirror briefly and pulls a face. Then she opens the cupboard, feels behind a pile of towels, takes out a multipack of razor blades, fifty of them, and puts them in. Then she goes.

He is waiting in Severinstraße, a few metres from the abbey entrance. He is wearing dark-grey salopettes and a fleece jacket which is completely felted. "Did it get washed on hot?" He nods. Irma, the housekeeper, refuses to have an operation on her cataract, which is why these things happen. "Sun cream on?" she asks. He laughs. "Orderliness personified," he says. You haven't got a clue, she thinks.

They drive along the northern edge of the lake, past Waiern, and shortly afterwards turn left towards Moosheim, through the village and up into the Lassach valley which heads south-west in the direction of Niedere Tauen. He has his elbow hanging out of the open window and is obviously enjoying it. "Like the old days," he says. She asks what he means by the old days, and he says, the time when he used to think nothing of driving a bit on the left, a bit on the right or weaving from one side to the other. "And now?" she asks. Now he drives only on the right, he says – at least that's what he tells the medical officer in his driving fitness assessment.

197

The car park is very full. Viennese, visitors from Graz, cars with Bavarian number plates. "Easter holidays," he says. "Probably just teachers." She puts on her ski boots. "No teachers, please!" she says, attempting a smile and realising that she is trembling. This happens sometimes. "You don't like the holidays," he says. "You don't either," she says.

The track takes them through open larch woods, past several towering, isolated boulders to a steep drop which they negotiate with some short traverses. At this point the valley widens into a trough, collecting the warmth like a parabolic reflector. The crust on the snow is holding up well, but in places the surface is starting to melt. Most of the time he is in front of her, sometimes he speeds up and sometimes he falls back, remaining beside her for a while to tell a story. She likes the ease with which he moves, never getting out of breath, the sound of his heels hitting the skis, and how naturally he talks about monastic poetry, the fear of dismemberment, and the smell that comes from between her earlobes and collarbone when she sweats – all in the same sentence.

There are patchy clouds in the sky. The light washes over the surface of the snow in waves. She listens to the scraping of the climbing skins and tries to stay in a steady rhythm. Gradually she starts to relax. He is singing away to himself. "Ain't talkin', just walkin'", over and over again. Another one from God's penultimate album; the final song.

The track veers to the right, to a flat col. Some way above them she can see a couple in yellow soft shell jackets. She remembers having to wear the same clothes as Nora, her younger sister. It was her mother who made her. "I need something to drink," she says suddenly and stops.

She looks across the foothills to the lake. He says how much he misses the children during the holidays, the sounds they make, their words, their rapid movements, how he can't resist talking to them when he bumps into them in the street, and how he begins to fall apart by the beginning of August at the latest. He talks about the routes he takes when he runs at night, sometimes under a starry sky, sometimes through rain and storms, and how he loves it most of all when bolts of lightning strike the lake and thunder crashes from the ridges of the Kammwand. That is far more likely to keep him in one piece than endless weeks of fine weather. At the beginning of the school year he is usually stuffed full of neuroleptics and yet all over the place like an asteroid swarm, in a frenzy and shattered into a thousand fragments. He takes a bar of chocolate from his rucksack, breaks it in two and gives her half. "Chocolate helps as well," she says. "Not with everything," he says. "Yes it does," she says, although she knows that he is right.

When the yellow jackets have vanished they proceed. She thinks of Natalie with her old-fashioned plaits, who has told her how expensive eggs are a number of times, and her mother, who wears woollen, pleated trousers and pushes Natalie's little brother around town in a pram with spoked wheels which must be forty years old. She thinks of Britta and Günseli, who are serious girls, too, and chubby Vanessa, who at least laughs once in a while. Then she thinks of Roswitha, her niece, who carried her train and scattered peony petals outside the church after the marriage ceremony. She was five at the time, dark blonde, in a white dress, and he had lifted her onto his arm, smiling for the photographer. That smile is imprinted on her memory, his eyebrows, his broad fingers and the question he asked her afterwards: "Whose is this little girl?"

"Some people are scary when they're thinking," he says, out of the blue. She gets a fright. He claims that there are people who hover a hand's width above the ground, she thinks, silently, as if on an air cushion, and in fact he's one of them. "You wander around like a ghost," she says. He laughs and pulls his shirt over his head. "Spirit on the water," he sings. "Pull your shirt back down," she says.

"Why?"

"I want to see your face."

"What are you frightened of?" he says. She shakes her head, says nothing, and speeds up. "You won't keep that up," he says. "Wanna bet?" she says. She knows she can be quick if she needs to be. Start by increasing the frequency, and only then the length of your strides, never the other way round. He keeps up with her easily. At the third sharp bend she slides back a little. "What are you running away from?" he says. "Not from you," she pants.

"What then?"

"I can't tell you." She gets to a certain point where everything just blurs, what is her and what is not, she can no longer distinguish between herself, the children and the people around her, and all of a sudden the whole of the world is at her back, an army of large, dark men.

"Him?"

She nods. She was far too young, she says, far too trusting, still a child, and he had this smile and these large, smooth hands.

She enjoys the moment when the view suddenly extends over the ridge and drops down to the south, to the limestone mountains of Upper Styria and the Tauern. The wind hits her full blast. She likes that too, having to brace her shoulders forward, the burning feeling on her chin and the cold which shoots up her nose like two icicles. They climb straight up the narrow spine, past an outcrop, bypass a cornice to the south, then they are at the top.

"Some people are like that", the psychiatrist had told her, and when she replied that she knew that, he said: "So why did you marry him?" She said she'd send him along, maybe he'd understand then, and at this the psychiatrist had apparently taken fright and said it wasn't necessary, he could imagine him well enough. She doubted that, she said, and the psychiatrist, offended, had replied, "You don't trust me one bit."

"*Whack*," she said. "There are a number of words for it. But *whack* seems to describe most accurately what he did to me: the slapping sound made when a sharply directed hand or leather belt meets bare flesh." "He whacked you?" he says. "That's what I call it," she says. "How badly?" he asks. She says nothing. When she screws up her eyes the glint of the snow crystals becomes multi-coloured. It is the small, childish things that make the world bearable, she thinks, like screwing up your eyes in the snow, monks who can't keep still, and certain phrases such as "You don't like holidays" or, "The sun makes the moon shine". He removes the climbing skins from his skis, adjusts the bindings into the downhill position, and checks that the screws on the telescopic sticks are tightly fixed. "Why do you always have to be doing something?" she asks. "Because the bells have flown away," he says, "and it's all so dreadfully quiet." She taps her head. And yet something is unsettling her. She does not know what it is. Sometimes there are things you just miss, she thinks.

Ten short thrusts, four long ones – the firm snow on the first slope beyond the end of the ridge is barely ankle deep. He skis ahead of her, pushing extremely close to the edge while singing "O Haupt voll Blut und Wunden" at the top of his voice. When her thighs start to burn she does a downhill turn and yells that he's a lunatic. He does not seem to hear a thing and skis on. She slips the rucksack off her shoulders, reaches into the lower of the two external pockets, pulls out the small pack of razorblades and sends it flying off into the distance, even though she knows this will not help.

The crusted snow is starting to melt at the spot where he is waiting. "Watch out for your bones," he says. "Something's annoying me," she says, gasping, "and it has to do with bells." He laughs: "Are you surprised?"

*

201

He is driving. She is clinging on in the passenger seat, shivering, and her lungs are burning. Racing down through refrozen snow over an altitude of three hundred metres, several falls, ending up on a goods path where the snow had melted away altogether. He is the same as he is after a run. "I run," he says, as if needing to apologise, "all the time, every day." She nods and says nothing.

They take the southerly route, the avalanche protection gallery between Moosheim and Sankt Christoph, the Kammwand tunnel. Somewhere in the bends that lead up to the western entrance she falls asleep. She dreams of her mother, in duplicate, standing beside a huge wardrobe, trying on clothes and chatting to herself. When something dark steps out of the wardrobe she starts awake and thinks that her mobile has rung. He says it might have been the brakes squeaking, "Where are we?" she asks. "I've got an idea," he says.

"Weren't we going to my place?"

"This won't take long."

He helps her out of the car. "You can leave everything here," he says. He walks in front of her, taking large springy strides. Her shoulders are aching, as are her calves and lower back. The iron gate, ajar, the plane trees beside it, the secret path, the opposite direction this time. Up the steps, the metal door with frosted glass. The flowerpots along the passage of the cloister wing, Christmas cacti, azaleas, a lemon tree. Twenty-seven paces, she knows that now. The window is wide open. One of his obsessions is to get a pair of birds to build a nest in his room, preferably swallows, he says.

He leads her into the middle of the room. "Stay there," he says. He kneels and opens the belt and zip of her salopettes. She can feel the anxiety welling up inside her. "What are you doing?" she asks, trying to push him away. "Not what you're afraid I'm doing," he says. "Promise." He pulls her trousers down to her knees, then her tights. "I'm cold," she says, putting her hands on her bare thighs. "Almost done," he says, pulling up one of the two chairs in the room. "Now sit." He takes all her clothes off, ski socks, trousers, tights. "One sec," he says, disappearing into the bathroom. She looks out of the window and suddenly the image of bells with wings appears before her, moving across the sky in formation like migratory birds. Then she tries to remember which coats her mother actually wore. She recalls a grey woollen one, coarse weave with large black buttons.

The enamelled washbasin he is carrying is white with a narrow, dark-blue rim. When he puts it down, soap bubbles slosh over the wooden floor. "What are you doing?" she says. He laughs, lifts her legs with one hand, pushing the basin towards the chair with the other, and gently puts her feet into the warm water. He pulls a bath sponge from his armpit, soaks it, and presses it against her calves. He used to have a wife who existed only in his mind, he says, "and now I've got one whose feet I wash on Maundy Thursday". She closes her eyes and imagines two small bells with wings building a nest in the corner between the wall and ceiling. "Why are you laughing?" he asks. "Because sometimes you can be seriously bonkers," she says.

EIGHTEEN

It was way past midnight, and Raffael Horn was longing for an island he had never been to before. He imagined the coastal road, hills of heather, streams that cut into basalt rock and, right by the sea, villages with the whitewashed walls of the distilleries: Port Ellen, Port Askaig, Bowmore.

He imagined endless herds of sheep, downpours, real fires, and himself standing by the surf in a tweed jacket, looking out at the Atlantic. "Naff male fantasy", Irene would say, and Tobias would mutter something about "escapism"; recently it had become his favourite word. Horn would pour himself another glass of Laphroaig and just let everything bounce off him.

Horn sat at his desk going through the report he had written up from the notes of his interviews with the three children. Two boys with a background of family migration, one a dreamy dragon slayer, the other with a hereditary disease and the ability to name all the capital cities in the world. A girl, shy, guinea-pig lover, with a certain talent for drawing. Nothing unusual in the basic make-up of any of them: of normal intelligence, emotionally responsive, adequate degree of human contact, reserved yet interested. All three clearly upset by a similar experience, wary of answering questions relating to the event, obviously frightened by something they called "the same thing", but refusing to say what this was. No visible pathological disorders, in particular no sign of post-traumatic stress disorder. He closed the document. Post-traumatic disorders sometimes did not show up until months or even years after the event; from that perspective, what he had just written was of very limited value, but only someone who was an expert in the field would know that. He stood up, left his study, and walked out into the open air. It was drizzling slightly. In the morning there would be fog over the Furth Basin. This was when the cat would usually be rubbing itself around his ankles. But she was with Tobias and Tobias was with Michael, still, as was the Volvo. He had been stupid enough to say that he didn't need the car. Sons tend to exploit things like that.

The light was on in the stable. Irene was sitting in one of the armchairs, listening to music. Somebody was singing Baroque arias, a voice that became open and raw in the lower registers. "But that's not a cello," he said. She closed her eyes and said nothing. He felt stupid.

"A countertenor?" he asked. "Kowalski? Scholl? One of the English ones?" She shook her head and pointed to the C.D. case on the speaker. A narrow face, short, dark hair, sticking-out ears, the face betraying a hint of scepticism. Marijana Mijanovic, he read. "Never heard of her." "Right up your street, though," she said. "The voice?" he asked. "Everything about her," she said. "Her ears, her critical look, her voice of course." She's right, Horn thought, it's obvious, who else could know what I like? He asked her why she was listening to it, and she said it was because she liked the woman, too, and also because she'd love to play the cello in the way that voice sang, softly and wildly, at times so untamed that you could hear the tongue vibrating.

She sat up and motioned him over. "I want to ask you something," she said, "very quietly." He perched on the arm of her chair and bent over to her. She whispered something to him. "What, now?" he asked. "Here?" She nodded.

"It's the only thing which will calm my nerves."

"But you're only playing Bruckner's 'Te Deum'," he said. She shook her head. "Not only. But when I talk about it, it makes me even more nervous." She shrugged her shoulders apologetically. He stroked the bridge of her nose with his index finger. "My silly little perfectionist," he said. She pulled him towards her. "Will you go and get some duvets?" she whispered. "It's chilly."

Marijana Mijanovic sang something about *vago e bello* and *fiore* and *prato*, while Irene lay on top of him in that way she called "full length": everything touching, toes, thighs, tummies, chests, hands, chins, mouths, noses, heads. The tip of his tongue traced over her incisors, he smelt the piquancy of her fragrance and felt her shivering gradually subside. "What do you want to play?" he said. She lay her head on his neck, nibbled at his collarbone and said nothing.

Later, they were lying on the carpet, one duvet beneath them, the other a cover, and he told her about Felix, Britta and Sen Wu, their openness, curiosity and the puzzles they presented. He said that justice in the world ended the very moment you compared children's histories, and she replied that he didn't have to tell her that. Tobias would ensure that the thing with Michael sorted itself out, he said, and she replied that Tobias hadn't been at home for several days, had he forgotten? "Talking of Tobias," he said, "will you come to Scotland with me in the summer?" "Talking of male fantasies," she replied, "do you know who Handel wrote all that music for that Mijanovic is singing?" He shrugged. "A castrato," she said. So he hadn't been totally off the mark with his countertenor guess, he said. A countertenor was not a castrato, thank you very much, she replied, "and by the way," she added in English, cutting off a boy's balls was far worse than hitting him. "If you look hard enough there's always something worse," he said.

While Irene's breathing beside him became ever calmer, he thought of meadows full of flowers, of Lisbeth Schalk and Leonie Wittmann, of the fact that certain of his colleagues referred to female companions at academic conferences simply as "symposium support", and of his sons, who at that very moment might be sitting together slagging off their parents, Michael with a glass of wine, Tobias with a joint between his fingers. He wondered when it was that the one had taught the other how to drive, and how close the contact between the brothers had been all this time, without him or Irene noticing anything. He looked through one of the roof windows at the sky. No stars were visible. He wondered again whether this was the right house for him, on the edge of a forest, in the commuter belt of a small town, and then he wondered who would think him conventional if they knew that he thought having sex with his wife was the best thing in the world.

The call came just before six o'clock. There was a white morning light in the stable. Irene had rolled onto her side and was snoring gently. He reached for his mobile which he had left on the bentwood chair. It was Christina. Günther had just called from the hospital, she said. Margot Frühwald had been having spasms for the past half hour. Gerlinde Schäfer, the most ambitious trainee doctor on the planet, thought as usual that she had to sort it out herself, but was not coping. Horn threw back the duvet. "Can you come and collect me?" he asked. "My son's stolen my car and I don't know whether Irene needs hers today." "I wouldn't mind having a son who stole my car," Christina said and hung up.

Horn gathered up his clothes. Immediately above him he heard a rustling in the pitch of the roof. A dormouse or a marten. Irene got along better with these sorts of animals than he did. Leave them alone, they're not doing us any harm, she would say if he started thinking aloud about traps or poison. They'll only eat our roof insulation, he would say, and you'll freeze again. She would just laugh, shrug and stroke Mimi, who seemed not to have any intention of messing with a marten either. "Women pacifists", or some similar phrase would then cross his mind. "Have a good dress rehearsal, break a leg!" he said softly in Irene's direction before he left. She grunted.

"How's Dolores?" Horn asked as he climbed into Christina's car. "She can write her first name and she'll be starting school in September," she said. Maybe she'll steal your car one day, too, Horn said. Christina replied that he should cut the crap; she didn't know anybody with Down's Syndrome who had a driving licence, and Horn said a lack of a driving licence hadn't stopped his son. When they came to the curves that led to the fast road he saw that he had been wrong with his fog prediction from the night before. Layers of high cloud were hanging above the basin. The lake was grey. Good Friday, he thought, and he thought of how the hospital would reek of fish at lunchtime. "Where's your daughter now, in fact?" he asked. Christina gestured behind her with her thumb. He turned. The girl was curled up on the back seat, asleep.

"Do you take her to kindergarten in her pyjamas?" Horn asked. "She stays with me in the office till noon," Christina said. "Then I drive her home. Today's a half holiday. And I do have some clothes with me, if it makes you feel better."

Christina carried her daughter across the car park and past the porter to the lift. The girl woke up and said, "Push". Like any other child, Horn thought, and Christina said, "What do you expect?"

*

Margot Frühwald was pale purple in the face and gasping for breath. "It could kick off again at any moment," Günther said, who was the first to spot Horn. Horn asked how long she had been like this. Günther said forty minutes, and Karin, who was also standing by the bed, said, "Maybe longer." Gerlinde Schäfer was putting the oxygen mask over Margot Frühwald's nose. If you subtracted the spasm-free intervals, the net time she had been in spasm was a maximum of twenty minutes. Horn gave her a searching look. She was pale and quivering. In truth the whole thing had begun just after midnight, Karin said. During monitoring Frau Frühwald had suddenly sat upright in bed, stared into the distance, and started counting in a loud voice: "Seventeen, eighteen, nineteen, twenty, twenty-one", different series of numbers. Occasionally she would say, "There's one's missing", or, "Gunde, there's one missing". She had also made erratic movements with her arms, sometimes wiping with her hands, sometimes as if she were trying to pluck an apple from the air, or as if she were waving to someone. "What does Gunde mean?" Horn asked. Friedegund Mayrhofer had been the head of the old town kindergarten, now called Kindergarten Furth I, Günther said, she had been known to her colleagues as Gunde. He knew this because she'd taught him at the kindergarten.

"What have you given her?" Horn asked. Schäfer remained silent. He saw tears welling in her eyes. "Infusomat, clonazepam ampoules, solvent, pulse oximeter," he said to Karin and Günther. When the two of them had left the room, the stocky young woman sat on a chair by the window and started to cry. "It's not your fault," he said. "Yes it is," she sobbed.

"Why?"

She thought that Margot Frühwald was hearing voices and seeing things, so she had given her risperidone, and not just a small dose, either. Horn started to understand. "And you think that sparked off the attack?" Schäfer sniffed up the tears and nodded. He felt the urge to kneel down beside her as if she were a little child and put his hand on her thigh. Frau Frühwald had evidently suffered a temporal lobe seizure, he said, which had gone on for a long time and had ultimately translated into a grand mal seizure. So although, psychiatrically speaking, the stereotypical movements and exclamations had nothing to do with hallucinations, he was certain that she had not set anything off with her antipsychotic drug either.

"Sometimes medicine is less harmful than it thinks it is," he said.

Schäfer gave him a doubtful look. "So she's not going to die?" she asked. "Not yet," he said.

They put Margot Frühwald on the clonazepam drip and administered her a dehydrating agent for the prophylaxis of cerebral oedema. Then Horn got on the phone and was put through to the neurological monitoring unit. There were two beds free.

Dolores was sitting on Christina's lap in the staff room, wolfing down a plaited bun. "Aren't you too heavy for your mum?" Horn asked. The girl shook her head. "She tortures Christina every time she's allowed here," Karin said. "No!" Dolores protested, spluttering a cloud of crumbs and sugar crystals around the room. "Oh, yes you are," Horn said. She kicked her legs at him. In fifteen years she'll take her driving test and drive a hundred and sixty on the motorway, he thought. "No," Dolores said. "She won't," Christina said. It's worse when I'm woken too early, Horn thought, putting his hand over his mouth.

"Are you going to send her home?" Christina asked. "Fräulein Schäfer? No. She's got to get over these things. Anyway, ambition and taking it easy don't go together," Horn said. He was harsh, she said. No, he wasn't, he replied, and if he knew his colleague Herr Hrachovec, that man would look after the poor girl when he arrived at eight. "The hero in the white coat," Christina said.

"Who saves the feeble woman."

It obviously still worked like that, she said – unless the feeble woman had a disabled child, then the number of heroes was quite clear. "One more," Dolores said, reaching for another plaited bun.

She has a disabled child and that Richard, Horn thought, no sign of a hero there. Richard Gassner from the I.T. department was definitely no hero. He was short, bearded and paid Christina the occasional visit to sleep with her. Otherwise he left her in peace. Which was the most important thing as far as she was concerned, she said.

*

At the morning meeting Gerlinde Schäfer was sitting near Hrachovec. She appeared to have regained her composure. Apart from the Margot Frühwald incident there were two things to report from the shift, she said. First, in the middle of the afternoon they had discovered Sabrina stark naked in Marcus's room. He had evidently found this rather embarrassing and had assured them that nothing had happened. She, on the other hand, had said that she'd been wanting a child for a long time and could not pass up the opportunity. Nobody could say exactly what had taken place, because Sabrina had ingeniously painted over the lens of the surveillance camera with nail polish. "Is she using contraception?" Horn asked. Nobody knew. "Is he using contraception?" Leonie Wittmann asked. He could not imagine that someone who had recently fallen from the ceiling with a noose around his neck would be thinking about contraception, Horn said. Nor a young woman who regularly slices through her skin with razorblades, she said.

On the topic of nooses, Schäfer said, the second noteworthy item was Marcus's goodbye letter. It had been brought in by a detective who'd said that she had been here recently with Felix Szigeti and Britta Kern. In fact it was the print-out of an e-mail Marcus had sent to his best friend. She had attached a note of his medical history. The friend was a certain Florian Weghaupt, a young man who'd recently died in a fall from scaffolding. It had even been on the television news. The letter was full of accusations aimed at the world, and clearly written after Weghaupt was already dead. It started with the sentence: "Flo, you were always the more consistent of the two of us." She couldn't remember any more of it.

Horn thought of Tobias and his own brand of consistency, the solidarity between the two brothers, and a new car. Then he thought of the early morning, the white light in the stable, the rustling of the marten in the roof insulation, and how Irene had nibbled at his collarbone. "Do you like Baroque music?" he murmured to Wittmann. "Not especially," she replied. "Why?" "No particular reason," he said.

They were in the middle of a discussion about people who wanted to be cared for, but who only got sex, when Kurt Frühwald suddenly appeared in the doorway. They all went quiet. Frühwald was ashen. His right cheek twitched incessantly. "Where is she?" he asked softly. Horn stood up and walked over to Frühwald. "Come with me," he said. Frühwald looked straight through him. "Where is she?" he roared. Horn took him firmly by the arm and pulled him out of the room. "In neurological intensive care," he said. "That's where they rang you from."

"Nobody rang me!"

"So why did you come?"

Frühwald stood there, fists clenched, and did not answer. The laughter of Christina's daughter rang out from her office. Horn pictured Dolores running down the corridor after a toy car, stopping, staring at the two of them, and then all of a sudden Frühwald would hold out his arms. He imagined her opening her mouth in astonishment, so you could see her tongue, forgetting to breathe for a short while and splaying her fingers like a little mermaid. Then he imagined Kurt Frühwald pausing, dropping his arms, and kicking the toy car with his right foot as if he had not seen it.

Frühwald did not say a word as they made their way to N31, not in the hallway, not on the stairs and not by the sliding door where they then had to wait. Horn thought of the lime tree outside Frühwald's house, of Margaret Frühwald's face with the peacock-feather bedclothes wrapped around it, and how her husband had undone the magnetic clasps on the white straps. The tall, dark-haired nurse who stepped out from behind the pane of frosted glass said she was sorry, but his wife was just having a venous catheter attached to her neck to give them better access in case of an emergency, he should not come back for at least another hour. Frühwald stared at the wall for a while, then turned to go. He pressed the button in the lift. "My wife's been taken away from me, every single day, for the past eleven years," he said. When they reached the ground floor he headed for the exit.

*

He gave them his word, he had not touched her, Marcus Lagler said, looking to Herbert for help. First she had climbed up on the table and painted the surveillance camera – quite a protracted job with the tiny nail-polish brush – then she had stood in front of him and removed one item of clothing after another, not like a stripper, but more as you do before going to bed. For a short while he had thought that her body was rather beautiful, but he had noticed those scars and cuts – lots of them – all over her body. He knew from magazines and the television that people did that sort of thing to their arms, but on her legs, stomach and breasts – he hadn't been prepared for that. So as far as he'd been concerned, sex was out of the question, and to be honest he never really was sure what she was after either, because she'd just stood there naked beside him, goose bumps on her thighs, giving him a stare which was provocative and sad at the same time.

Horn put the piece of paper on the table. "This is what I'm here about now," he said, they had already figured out the Sabrina thing. Marcus looked up at the ceiling for a few moments. "Where did you get that from?" he asked. "From Florian's mother in the end," Horn said. "Silly cow," Marcus said. "I beg your pardon" Herbert said.

"Nothing. That's what mums are like."

"What are mums like?"

"Ignorant, moronic, poking around in people's e-mails."

"Like your own?"

"Yeah, like mine."

"And not interested?"

"What do you mean?"

He had written that too, Horn said, that not even his closest family members were interested in his music. "In our music," Marcus said, "in our worthless, good-for-nothing, derivative music." What he had heard him play was not in the least worthless, Herbert said. Unfortunately his opinion was not worth a damn, nor the opinions of friends or guitar teachers, Marcus said, and Palkovits, the producer they had worked with, had said that they were decent rip-offs but nothing more. Florian had had the courage to ask who, in the man's opinion, they were ripping off, and this drugged-up bloke with greasy hair said that was beside the point, it sounded derivative, end of argument. Months of intensive rehearsal down the drain, not to mention the work composing the lyrics and music. The man hadn't even let them play for him, he just said that he had heard enough on the demo C.D., end of story. "And a few days later Florian fell to his death," said Herbert. Yes, when that happened it was all over, Marcus said, after that he looked at the world as if he were viewing a series of video clips he no longer had anything to do with, and that's the state he was in when he wrote the letter to Florian, the only person who'd really meant anything to him. "And then . . ." Herbert said. "I hanged myself," simple as that. He'd gone down to the basement when it was quiet, chopped off a piece of an old climbing rope with a hatchet, two, maybe three metres, and tied a noose. He had no idea where the rope came from, it had been there for ever and, no, as far as he knew his mother had never gone climbing, nor had any of his various stepfathers. "Various step-fathers?" Horn asked. There had been four so far, Marcus said, the last one had been on the scene for two and a half years. The moment he, Marcus, was born, his biological father had buggered off to the South Tyrol where he originally hailed from, but he'd already told them that about a hundred times. At that moment Horn suddenly saw all the questions that needed to be asked lined up before him, as if on a school blackboard. Have you tried to get in contact with your father? How do you imagine him? Do you have a photograph of him? Which of your stepfathers did you have the best relationship with? Do you still see him? Did your first stepfather beat you? The second? The third? The fourth probably not any more. He felt ridiculous and only asked one question: "Why under the chandelier?" Marcus Lagler again turned his gaze to the ceiling, then looked at Horn. It sounded a bit childish, he said, but he had formed this nice image in his mind: his mother turning on the light and him hanging there peacefully, the light above his head like a halo.

*

Sometimes Raffael Horn felt the need for a drink in the middle of the day, and this disturbed him. It happened when there were arguments within his team, when Irene was in one of her detached phases, and when Krem, the commercial director, threatened redundancies. There was also this strange, mental sluggishness, the feeling of having missed something important, without there actually having been anything that he could have missed. You're going mad, he told himself, there's no more to the world than what exists. Still, in situations like this he was pleased not to have a beer to hand or schnapps. He went to the tap and drank until his stomach ached. Then he opened the window hoping to smell something strong, such as lilac or rotting reeds. But he could not smell anything at all.

"There's always more to the world than what exists," Leonie Wittmann said, leaning with her shoulder against the wall. This happened from time to time: after the rounds, someone would lean against the wall, a group would form, and weird sentences would be uttered, plucked right out of everyday hospital life. Hrachovec wondered whether that comment about the world wasn't banal, and Wittmann said, yes, it was to an extent, but on the other hand it was the banal things in life which provided relief, such as realising that you'd never be able to deal with everything and would always overlook something, or that all concrete things in life were symbolic, too, the noose hanging from the chandelier hook, cutting your own skin or showing your naked body to another person. Or slapping a child in the face, Horn thought. "Exactly," Wittmann said.

They discussed body imagery, the question of how badly a child would have to be treated for it to indulge in self-harming later on, and the pleasurable notion of punching Sabrina's father's lights out. At the end they talked about subconscious motives for choosing a particular musical instrument. In his view, Hrachovec said, music should never be the reason for a suicide attempt, and Herbert replied that this was the romantic, sentimental drivel of someone who was absolutely clueless. Musicians were always topping themselves, especially guitarists – in fact people expected them to. Horn thought of his wife's emotional transparency, her red cheeks when she practised, and how she always said that to be really believable a musician had to play as if their life depended on it.

"Has your strange feeling gone now?" Wittmann asked before they parted company. He listened to his inner self for a moment, then shook his head. It probably had something to do with his obsessive Scotland fixation, he said, nothing else.

The grey-haired man was waiting for him by the steps. "Possner," he said, "Armin Possner". Horn needn't worry, he evidently had a very forgettable name; by now he knew the face people made, some of them would say Possnik or Posch. He had called his company Apollo, A because of Armin and Po because of Possner, Apollo Recruitment, people didn't have such difficulty with that. Occasionally he was also called Herr Apollo. He knew he ought to have telephoned ahead, he apologised for this oversight, but he needed some quick advice.

Horn looked at the man, the neat haircut, the polished shoes and the piece of paper folded many times over. A schizophrenic wife being treated in Graz was what came to mind, and suddenly he wondered whether stripes on ties always went downwards from left to right.

His daughter had vanished the day before, the man said, like a ghost, without leaving anything behind, no clue, nor any message. She was thirteen and had been very difficult for the past six months – he had briefly mentioned that the last time they met. All he knew for sure was that she had taken money from his office, several thousand euros, which was not that significant as she had always been a thief. He was more worried by the accusations she had been obsessively levelling at himself and his wife: that at the time they had not in fact put her into care, but bought her from her Indian parents, with the intention of "sub-letting" her for short periods – that's what she called it. He was trying not to get worked up about it, but rather to think about the traumas of her childhood, years in an orphanage, time on the streets, and everything that had happened to her there. This allowed him to come to terms with her behaviour to an extent; his wife, on the other hand, was all over the place, no longer sleeping, talking to the television, and since yesterday insisting that her daughter was dead.

"What's her name?" Horn asked.

"Who? My wife?"

"No, your daughter."

Fanni, the man said, his foster daughter was called Fanni. To begin with she had been a quiet, well-adjusted little girl, but that had gradually changed. Now he didn't think he could cope with the matter on his own and wanted to report it to the child welfare office, her going missing and the accusations she was likely to be making. That was the first thing he wanted to ask Horn, the name of a contact at the local child welfare office, somebody you could safely tell a story like this to. "Safely?" Horn asked. "You know what I mean," the man said. "Without the usual prejudices." After all, they were talking about a foreign girl who looked pretty exotic. Which shouldn't be a problem, even in Furth, Horn said. "Let's hope you're right," the man replied.

"And the second thing?" Horn said.

"Would you treat her?" the man asked.

"But she's not here."

"When she's back – would you treat her? She's quite unstable. You've got to believe me."

The man looked exhausted and worried. Some people had to shoulder the burden of a schizophrenic wife, add to that a foster daughter who ran away from home, and yet they still managed to iron razor-sharp creases into their trousers. Horn looked at the baggy knees of his jeans and thought about the fact that Tobias crushed eggs, abducted cats and drove vehicles illegally. Then he thought of Irene, who would go through periods of hardly sleep-ing, who definitely talked to her cello, and repeatedly saw the deaths of her sons played out in her head. In spite of all this he had it good, of that he was certain.

"What sort of staff can one recruit from your firm?" he asked. The man gave him a look of surprise, then smiled. Mainly builders, he said, bricklayers, joiners, crane operators, and plenty of them if necessary, several hundred at a time. But he also had highly qualified staff on his books, software developers, I.T. engineers or security experts for the protection of property and people. Should he ever need it, he could recruit someone to build a stage, write a speech or weld a shark cage underwater. I'd like the shark cage, Horn thought. Then he asked where he got all these people from, and the man said from all over the world.

*

Horn turned around, went into the office and picked up the

218

telephone. Leuweritz answered. "Don't you ever operate?" Horn asked.

"Are you phoning me to revel in the laziness of casualty surgeons?"

"More serious than that. You've got schnapps in your department, haven't you?"

"Sure do!" Leuweritz said. Horn hung up. A trace of Andrea Elmer's perfume hung in the air – Miyake, if he remembered correctly. A fragment of one of Leuweritz's phrases came into his head: *the tip of a fence post touching their pericardium.*

NINETEEN

The first thing he saw was a yellow Playmobil island with palm trees. It was on the concrete path by the door, a few metres from the garden wall. It was cracked from the edge to the middle, and a wedge-shaped piece had broken off. Somebody must have stepped on it. In the juniper bushes to the side of the path was a raccoon cuddly toy and a red doll's bed. Ludwig Kovacs picked up the raccoon and took it with him.

Two women were standing by the entrance. One of them – thin, grey-haired, slightly odd hairdo – was crying. The other, short and round, and wearing a mint-green poplin coat, was holding her hands, trying to calm her down. "Which of you called?" Kovacs asked. "I did," said the shorter one. "Are you from the police?" He nodded. "And who are you?" The thin lady sobbed. Her name was Lea Wirth, the head of the kindergarten, the other woman said. She had heard about it from her.

At 6.34 a.m. a call had come through to the out-of-hours office of the Furth police, and been logged in the usual way. Her name was Erika Oleschowsky, the woman had said, and she was a notoriously early riser, no matter whether it was a weekday, a Sunday, or even Easter Saturday. She lived in one of the terraced houses in Zsigmondygasse, number eighteen, and her bedroom window looked directly onto the rear of the town kindergarten, the playground and the outside terrace. When she had gone out onto her balcony that morning, all she had felt at first was a vague inkling that something was different from normal. Then she had seen that all the ropes on the climbing frame in the playground had been cut. Rope ladders, swings, rings – they were all on the ground. The wind had strewn all across the lawn a mass of brightly coloured scraps of cloth, irregularly shaped, different sizes, she hadn't been able to identify them. And the door out to the terrace was wide open. As the whole picture looked as though the place had been burgled, she had telephoned the police without delay.

Jürgensen, a complete newcomer to the service, had been unable to cope and had called Töllmann, and Töllmann had said that since it concerned children it was clear whose responsibility it was.

Kovacs had rolled away from Marlene's embrace, wiped a dribble of saliva from her face, and snuck out of the flat. On the stairs he had paused briefly, thought of Charlotte, who was asleep on the gallery, and for some unfathomable reason had pictured the fine veins on Marlene's breasts. He had felt good and this surprised him. It was, after all, early in the morning on Easter Saturday, and he could now forget about his breakfast *à trois*.

"Would you like me to open up?" Lea Wirth asked. The key was sitting in the palm of her hand. She looks like a shrunken Prince Valiant somehow, Kovacs thought. He took the arm of the kindergarten teacher and led her to the door. Yes, he would like her to open up, he said. Kovacs felt her quiver when she put the key into the lock. "It's not locked," she said. "Why on earth is it not locked?" He did not say anything and pulled open the door.

In the hallway two smashed basins were lying side by side, along with several overturned lockers and a large brown floor-vase with willow branches. Lea Wirth gasped. "Are you going to be alright?" Kovacs asked. She stared at the room, making tiny circular movements with her hands. He let go of her and lifted one of the }lockers upright again. "Sit down," he said. "Frau Oleschowsky will stay with you." He asked how many rooms there were in total, and

Erika Oleschowsky said there were two classrooms, the office, the lavatories, a meeting room, and a quiet room for the little ones. Lea Wirth sat there trembling.

Mauritz answered straightaway. "Who's ruining my peace?" he asked. "Who do you think?" Kovacs said. He realised that Mauritz was probably just about to tuck into his second fried egg, and that he and his wife were congratulating each other on the fact that Nikolaus had finally gone off to sleep, but regrettably it looked like a case for forensics. Another scaffolding incident? Mauritz wondered, and Kovacs said no, a kindergarten, sorry to disappoint, all on the ground floor, four steps up to the front door, but there was a wheelchair ramp.

"Can I finish reading the sports section?"

"No," Kovacs said, and he shouldn't forget the police tape or the spare battery for the camera. "Blood?" Mauritz asked. No blood, as far as he could tell, just lots of broken stuff, Kovacs replied. "Who on earth would wreck a kindergarten?" Mauritz said.

Kovacs went slowly from door to door. It was as if a tornado had passed through the rooms, or a gang of hooligans. Overturned shelves, the contents of cupboards tipped out, emptied Duplo and Lego boxes, drawings ripped from the walls, a pirate ship with a real skull-and-crossbones flag trampled to bits, a family of dark-grey corduroy hares with all their ears ripped off. In the lavatories the third basin along was hanging downwards from its left-hand fitting. The mirrors had been smashed, the children's footstool, which had clearly been used as an implement, was beside the door. Only in the office and meeting room did everything appear to be untouched. Two folders labelled PERSONNEL lay on the desk. In a water jug stood a forsythia branch, hung with a few painted Easter eggs.

"I found these in the garden," Kovacs said, showing Lea Wirth several strips of coloured plastic. "Have you any idea what these are?" The teacher nodded. "From our paddling pool," she said. "But we don't usually bring that out until the middle of May." It's been cut up, Kovacs said, probably with a Stanley knife. Lea Wirth thought for a moment, then shook her head. "What is it?" Kovacs asked. Nothing, she said, the paddling pool was folded away in the garden storage room, behind the·hose reel and terracotta flowerpots, but hardly anybody knew that. Had that room been broken into as well? "Broken into? What do you mean?" "Well, what else?" Lea Wirth asked. There was no sign of a break-in on the terrace door, and she had seen the front door herself. "Do burglars have keys?" she asked. Duplicate keys, skeleton keys, everything, he said, and Erika Oleschowksy asked how nutty someone had to be to cut a paddling pool to bits.

Kovacs asked Frau Oleschowsky to make them all a cup of coffee. In truth her curiosity and green coat were getting on his nerves.

"Incidentally, do you know Felix Szigeti?" he asked. Of course she knew him, Lea Wirth said, and Britta Kern, too, if that was what he was driving at, Sen Wu was the only one she didn't know, he'd gone to the kindergarten in north Furth. Anyway, Felix and Britta had been delightful children, both a bit eccentric, and Felix could be a little impulsive sometimes. In her view, only someone who was seriously mentally disturbed would go around beating up children. She hesitated for a moment. "But you don't think that the two are ..." "No, I don't," Kovacs said.

He asked all the usual police questions, even though he knew they would not get him anywhere. Is there anybody you think might have done this? Have you or any of your colleagues been threatened recently? Maybe in the past? Any unpleasant scenes with parents? Grandparents? Do the neighbours feel disturbed by the noise the children make? Lea Wirth kept shaking her head. The last time there'd been a disagreement was the previous week, she said eventually. A four-and-a-half-year-old boy had invited a girl to touch his penis while they were playing doctors and nurses in the dolly corner. The girl's mother had reacted with indignation, going on about sexual abuse and teachers neglecting their responsibilities. Funnily enough, in the end what pacified the woman most of all was the argument that it did no harm if a girl discovered early on what it felt like to touch a penis; it was said to increase self-confidence. Kovacs found himself getting irritated by the well-rehearsed way in which this elderly kindergarten teacher spoke about sexuality.

Mauritz came in with Erika Oleschowsky. His face was bright red. "What's up? You seem to be even more out of breath than usual," Kovacs said. "A quick coffee will fix it," Mauritz replied, supporting himself against the wall. He'd rather not hear any more talk of lateness or a *second fried egg*, please, quite clearly this was going to be one crappy Easter Saturday. The two ladies nodded in agreement. Erika Oleschowsky poured coffee into plastic beakers. Children normally drink out of these, Kovacs thought, and then they make Lego houses, brush dolls' hair and have battles between their Pokémon figures.

He had been driving along Seestraße towards Rathausplatz, Mauritz said, at a leisurely speed, appropriate for a holiday, as it were, and suddenly there was this car in Ellert's toy shop. It wasn't unusual for cars to be found in toy shops, Kovacs said, he had even bought a green Matchbox Lamborghini when he was a boy, from Heinisch's toy shop in Bruck an der Mur. He had paid with a twenty-shilling note stolen from his father's wallet, and although he never stopped being plagued by feelings of guilt, he loved the car. "Some kind of minivan," Mauritz said, stirring sugar into his coffee, "terrible bodywork, ghastly colour, disabled badge, hydraulic platform at the back." The car was going backwards and must have crashed through the glass frontage with huge force, only coming to a standstill in the middle of the shop. It seemed to have destroyed all sorts of things, but he hadn't had the time to inspect the damage in detail. He'd wound police tape around the area several times over and had called the station. "Accident?" Kovacs asked. "Accident, incident, break-in, who cares?" Mauritz said. Jürgensen had come, he'd contacted him before he went off duty. He was now hanging about the crime scene, half asleep, waiting for someone to take over. First an accident, then a crime scene, that was inconsistent, Kovacs said. Mauritz drank up his coffee and put the cup into Frau Oleschowsky's hand. "You're such a pedant!" he said. "Do you want to see it?"

"What?"

"The crime scene."

"There are some things that are never coincidences," Kovacs said before they got into Mauritz's Renault. "You mean the kindergarten and the toy shop at the same time?" Mauritz asked. "Who does things like that?" Kovacs thought of the freshly ironed shirt in the renovated house in Sankt Christoph, the purple marks left on the girl's face, and Relaxo. Then he thought of the precise edging of the flowerbeds in the front garden and how Sabine Wieck had needed to wash her hands afterwards. "Someone who's had problems in their childhood," he said.

"I was always the fat one," Mauritz said after a time. "What do you mean *was*?" Kovacs asked. Mauritz laughed. He meant when he was at kindergarten. He had always been the fat one and from day one *Mauritz*, as if that were his first name. *Mauritz can't walk that quickly, please wait for Mauritz* – those were the sentences he had hear the two kindergarten teachers utter on a daily basis. Tante Frieda and Tante Berta, that was it. What the hell was his first name again? Kovacs wondered. Of course it had bothered him sometimes, Maurtiz said, but there had never really been any question of taking his revenge by laying his kindergarten to waste. Anyway, once he'd made it up the climbing frame faster than Christian Rametsteiner. Christian's trousers had got caught on some wood, he'd just been unlucky. Engelbert, Kovacs thought, that's his name, Engelbert.

They were still trying to trace the owner of the vehicle, Mauritz said, there were the usual holiday-related complications. Apart from that they could assume with some confidence that the car was stolen. "How so?" Kovacs said.

"Would you park your own car in the middle of a toy shop?"

"An apple-green Lamborghini Miura," Kovacs said.

Only a handful of people had come to gawp at the scene. The Jürgensen boy was strutting up and down, trying to look authoritative. When he saw Kovacs and Mauritz he pulled a piece of paper from his jacket pocket. First of all, the shop owner was on his way back from holiday in Italy and would be arriving that evening, a neighbour had told him that. Secondly, although the computer system still wasn't working, one of the bystanders had identified the vehicle. It belonged to Kurt Frühwald, an insurance broker whose wife was paralysed from the waist down, hence the wheelchair platform at the back. He had asked the man to wait in case Kovacs wanted to know any more.

The man was sitting inside the shop on a blue children's chair, concentrating hard on a wooden puzzle. He was absolutely certain it was Kurt Frühwald's car, he said. He had insured his two horses with Frühwald a week or so ago, and had driven to the stable with him in that same mustard-yellow car to get the insurance company's expert opinion. Frühwald had told him about his wife's needing a wheelchair and also that she wasn't quite right in the head at the moment. "Have you got all of that?" Kovacs asked. Jürgensen nodded eagerly. The man looked at the puzzle in his hand, seemed to consider for a moment whether to pocket it, but then put it back on the shelf. Who would have thought that you have to insure horses as well? Kovacs thought. He reached for his mobile.

Was he disturbing him?

He was painting Easter eggs? Of course!

Wasn't he the expert in people who weren't right in the head?

He should get to the point? Yes, he understood. Did he know anybody by the name of Frühwald? That's the one, with the wife who was paralysed.

Oh Christ? What did *Oh Christ!* mean?

Why all these questions? Did he know what car Frühwald drove?

Wrong to answer a question with another question? Not for the police.

A mustard-yellow minivan. Why was it only other people were able to come up with the phrase *mustard-yellow* so readily?

Psycho-*what* fits? O.K., he didn't need to understand. Who? The wife? The man was what? Feeling hemmed in?

What did he do with her? Magnetic clasps? He couldn't understand a word.

An accident? Eleven years ago? Where?

Awkward relationship with children?

"Did you say over the rim of the paddling pool? . . . Concrete plant troughs? They're gone."

Kovacs pictured the pirate island, the hares with their ears cut off, and the scraps of coloured plastic which the wind had blown about the lawn. He imagined the woman with the Prince Valiant haircut sewing buttons onto dolls' clothes, building castles, catching children playing doctors and nurses, but remaining quite calm about the whole thing. Then he imagined children running around the garden, straight through the paddling pool, laughing and screaming as they went.

Yes, only the car. Kurt Frühwald himself was nowhere to be seen.

Did he have any idea . . .? Yes? What was he doing?

Could he repeat that, please?!

*

Of course biologists were friendly people, Veronika Bayer said as she unlocked the boathouse. All that fresh air and regular contact with plants and animals, none of which put you under pressure – it was enough to bring a smile to your face even if you were dragged out of bed early on Easter Saturday. She was a tall woman with broad shoulders and a prominent nose. Her particular area of expertise was owls, she said, but recently she had been focusing on anomalies in the bird population, vagrants from the east such as waxwings, the impact on the settlement of golden eagles in the Lungau and migration dodgers. "What?" Kovacs asked. "Migration dodgers," she said. More and more individual birds or small groups were not migrating, for different reasons. Most of them wouldn't survive the winter, but some developed astonishingly adaptive mechanisms. "You don't bring them inside?" Kovacs asked. Veronika Bayer laughed. No, she said, that wouldn't help anyone.

"So you watch them die?"

Dying went with her job. With a pole she pushed open the door on the water side. A pair of mallards cursed in protest.

Mauritz eyed the boat. "Wouldn't it be better if I waited here?" he said. The boat was licensed to take eight passengers, Veronika Bayer said, unplugging the cable from the charging unit. Anyway, there were life vests under the seats. "They never fit me," Mauritz said.

They went along a section of reeds, then out into the lake, moving in a wide arc. The sky was overcast, the lake a bluey grey. The sun's reflection danced here and there on the water. Kovacs sat with binoculars at the bow and felt the occasional spray of water on his face. He liked that.

There had been times, Veronika Bayer said, when Frühwald had gone swimming every day, and as he had always set off from the jetty at the wildlife observation centre, they had seen each other all the time. Got to know each other? That would be stretching it, he hadn't ever said much. They'd sometimes met him on the lake, too, so yes, he would be familiar with the electric boat. But Frühwald might still panic or try to escape if he sees me, Mauritz said. Then duck, Kovacs said. "Duck? Me?" Mauritz said, tapping his head.

They talked about the fish population, about how beautiful the char was, about the school of whitefish at Waiern, and how every year at the end of May the graylings migrated from the river into the lake at the Moosheim end. Kovacs mentioned his chub catch, and Mauritz said that as soon as Nikolaus could hold a rod he would have a go with him.

Kovacs imagined Charlotte at the stern of the boat, a short spinning rod in her hand and her mohican shining far across the lake, then Marlene with her look of disdain, and finally the two of them sitting together at breakfast, eyeing each other mistrustfully.

"Do you trust this psychiatrist, then?" Mauritz said.

"Do I look like someone who trusts psychiatrists?" Kovacs replied.

"So why are we here?"

Because he saw two possible alternatives, Kovacs said, either the man was hanging from a rope somewhere, or beating up a child. Veronika Bayer gave him a horrified look: "You mean he . . .?" Kovacs shrugged. "Maybe it was him, maybe it wasn't – I don't actually have a clue," he said.

"Do you have children?" she asked. Kovacs nodded. One daughter, he said, and yes, he had hit her once. Recently he felt as if the whole world wanted to know whether he had ever hit his daughter. But she didn't, Veronika Bayer said – she was sure his daughter must be wonderful. Yes, she is, Kovacs said, used to be a sack of potatoes, now she's a Red Indian.

"Mine's called Nikolaus," Mauritz said, beaming.

"Look ahead to the left," Veronika Bayer said. It took Kovacs a while, then he was amazed by how close they had got to the man without noticing him. He looked through the binoculars. "Bald head and goggles," he said, "and he's already on his way back." Frühwald was swimming breaststroke, long, relaxed strokes, and every time he pushed his arms forward he immersed himself as far as the lower rim of his goggles.

They steered towards the bank at Fürstenau and closed in on him from behind. "Have you actually got a gun on you?" the biologist asked all of a sudden. Kovacs shook his head. "Are you scared?" Mauritz asked. She grinned. "No," she said.

When they were right beside him, Frühwald shot them a brief glance. Kovacs was sure he knew who they were. "What are we going to do?" Mauritz asked. "Nothing for the next few minutes," Kovacs said.

At a distance of five or six metres they accompanied Kurt Frühwald until they were almost at the shore. In the end Veronika Bayer turned the dial up to maximum so that they arrived at the jetty shortly before him. She let Kovacs and Mauritz disembark and then moored the boat.

Frühwald was wearing a knee-length wetsuit with short sleeves. He knew that it looked faintly ridiculous on a man of his age, but it was perfect for Easter, a bit of insulation and a lot of freedom of movement. He took off his goggles. "I assume you're from the police," he said. Kovacs nodded. Mauritz gave an embarrassed cough. He wasn't going to deny anything, Frühwald said, he was responsible for it all, the kindergarten stuff and the toy shop, and he realised that he ought not to have done it, but he just couldn't help it. He had stayed silent for eleven years, and then he had spent half an hour being very loud indeed. "My wife was taken away from me eleven years ago, you see," he said, "and now they're taking her away from me again." He stood there, dripping, red goggle-marks around his eyes. Did they mind if he got a towel? His bag was under the boathouse jetty.

They walked behind him. Bandy legs, varicose veins and he walks like someone who has carried a lot on his shoulders, Kovacs thought. "It's been quite a struggle for you," he said. Frühwald bent down and pulled out the bag. "Yes," he said, "three and a half kilometres at a maximum of fifteen degrees." He rubbed his head, arms and legs dry and folded the towel again. "You can get changed inside," Veronika Bayer said. He would rather do it here and now, Frühwald said, starting to peel off the wetsuit.

"So why the children?" Kovacs asked abruptly. Frühwald paused. "What do you mean?" he asked.

"Why Felix Szigeti, why Britta Kern, why Sen Wu?"

Frühwald dropped his arms and gave Kovacs a baffled stare. Then he burst out laughing. "Do you know," he said eventually, "you may be an idiot, but I'm not a psychopath."

It was not often that Ludwig Kovacs felt a profound satisfaction when someone called him an idiot. But on this occasion he did.

TWENTY

I explain the way to her. I say, "Faistauersgasse, Ruderclubweg, Fürstenaustraße," and she says, "True." I say, "There's a train going through the mountain." She stops, listens and says, "False." I say, "The rock looks like an owl," and she says, "I've never seen it." Then we laugh. I say, "Past the mattress house." She says, "Funny name." I say, "Escape route number one, florist's, dead end." She sniffs the air and says, "Florist's is right." I say, "Findus, a wombat." She says, "Nonsense." I say, "Yellow factory building," she asks me why a dead end is called a dead end. I say, "Wire factory, scythe production, galvanising plant," and she asks why escape route? At one point I say, "Moped, edge of the pavement, billboard." She says, "You're lying." Sometimes I say, "Volvo," just for the hell of it, and she says nothing.

Lara is my herald. I chose her for the job. If I committed seppuku she'd be my kaishakunin. She's got her own bodyguard, another kind of kaishakunin. So there's a little chain. I like that. Lara sat in front of Switi in class. Switi breathed onto her back or spat crumbs into her neck. That's why I took her. She knows what Switi smelled like. And apart from that she's more attentive than anyone else in the world.

The elder shrub, the tin barrel, the three wooden boards. The bodyguard whines softly. "Quiet," she says. We go down the narrow steps. She holds the lead in her right hand, and with the left she supports herself on the wall. "Don't worry, it's light down below," I say. We both laugh.

I take her to the workbench. She puts her hand on the edge. I show her my tools, the hammers, the files and the lubricated grindstone I bought myself. She turns the crank. The stone turns very gently. "There's no electricity down here," I say. I've managed though.

Longbottom looks for a spot under the window and lies down. I push the old iron-framed chair over to her and say, "Sit down." She runs the tips of her fingers along the keyboard, over the touchpad, along the edge of the screen. "I bought that, too," I say, "the grind-stone and the Notebook. It's got a built-in D.V.D. drive and a battery that lasts six hours."

"Wait a moment," I say. I go behind the wooden screen and pull on the cuculla. When I return Longbottom gets up and grumbles. Then he lies down again. "You've changed," Lara says. I go over to her, take her hand and place it on the material. She makes tiny movements with her fingers. "Folds," she says, "so many folds. Really lovely." I tell her it's a gown for feast days and that I just took it because I liked it. "Who from?" she asks, and I say from someone who doesn't need it any more. Then I test her and ask, "What colour?" She feels it with great concentration and says, "Dark blue, purple or black. Dark, anyway." "Black," I say. I don't know how she does that.

I put the double D.V.D. box on the workbench. I tell her every-thing. One side is yellow, the other's red, I say, and there's another D.V.D. under the red one." I also tell her that the film is thirty-three minutes and forty-eight seconds long and that there aren't any breaks, it's non-stop. I tell her she's got to sit through the whole thing if she wants to be Switi's friend and my herald, and I say that she has a bodyguard and she has me. Before I press *play* I tell her that I'll be standing behind her all the time.

*

That's it. It's the bit when all you can see of her is the white froth with the bubbles. In the top left a bit of the concrete slab with the iron ring. A few blades of grass. Everything is still.

Longbottom is standing beside Lara, licking her hand. Her face is deathly pale and she's jiggling backwards and forwards on her seat.

"Who is that?" she asks. "Who is that?" "There are three of them," I say and I tell her that she doesn't know them and they're on a list.

"One of them's giving instructions," she says. "That's the one I stole the cuculla from," I say.

I bend down and fetch the bamboo stick from under the workbench. "Turn to me," I say. I pull the hood over my head. Longbottom grumbles again. "Quiet," she says, putting her hand on his head.

"You will be my herald," I say. Then I say that I'm proud of her because she's Switi's friend and only asked *What are they doing now?* eleven times and didn't try to run away like Sen Wu, or puke like Britta Kern. I tell her she's got a special job to do and that it's going to get a bit unpleasant now, but it has to happen.

When I raise the bamboo stick Longbottom growls. I've never heard him growl before. She closes his eyes with her thumb and forefinger. "Nothing's going to happen," she says.

I walk around her and hit her on the back, on the shoulders and on the head, alternating between the stick and the palm of my hand. I give her medium-hard strokes and say: "I am the black cowl, dark snow that covers everything." I say the phrase nine times, then three times, then again three times with not much interval between. That's the ritual.

Lara flinches a little, but that's all. By the end Longbottom is barking. She puts her hand around his muzzle. I tell her it's over.

She asks whether she can touch the cuculla again. I hold out a sleeve to her. Her fingers do the same tiny movements again. "Cowl," she says. "Everybody thought it was owl."

234

I open the D.V.D. player. The picture with the white froth and the bubbles disappears. I take out the D.V.D. and put it under the yellow one. That's the most important part, I say. I take off the cuculla, fold it up, then take the book with the brown cover and the four pieces of paper out of my coat pocket. "The book with the pelican stories," I say. "That's part of it, too. And the list." I shove the four things into a dark-blue nylon canvas shoulder bag with the word *Apollo* printed on it. Apollo is the god of youth and poetry, I say. Lara asks if I will read her a pelican story and I say maybe later.

No, nothing's going to happen to her, it's all over now, and I say that she should tell the other three it's not going to happen to them any more. "You are the four that know," I say, "and I'm the black cowl, the dark snow." Then I say that I'm going to do what snow usually does – melt away.

I put the bag on her shoulder and repeat what she has to do. She knows. "I can't feel anything any more," she says. Longbottom looks at me with mistrust.

Before we go I fetch the Hattori Hanz sword from the tool drawer, lay it on the workbench and undo the towel I wrapped it in. "Now it's perfect," I say. I tell her how difficult it was to sharpen the outer edge of the blade, how it didn't work with the blowtorch, and how in the end the lubricated grindstone was the answer. "Razor sharp on both edges," I say, taking her hand. "Do you want to touch?" I ask. She recoils, shaking her head. She asks whether she has to take the sword with her, too, and I say, no, she doesn't have to.

*

Outside, Longbottom noses the *Apollo* bag. "It's something new to him," Lara says. Then he starts snuffling madly around the elder bush that grows alongside the shed. "He can smell Findus, the wombat," I say. "Nonsense," she says.

235

TWENTY-ONE

He reserved a space for her in the choir stalls, only a few metres from the orchestra. If the lardy-arsed, mouthy parish councillors can sit there, then so can she, he said. No doubt someone will bitch about it, but she does not care. He turned up at the last minute, as always, during the opening bars of Mozart's "*Requiem*" to be precise, an iPod headphone in his left ear, and she felt embarrassed for him as if she were his wife. "Take it out," she whispered to him, and he grinned, humming "Spirit on the Water", and obeying her for the very first time.

To begin with the issue had been controversial, luring the fundamentalists in the parish out of their holes. Even the papers had reported on it: "Church as Marketplace?" The critics were only silenced when Clemens wrote a circular in which he put himself at the centre of the whole thing, saying he thought there was nothing nicer than celebrating the Resurrection in a full church and so, to his mind, a concert before the Easter vigil was a brilliant idea.

"Do you know the soloist?" she asked him before the middle piece, a Benjamin Britten cello sonata. "You bet," he said, grinning. The piece, two short, wild movements beginning with a pizzicato section that sounded like tiny explosions, followed by a sequence of martial marching rhythms, practically overwhelmed her. The cellist had sat there with glowing cheeks, the tip of her tongue between her teeth, and she had found it wonderful that someone with ears that stuck out like that could be so beautiful.

She was the psychiatrist's wife, he whispered to her before Bruckner's "*Te Deum*". The church was probably full of his cronies, she replied, and he said she should just enjoy the men, the black-haired tenor and the bearded bass-baritone who had sung the "*Tuba mirium*" as if he were a trumpet himself. She tried but it did not work. The truth is, I'm only interested in him, she thought, and suddenly she felt very vulnerable.

After the foods have been blessed, she squeezes past the people to the side altar on the left, to look for her basket with ham and eggs. Something prods her in the back of her knee. She thinks it must be Bauer and does not react. She is prodded again. "Stop that, I'm looking for our dinner," she says. "Stella." She turns around. It is Lara.

"Have you got a basket up here, too?" she asks. Lara shakes her head. In the last lesson before the holidays she, Stella, had said "Happy Easter", she says, and "Maybe we'll see each other, on Palm Sunday perhaps, or at the Resurrection concert", which is why she knew that she would be here. Longbottom finds people he knows easily. Lara takes off the bag hanging across her torso and holds it up to Stella Jurmann. APOLLO, she reads. It does not mean anything to her. "I'm to give it to you," Lara says. "What is it?" Stella asks.

"You're not to look at it until you get home," Lara says.

"Who gave you this bag?"

"Fanni."

Which Fanni? she asks, and Lara says Susi's sister. "Our Susi?" Stella Jurmann asks. Lara nods and says nothing. Stella starts to open the bag. "No!" Lara says, "Please don't!" "It's O.K.," Stella says, resting her hand on Lara's shoulder, "I won't look at it till I get home." Longbottom grumbles. He always does that when someone touches Lara.

*

Bauer is waiting outside on the steps by the railings. "What took you so long?" he says. She had been looking for their dinner, she says, and then Lara gave her a present. She raps her knuckles against the bag hanging over her shoulder. "APOLLO," he reads. "What's inside?" He reaches for it. She turns away. "Not till we get home," she says. "I want a present too," he says. She laughs. "Where's your iPod?" she asks. He shrugs. He never needs it after the celebration of the Resurrection, he says.

The southerly wind drives her onwards. She can see the odd star in the sky. She thinks of how assuredly Lara moves, of her position in the class, and wonders whether it is only in the minds of sighted people that being blind from birth is so terrible. "The world is unjust," she says. "Lara sees too little, you hear too much." He gives her a poke in the side. "Cheesy joke," he says. "I know," she says.

*

She comes out of the kitchen with a tray and gets a fright. "What on earth?" she says. "It's not Carnival time." He stretches out his arms and spins around. It was in the bag, he says. He's got an identical one in his cupboard – a cuculla. "A what?!" she asks. He looks like a ghost and anyway, what was he doing opening her present? He says he's sorry, sometimes things still get the better of him. Then he says, "Cuculla, the cowl, a monk's robe for feast days," and points at the table. Those were also in the bag – a book, a few pieces of paper and a double D.V.D. "Take it off," she says, and he does.

When she opens the book and reads the first page she begins to feel ill. "What's wrong?" he asks. She pushes it over to him. "*Switi and Fanni in the mattress house*," he reads out aloud. "And the second sentence: *I am the black cowl, dark snow that covers everything.*" He leans back. He says he doesn't understand.

"Britta," she says after a while. She drums her fingernails on the table. "Sorry?" he asks. Britta Kern said "plack awrl", it was that simple.

238

He leafs through the brown book. "Just pelican stories," he says. "One to nine, and one other text at the end." She asks him to read her a pelican story. Which one? he asks, and she says the first one.

He reads about a pelican who has a small elephant for a friend. The elephant is a bit clumsy, like all elephants really, and is frequently responsible for the failure of the pelican's ambitious projects. Amongst other things he swims terribly slowly, he doesn't like eating fish, and he can't fly at all, even though the pelican has heard of a small elephant who could fly perfectly well by flapping his enormous ears. The small elephant gets sad because he realises that he's not up to the pelican's high expectations, so he decides to swap his pelican friend for another elephant.

"That's it," he says. "What?" she says. Sorry, but that's how the story ends, he says. "Another one," she says.

The parents of a small pelican are killed by a ravenous sea lion. The pelican decides he wants to live somewhere else and so moves to Africa. There he meets a wise chimpanzee who reveals to him that he will not find peace until he avenges his parents' death. So the pelican learns a variety of martial techniques and transports an entire arsenal of weapons back to his beach. He starts fighting the sea lion, attacking with his beak, missiles and poisoned fish. Nothing works. In the end a cormorant recommends that he should ask the sperm whale. The sperm whale listens to his story, swims to the pelican's beach, and eats up the sea lion.

"And that's it." Better, she says, which number was that one? "The ninth," he says. "The last one." "Now read what comes afterwards," she says. He looks in the book. "It's called 'What I'm going to do to him'," he says. "To whom?" she asks. No idea, he says.

*

I've studied them, both of them. I've had long enough. I know the medicines she takes and I know when he drinks coffee. I walk up to him and whisper into his ear that I want to go upstairs with him. He's surprised and asks why, and I say because I'm going to be a woman soon and I want him to give it to me, he owes it to me. He grins and stands up. "Alright then, let's go on up," he says. "Like the old days." The mad woman is sitting on her sofa, just gaping into the distance. Up the stairs, into the bedroom, I hold my breath, the wardrobe, the picture with the eagle and the owl, the keyhole. "You open it," he says. I run through the rooms as if I'm having a look around. Then I say, "Let's go into the white one." "Wherever you like," he says. He leans against the doorframe. I get undressed. I make sure the cameras are turned off. What's going to happen now is for me alone. I point my finger between my legs and say, "I've made myself smooth especially for you." I go up to him and let him have a good look. He puts his hand on me. I don't care. He wants to lie down. That means the sedatives are working.

He lies on his back, I put him inside me. I bend forward, a little to the right, and pull out the Hattori Hanz sword from under the white mattress. "I am your kaishakunin," I say. He looks at me with huge eyes and doesn't understand anything. Hilt at the top, I raise the sword as high as I can and then thrust it straight downwards. It makes a crunching sound as the tip hits his spine. He lets out a short groan. I draw the blade down in a curve to his liver, a swift and rapid movement, then I pull it from his body. That's when the blood appears. I bend forward and, fingers outstretched, shove my hand onto his chest. He has a crooked smile and tries to raise leg. He can't. I lift myself off him and stand up. I don't look at him any more. I don't say anything.

*

"What's all that about?" he asks. She does not reply. He grabs the D.V.D. box and goes out of the room.

She takes one of the blessed eggs from the tray, knocks it against the tabletop and starts peeling it. She gets this cold sensation in her lower jaw that she has not felt for a long time. She sprinkles salt onto the egg and takes a bite. It tastes good. This surprises her.

He calls her as she is cutting some ham. She goes into the bedroom. "I've found something," he says, holding up a D.V.D. "Eating Sweet Brownie".

*

A girl has an orange tube inserted into her body. That is how the film begins.

Bubbling white froth. A concrete slab. A few blades of grass. That is how it ends.

*

She runs into the bathroom, smashes the toothbrush glass against the basin, and picks up the largest shard. She slashes her arm from elbow to wrist, again and again. And screams.

TWENTY-TWO

"Move away!" he said, with an authority they have never heard before. Horn took a step backwards and leaned against the window-sill beside Irene.

Tobias opened two break-seal ampoules, one containing solvent, the other a white powder. He drew the solvent up into a five-millimetre syringe, letting it slowly run over the powder. He pricked the stopper on a bottle of saline solution and injected the mixture into it. Then he attached an infusion set and gave the bottle to Irene. "At eye level, please," he said. She raised her arm obediently.

He lifted the cat from the bench and laid her on the kitchen table. She tried to bolt. He held her down with his forearm. "That looks brutal," Irene said. Tobias replied that she didn't have to watch. He stuck a subcutaneous needle onto the infusion set, removed the protective cap, squeezed up a fold in the cat's neck with two fingers, and inserted the needle. The cat hissed. "On," he said. Horn turned the dial. "Slow or fast?" he asked. "Fast," Tobias said. He tickled the cat between her ears and carefully relaxed his grip. He can drive a car without my knowing a thing about it, and he knows how to prepare an infusion, he thought.

"How do you know how to do this?" Irene asked. "Dopeheads need to know," Tobias replied. "After all, they'll need it later on."

"Don't be so silly," Horn said.

"Who's the silly one here?"

They had showed him how to hold the cat at the vet's, Tobias said, straight after the M.R.I. The vet had looked at the pictures, said what had to be said, that the growth itself could not be halted, but that the swelling of the brain around it could be reduced with cortisone infusions, for example. He had asked how to do it, the vet had taken the stuff out of the cabinet and let him try it there and then; he could take his time because the cat was still under sedation. How on earth did he hit upon the idea of an M.R.I.? Horn asked, and Tobias said, a bit of Googling, plus he was the son of a doctor don't forget.

She would probably behave normally after the infusions, the vet had said, eat, run around, wash herself, nothing else. Tobias held the cat between his hands until the bottle was empty. Then he pulled out the needle, lifted up the cat and left.

*

Strange times, Horn thought, picking a red slug off the lawn, my son steals my car, my wife plays pieces of music I've never heard before, and my perception is failing me. "What do you mean by that?" Irene asked.

"By what?"

"That your perception is failing you."

"Nothing in particular," he said. "There are things I'm not seeing or hearing, and I'm judging people wrongly." She asked who, and he said his two sons and certain men who were worried about their wives.

"Is that something you do, too?" she asked. What? he asked, and she said, worry about your wife, and he said no longer now that he had seen the tenor. She laughed. "Just throw the slug away," she said.

They talked about the concert, his surprise when he had seen the programme, how the second violins had come in at the wrong point during the "*Lacrimosa*", and the tenor's over-the-top warbling in "*Sanguine, sanguine*". Then they discussed the fact that there must

243

be something between siblings which parents could not grasp, a sort of secret relationship which involved some kind of awareness and duty. She said that as she was an only child she lacked this direct relationship, and he thought of his sister's diary which he had opened and where he had found a passage in which she was debating whether she should give names to her breasts. He had never opened it again.

"Do you know where Tobias has gone?" she asked. As far as he knew he was lying on the carpet in the stable, the cat on his tummy, listening to some ghastly music. Why was she asking? "I'd like to take a peek in his room," she said. Why, he asked, and she replied she had the feeling that it was something she wouldn't be able to do in the future. "You just want to have a sniff to see whether he's been smoking a joint, don't you?" he asked. She grinned. "He doesn't smoke dope," she said.

They walked between the rhododendron bushes and the peony bed to the yard at the back. They looked around at the same time. "He's not coming," Horn said.

Irene turned around slowly in the middle of her son's room. The bed was made, there was no smell. On the desk was a box made of pine boards. It was big enough to fit a curled-up cat in. "Who made that?" she asked. "Michael, I assume," Horn said.

"Do you know what it's for?"

"No, I don't," he lied.

TWENTY-THREE

The sky was bright blue. Spring has no idea, Kovacs thought, about fathers and their daughters, or about the really bad things in life. With his thumb he traced a line across the condensation that had formed on the outside of his beer glass. Then he reached into his jacket pocket and switched off his mobile. He had had enough.

First, Mauritz had called to tell him that the result of the chemical analysis of the sweet-like thing they had found in the victim's mouth had left them totally baffled. This was because it consisted predominantly of snake venom. He had answered, yes, of course, just like he, Mauritz, consisted predominantly of muscle, and Mauritz had said he was being serious.

Then Demski had been on the line from Berlin, without giving the least indication that he felt at all guilty. "We've got him," he had said. "He's a minor player." Kovacs had answered, "The chap we've got is no minor player," and Demski had said that the man he was referring to went by the name of a Greek god. I'm going to steal his tin duck, Kovacs had thought all of a sudden, and after a while the thought of this made him terribly happy.

*

Marlene came out onto the terrace with Charlotte and another girl. It was a few moments before Kovacs recognised her. "Let me introduce you to Isabella," Charlotte said. "The school ghost," Kovacs said. Sack of potatoes, school ghost – he could be pretty rude at times. The school ghost grinned.

How was his gash? Marlene asked, sitting down beside him and taking a sip of his beer. Kovacs did not reply. "Do you know what the worst thing is?" he said. "It's not having a clue. About anything. And then you sit there and wonder when you started to overlook things. In the end you realise that you weren't there from the very beginning. Then you start creating your own story, any old story, and trying to imagine how it must have been."

Marlene said she didn't understand a thing at the moment, and Kovacs said that wasn't a problem.

He sat there, his hands around his glass, taking the odd sip of beer. Beside him two girls were chattering away, one with a green mohican, the other who did not go to school. Marlene was waiting for her coffee and was silent. On the railings in front of them a bullfinch was working away at something with its beak, the remnant of a cake or a seed.

*

He imagined the girl sitting in an aeroplane, looking out of the window, drinking orange juice and reading the in-flight magazine. He imagined her looking at her passport and boarding card again and again, and being pleased with herself because she had kept her seat-belt fastened the whole time. Then he imagined her seeing the town for the first time, and saying "Dabhol, Dabhol", as if she had to give it a new name. Finally he imagined her taking the bus into the town centre, and the bus stopping to let her off, and her walking the last bit to the beach.

"What are you thinking about?" Marlene asked.

"Why?"

"You look so strange."

"I'm thinking about a pelican," he said.